Prai

Vuln

Here's what some readers have to say about the first book in the McIntyre Security Bodyguard Series...

"I can't even begin to explain how much I loved this book! The plot, your writing style, the dialogue and OMG those vivid descriptions of the characters and the setting were so AMAZING!"
– Dominique

"I just couldn't put it down. The first few pages took my breath away. I realized I had stumbled upon someone truly gifted at writing." – Amanda

"*Vulnerable* is an entertaining, readable erotic romance with a touch of thriller adding to the tension. Fans of the *Fifty Shades* series will enjoy the story of wildly rich and amazingly sexy Shane and his newfound love, the young, innocent Beth, who needs his protection." – Sheila

"I freaking love it! I NEED book 2 now!!!" – Laura

"Shane is my kind of hero. I loved this book. I am anxiously waiting for the next books in this series." – Tracy

Praise for
Fearless

Here's what some readers have to say about the
second book in the McIntyre Security Bodyguard Series...

"Fearless is officially my favourite book of the year. I adore April Wilson's writing and this book is the perfect continuation to the McIntyre Security Bodyguard Series."
– Alice Laybourne, Lunalandbooks

"I highly recommend for a read that will provide nail biting suspense along with window fogging steam and sigh worthy romance."
– Catherine Bibby of Rochelle's Reviews

Books by April Wilson

McIntyre Security Bodyguard Series

Vulnerable

Fearless

Shane (bool 2.5)

Broken

Shattered

Imperfect

Ruined

Hostage

Redeemed

Marry Me

Snowbound

Regret (early 2019)

and lots more to come…

REDEEMED

McIntyre Security
Bodyguard Series
Book 8

by

april wilson

Wilson Publishing
P.O. Box 292913
Dayton, OH 45429
www.aprilwilsonauthor.com

Visit www.aprilwilsonauthor.com to sign up for the author's e-mail newsletter to be notified about upcoming releases.

ISBN: 9781795002110

Published in the United States of America
Second Printing January 2019

Dedication

To Barbara and Herb Wilson
for bringing me into this amazing world.

1

Annie Elliot, 2004
Senior year in high school

J ake leans close to me in study hall on a Friday morning, nudging my shoulder playfully as his lips graze my ear. "Let's go away for the weekend," he whispers, making me shiver. "Just the two of us."

I shoot him a cautious side glance, keeping one eye on our teacher, Mrs. Bates, who's deeply engrossed in a romance novel. "Go where?" I mouth back to him.

"To my dad's cabin in Harbor Springs."

"Are you crazy? You know my parents would never let me—"

"Tell them you're spending the night at Stacy's. They'll never know." His eyes glitter with a challenge. "Come on, Elliot, say yes. I dare you."

I roll my eyes at the pouty expression on my boyfriend's handsome face and find myself fighting a grin. I'm so tempted to say yes. The idea of spending a whole night alone with him is temptation beyond belief. With my parents breathing down my neck all the time, Jake and I don't get a whole lot of alone time, so every hour we have to ourselves is precious. A night away, alone with him? I can't even imagine.

He reaches beneath the table and squeezes my thigh. "I'll tell my parents I'm spending the night with Cameron."

"But I have a ton of homework this weekend," I whisper, thinking of the many reasons why I shouldn't agree to this crazy scheme, starting with the fact that my parents would kill me if they found out. "And I have my calculus exam to study for."

He shakes his head. "Not a problem. You can do your homework and study all you want. I won't interfere—I promise."

I sigh, so torn between what I *want* to do and what I know I *should* do. "Jake...."

My parents think Jake is a bad influence on me. And to be honest, they're right—he is a bad influence. He's always talking me into doing things that will get one or both of us in big trouble. But I've also never been happier in my life. He makes the ordinary seem extraordinary.

He lays his head on my shoulder, gazing up at me with these big puppy dog eyes. "Please? Think of all the back rubs I'll be able to give you."

I am such a sucker for back rubs. Just the thought of his hands on my body makes me shiver with anticipation. "Okay!" I whisper back. "I'll do it."

He gives me a devastatingly handsome smile, his dark eyes lighting up. "I'll pick you up tomorrow morning at ten o'clock."

The class bell rings, signaling the end of our study hall period. This is the only class period we have together. All of my courses are advanced placement pre-college courses, and Jake's classes—well, academics aren't really his strong suit. He's more a man of action. He struggles a lot with academics, but on the football field... he's a god. His lack of interest in school is one of the things my parents dislike about him, but I don't care that academics aren't his thing. I love him anyway, for who he is. My parents, on the other hand, aren't quite so forgiving.

Jake walks me to my locker—actually it's *our* locker now. We decided to share a locker so that we'd have more time together during the school day. As usual, he carries my heavy textbooks along with his own. I'm not oblivious to all the longing glances he gets in the hallway. At over six feet tall with muscles that won't quit, he's the epitome of tall, dark, and handsome, and he stands out in any crowd. The girls can't help following him with their eyes. I'm used to it by now, and it doesn't bother me because I know he's not returning their come-hither stares.

No, for some completely unfathomable reason, my hot-shot boyfriend has eyes only for me. Go figure.

Jake stands guard like a dark sentinel as I quickly work the combination lock and open the locker door. He shelves the text-books in his arms and pulls out the ones we need for our next classes. He hands me my ancient civ textbook, along with my class notebook. Then he grabs his remedial math book.

After closing the locker door, he glances around to make sure the coast is clear—that is, there are no teachers within sight—and then he kisses me in front of a dozen pairs of watchful eyes, a full, on-the-lips kiss that makes my head spin. Wicked boy.

"I'll see you after class," he says, giving me a gentle push in the direction of my next class. "Go kick some ass, Elliot."

Elliot. Somehow, my last name became his favorite nickname for me. When he calls me that, I go weak in the knees. With a stupid, sappy grin on my face, I head to my next class, ignoring the snide looks I get from some of the girls on the cheerleading squad as they ogle my boyfriend.

The popular girls resent me for stealing the football quarterback. Apparently, he's supposed to be dating hot girls, not a nerdy, introverted bookworm like me. They don't get the attraction. Honestly, I don't get it either. I often wonder what he sees in me. I mean, he could date any girl he wanted, and for some crazy reason, he wants *me*.

Jake and I buck all the stereotypes, but we don't care because we're happy together. Ridiculously happy.

I can't help grinning all the way to class.

* * *

When Jake drives me home from school that day, my mother ambushes me at the front door with a sour expression on her face. She watches with obvious disapproval as Jake drives away in his late-model Ford pick-up truck.

"I wish you wouldn't let that boy drive you home from school," she says. "He's so reckless. You'd be much better off riding the school bus, not in that awful death trap he drives."

"Mom." I sigh, tired of this old argument. "Jake is a very good driver. His truck may be old, but it's not a death trap. He takes very good care of it. You have nothing to worry about."

She gives me a look that makes it perfectly clear that she doesn't believe me for one second. Then, her expression transforms from sour to pleased as she hands me a fancy white envelope. She eyes me expectantly as I glance down at the envelope, which is addressed to me. The words *Harvard University* are embossed in the top left corner, along with the address of the most prestigious university in the country. My heart starts pounding, and I can barely hear my mother talking over the roaring sound in my ears.

Oh, my God, this is it! I applied months ago to Harvard, as well as to another half-dozen top universities in the country, including Yale, Stanford, and Princeton. I've received acceptance letters from everywhere I applied, as well as scholarship offers. Except for Harvard. I haven't heard anything from them yet... until now.

"Well, hurry up and open it!" my mother says, practically ringing her hands in anticipation.

I stare at the envelope, suddenly afraid to open it. I'm nervous, yes. Harvard's acceptance rate is just a little over five percent, so the chances of any one person getting accepted aren't that good. But more than that, I'm not sure I want to go to Harvard any more. It would mean moving eight hundred and forty miles away from my home in Chicago to Massachusetts. *Eight hundred and forty miles away from Jake.*

Suddenly, I feel sick.

"What are you waiting for, Anne?" my mother says, clearly losing her patience. "Open it!"

It's always been my dream to attend Harvard, ever since I was a little girl. My father is a Harvard alumnus. He majored in business and economics, and now he has his own accounting firm in Chicago. I take after my dad, I guess, in that I love numbers too. I love equations and calculations. It's always been my dream to go to Harvard and then come back to Chicago to work in my father's firm. But now... I'm not so sure. So much as changed since I met Jake. Going to Harvard would just take me away from him. He's sort of my dream now. Shoot, in the past year, he's become everything to me. He's not just my boyfriend... he's my best friend. The idea of attending Harvard pales into comparison to that.

"For crying out loud," my mother says, grabbing the envelope from me. "I'll do it!"

She opens the envelope and pulls out a matching sheet of crisp linen paper. As she scans the contents of the letter, her lips curve in a satisfied smile. I know what that smile means. My stomach drops like a stone.

"I knew you could do it!" she says, hugging that letter to her chest.

She hands me the letter, which is a bit wrinkled now, and I glance at it briefly, barely registering more than the words *Dear Anne Elliot* and *Congratulations.* The old me would have been ecstatic at the news. The new me isn't.

"I have to call your father!" Mom says, rushing to the library to grab the landline. "Go get ready, Anne! We're going out tonight to celebrate!"

Celebrate? But I haven't even decided where I'm going to college. What I really want to do is stay here and go to University of Chicago. It's a fine school too.

I don't feel like celebrating. "I have homework, Mom."

"Fine. You can work on your homework until your father gets home. But be sure to put on a nice dress because we're going to the club tonight for dinner."

As I head up the stairs, my mind starts racing. *Harvard.* My life-long dream come true—or at least it used to be.

Now it feels more like a nightmare.

* * *

Saturday morning, I'm sitting on the front steps of my house five minutes before ten, my backpack filled with a change of clothes and my toiletries. My dad is golfing at the club, and my mother went to brunch with her friends, most likely for the purposes of bragging about my acceptance and scholarship offer from Harvard. I told my parents I was spending the night at my friend Stacy's house. Still in euphoria over my Harvard acceptance news, they didn't bat an eye.

Right on time, Jake pulls up the circular drive, to the front of the house, and parks his slightly battered pick-up truck. He hops out of the truck and meets me halfway, swinging me up into his arms and off the ground as he nuzzles my neck.

"Hey, babe," he says, setting me down gently and leaning down for a kiss. "Did you miss me?"

His smile is infectious, despite my anxious mood. "Hi. Yes, I missed you."

He looks at me, frowning as he cocks his head slightly as if I'm a puzzle he needs to figure out. "What's wrong?"

"Nothing." I shake my head, hoping he believes me. But I'm a terrible liar.

He gives me a look. "Come on, Elliot. I can tell when something's wrong. Spill it."

"It's nothing, really. Let's go before I get cold feet and change my mind."

Jake gives me a look that says he doesn't believe me, but he'll roll with it for now. Then he opens the front passenger door and lifts me up onto the seat. He stows my backpack on the floor in front of me.

"How far is it to your dad's cabin?" I say, when he puts the truck in gear and pulls out of the driveway.

"Two hours. Sit back and relax, baby. Enjoy the ride."

He's clearly happy about our little trip, so I paste a smile on my face too. Not wanting to spoil our overnight trip, I shove the thought of Harvard to the back of my mind and try to forget it.

He reaches for the radio dial, then hesitates as he looks at me.

"Do you want to listen to music?"

"Sure."

He switches on the radio to a popular station, then reaches for my hand. His big hand is warm and comforting, and we lace our fingers together and rest our hands on my thigh.

"There's a little grocery store right on the edge of town," he says. "We'll pick up food and snacks and drinks. I'll grill some burgers on the back porch for us tonight, and we can make 'smores at the campfire."

"That sounds perfect. Thank you."

"Anything you want, babe," he says, bringing the back of my hand to his mouth for a kiss. He gives me a sly grin. "I also brought a brand-new box of condoms, and I hope to use every one of them this weekend."

"That's pretty optimistic," I say, laughing.

He kisses my hand once more, the feel of his lips on my skin sending shivers down my spine. I'm both nervous and excited about spending the night alone with him. It won't be our first time together. We've had sex before, but it'll be nice to do it in a real bed for once. It would be nice to have a little privacy so we can relax and not have to watch over our shoulders all the time.

"Are you sure everything's okay?" he asks me, his brow furrowing with concern.

I smile. "Yes, I'm sure. I'm just thinking about my calculus exam Monday. That's all."

He squeezes my hand. "Don't worry, you'll do great. You're my beautiful, smart, brainiac girlfriend, and I love that about you. I have absolutely no doubt you'll ace that exam."

* * *

After a quick stop at the little grocery store for food and snacks, we drive the rest of the way through the small rural town to his father's cabin, which sits far back from the road in a clearing in the woods. We're all alone out here, surrounded by nothing but trees and birds and squirrels. The cabin is small, rather rustic, with a quaint wrap-around porch. It's perfect.

Jake jumps out of the truck and comes around to open my door, lifting me out. Instead of putting me on the ground, he puts me over his shoulder, making me squeal as he carries me across the yard and up the porch steps.

"Home sweet home," he says, unlocking the wooden door and carrying me inside.

It's cool and dark inside the cabin, which smells a little musty after being closed up for a while.

"Why don't you open the windows to get some fresh air in here while I carry in our bags and the groceries. Have a look around. There are two bedrooms. Pick one for us."

While he goes outside to get our things, I walk through the small, barebones structure. Besides a small living room with a stone fireplace, there's a kitchen, two bedrooms, and a bathroom. I can see through the rear windows that there's another porch on the back of the house. The two bedrooms are identical, each with a double bed flanked by a pair of nightstands, a chair, and a small closet. I'm standing just inside the back bedroom when Jake walks past me and deposits our bags on the bed. "Is this room okay with you?" he says.

"Sure."

He pauses briefly on his way out to give me a quick kiss. "I'll bring in the groceries. Why don't you unpack, then get started on your homework while I go out back and chop some wood for the fire."

As I watch him walk away, I'm struck by how domestic this is. Just the two of us, away on a trip. This could almost be our honeymoon. The thought puts a smile on my face, and I feel the beginnings of butterflies stirring in my stomach. Tonight is a rehearsal for our honeymoon night.

We put the groceries away together, and then I sit at a picnic table on the back porch and do my homework while he splits logs out in the yard. I feel so achingly at peace watching him working in the yard while I do my homework.

He takes his shirt off, wielding that ax bare chested, creating quite a distraction. He's dressed in jeans and hiking boots, his upper torso gleaming in the sun as he swings the ax with tremendous force, his arm muscles bunching and releasing with each movement.

After splitting an impressive stack of logs—certainly more than we can use in a twenty-four-hour period—he stops to take a break, wiping his sweaty face on a towel before he guzzles a bottle of water. At eighteen years of age, he's more man than boy. His chest and arms are sculptured muscles, and the dark hair on his chest arrows down temptingly to disappear beneath the waistband of his jeans.

He catches me watching him and gives me a smile.

I smile back and then force myself to return to what I'm supposed to be doing. Good grief, how can I focus on schoolwork when he's walking around half-naked?

By late afternoon, my stomach is starting to growl.

Jake walks up onto the porch and leans across the picnic table to kiss me. "Sorry, I'm a sweaty mess," he says. "I'll grab a quick shower, and then I'll put the burgers on the grill. You getting hungry?"

I nod, thinking I'm hungry all right, and not just for food. "Starved."

"Good. Be right back."

I practice for my calculus exam while he puts the food on the grill for us. It's so much fun watching him prepare our supper while I solve math equations. I can almost picture us in the future... he'll be outside mowing the grass, while I'm helping our kids with their homework.

While the burgers are cooking, he sits beside me at the picnic table, looking ridiculously sexy in a pair of ripped jeans and a sleeveless T-shirt. He hands me a cold bottle of Pepsi while he chugs a beer he'd brought—or rather, stolen—from home.

For several minutes, he watches me solve differential equations. "I have absolutely no idea what you're doing," he says, shaking his head. He tugs on my ponytail, then traces the shape of my ear with a gentle fingertip. "I love how smart you are. They say kids inherit their intelligence from their mothers. I hope that's right, because then our kids will be geniuses."

I smile as he kisses me. He really means it. He is proud of me. I'm in running to be this year's class valedictorian, and Jake says he gets a kick out of the fact that he's dating possibly the smartest girl in our senior class.

"Ready to take a break?" he says. "Dinner's ready."

I lay down my pencil and close my math book. "Yes, thank you. It smells delicious, and I'm starving."

* * *

That night we lie on the sofa together, the cabin dark except for the flickering light coming from the fireplace. We put a movie on, but pretty soon the movie is long forgotten as we lose ourselves in each other.

My shorts and PJ top end up quickly on the floor, as does Jake's shorts and T-shirt. He slides his hand beneath the waistband of my panties, teasing me as his fingers slowly glide between my legs.

When his finger touches my opening, I gasp, arching my back.

"God, baby, you're so wet," he says with a groan.

Even though we're alone, we whisper to each other out of habit, so used to having to sneak around for some alone time.

His finger slides between the lips of my sex, and I whimper and tremble beneath his touch. When he kisses me, his mouth is hot and demanding, and he greedily swallows the high-pitched sounds coming out of me. Before long, my panties end up on the floor too.

"Bed," he says, standing and lifting me into his arms.

He carries me to the back bedroom and lays me down on fresh, clean sheets. I watch him dig a box of condoms out of his duffle bag, setting it on the nightstand within easy reach. Then he grins at me as he crawls onto the bed, between my legs, using his broad shoulders to wedge my thighs apart so he can settle between them.

For what seems like hours, he makes me shiver and shake, cry out, whimper, and gasp. He's relentless, using his mouth and his finger to make me come until I'm breathless.

My sex is wet and aching, more than ready for him when he finally kneels between my thighs and rolls a condom onto his erection.

He looms over me, our gazes locked, as he carefully wedges himself inside me. Gently rocking, he sinks deeper and deeper, just a bit at a time, stealing my breath with each inch. I grab onto his muscular arms, clutching them as if they're a lifeline.

Once he's fully seated inside me, he begins to move, slowly at first, giving me a chance to get used to him inside me. But it's not long before he's overwhelmed with pleasure and begins thrusting faster, harder. He grits his teeth, his expression tight and fierce as he takes us both higher and higher.

Every muscle in his body tenses as he throws back his head with a hoarse cry. "Elliot! God!"

His movements slow, but even with the condom in place, I can feel his erection pulsing and twitching deep inside me. Finally, he sinks down on top of me, his lips nuzzling the side of my neck as he sucks on my damp skin. "God, I love you," he groans, drawing me close.

I stroke his back and his hair, smiling when I feel him shiver beneath my touch. "I love you, too."

Finally, he pulls out and heads to the bathroom to deal with the condom. I hear the water running, and then a few minutes later, he's climbing back into bed with me, pulling me into his arms.

"I meant what I said, you know," he whispers in the dark. "I love you. Forever."

My heart stutters in my chest, seizing painfully, and I'm having trouble breathing. "Me too."

He chuckles. "You'd better. You have me under your spell, Elliot, and you're stuck with me."

I laugh too, because now he's tickling me, and pretty soon I'm squealing like a baby pig. "Stop it!" I gasp, trying to catch my breath. I bat at his hands. "Jake, stop it!" One of these days, he's going to make me wet myself.

He finally relents and pulls me into his arms. I lay my head in the crook of his shoulder and sigh as I breathe in his warm scent.

"Marry me, Elliot."

My heart stops. "What?"

"Marry me. I'm going to spend the rest of my life with you, so you might as well marry me and make it all legal."

I swallow hard as my heart starts galloping, sending blood rushing through my veins. "Okay."

He raises up on his elbow and looks down at me in awe. "Yeah? You will?"

"I said yes, didn't I?"

"You promise?"

I laugh. "Yes, I promise."

He nods, looking quite satisfied. Then he lies back down and squeezes me so tightly I can barely breathe. "We have to get married on March fifth, our day."

Our day. Our very first date was on March fifth. Ever since, that's been our day. It's our anniversary. We've celebrated that date every year since we met.

Later, as we're both drifting off to sleep, he nuzzles the back of my head, his breath warm on my neck and shoulders. "Remember, you promised. I'm going to hold you to it. As soon as we graduate, you'll be mine, forever. Mrs. Jacob McIntyre."

I smile sleepily. *Mrs. Jacob McIntyre.* There's nothing I'd like better.

* * *

Sunday morning, I awake feeling like someone has split my head open with a sledgehammer.

Oh, no. A migraine.

What awful timing.

Feeling sorry for myself, I let out a long, soulful whimper.

"What's wrong?" Jake says, sounding groggy as he presses closer to me.

"Migraine."

"Ah, shit," he says, sitting up with a groan. "I'm sorry, babe."

He gets up and walks to the window, laying a thick blanket over top the sheer curtains to darken the room. Then he leaves the room and returns a moment later with a small plastic tub, which he sets on the nightstand next to my side of the bed. "In case you get sick. Is there anything else I can do?"

When I start crying, he sits beside me on the bed and strokes my hair. "I'm sorry you're hurting."

I am hurting, but that's not why I'm crying. I'm crying because he knows me so well. This isn't the first time he's seen me having a migraine. He knows what to do, and he so good at taking care of me. He's so selfless.

"Turn over," he says quietly, helping me roll to my stomach.

He pulls the bedding down and begins running his fingers up and down my bare back, slow and soothing. The gentle, hypnotic movement lulls me into a quasi-sleepy state. Then he starts massaging my head, squeezing my scalp, which miraculously alleviates the pressure and the pain. Finally, I'm able to relax enough that I can drift back to sleep.

When I awake a couple hours later, he's lying beside me in bed, tracing letters on my back with his fingertip.

I
Love
You
Elliot

My heart breaks in two. How can I go away to school and leave him behind? I know it's only for four years, and not a lifetime. But how can I bring myself to leave him for a single day, let alone weeks or months at a time?

Will
You
Marry
Me
?

"Yes," I whisper in the darkness.

But even as I say the word, in my heart I know it's just a dream. A lovely, wishful dream.

2

Jake, 2004
Senior year in high school...
and beyond

When I arrive at Annie's house to pick her up for Prom, her father comes out of the house, alone, and walks up to the driver's door of my truck. The expression on his face doesn't bode well.

I roll down my window, forcing myself to smile. "Hi, Mr. Elliot."

He looks at my rented tux and scowls. "Annie's almost ready. She'll be out in a minute."

Annie's parents hate me. I know they do. They think I'm no-where near good enough for their daughter, and they're probably right. I can only imagine the grief they give Annie about me in private.

Mr. Elliot eyes me directly. "Has Annie told you she's been accepted to Harvard? She received a full scholarship, tuition, room and board, everything. She hasn't told you, has she?"

I stare at him, feeling like I've just been kicked in the gut. The air around me becomes thick and heavy, and I can't breathe. *Harvard?*

He frowns. "I didn't think so." He shakes his head with what looks like disappointment. "She's known for a month."

My mind is reeling. I know how huge this is. I know how hard it is to get into Harvard in the first place, let alone to be awarded a scholarship. Why the hell didn't she tell me?

"It's always been her dream to go to Harvard, just as I did." Frank Elliot looks me hard in the eye. "Are you going to be responsible for holding her back from reaching her potential? My daughter is gifted, Jake. She's brilliant. And unfortunately, she has a crush on a boy with no future. What are your plans after high school, Jake? What are your aspirations? How are you going to support my daughter in the lifestyle she's accustomed to?"

He waits, as if expecting me to reply, but the truth is he knows I've got nothing. I have no idea what I'm going to do with myself after high school. Maybe get a job. Maybe become a firefighter like my dad. Or maybe I'll follow in my two older brothers' footsteps and join the military.

Hell, I have absolutely no idea.

"You have no plan," he says when I don't answer. He gives me a cruel smile. "Instead, you intend to drag my daughter down to your level. If you truly care about her, you'll think twice about that. Annie has a stellar future ahead of her, a prestigious education at one of the most preeminent universities in the country and an outstanding career in my firm. What can you possibly offer her to match that?"

Caught completely off guard, I just stare at him like an idiot as my mind races for a suitable answer. But the truth is, I've got nothing to offer her. I hate school, and I have no desire to go to college. I want to get out in the world and actually *do* something. I just don't know what yet.

The front door opens, and Annie hurries out. She's dressed in a knee-length, pale blue sparkly dress. Her dark brown hair is up in a fancy hair-do with a few long curls hanging down to her shoulders. She's so pretty it makes my heart hurt.

Mr. Elliot wipes the smirk off his face when his daughter approaches. He meets her at the passenger's side of the truck and kisses her cheek. "You look lovely, sweetheart," he says. "Have a good time tonight."

Then he looks at me through the open passenger window, his gaze icy. "Her curfew is eleven o'clock, and not a minute later. Is that clear?"

"Yes, sir." I hop out of the truck and walk around to open Annie's door and help her up into the seat. This old piece-of-shit truck looks pathetic next to her beauty. I feel like I'm transporting

Cinderella to the ball in a rust bucket.

Annie's dad walks away without another word, climbing the stone steps to the front door of their home.

"Is something wrong?" she asks me as she buckles her seat belt.

I shake my head, pasting a smile on my face. *Why didn't she tell me about Harvard?* Did she think I wouldn't want her to go? Of course I want her to go! This is a chance of a lifetime, and she's worked so hard for it. She deserves this. I would never want to hold her back.

"Jake?"

Tonight's a big night for us, and I don't want to ruin it. I force myself to smile as I reach for her hand, bringing it to my lips to kiss. I breathe in the sweet, delicate scent of her skin—a scent I've become rather addicted to. "You look beautiful, Elliot. You'll be the prettiest girl at the dance tonight."

She frowns. "Are you sure—"

I close her door, maybe a little bit too forcefully. "Hey, we'd better get going. We don't want to be late, right?"

I try really hard to act normal, but I must not be doing a good job of it, because Annie's quiet all evening. She's undoubtedly picking up on my mood—I feel like I'm drowning. I'm swamped with a sense of dread that I just can't shake. She has to go to Harvard. That's not in doubt. But when she goes, what will happen to us? I feel sick to my gut, but I do my best to hide it from her.

We dance a few of the slow dances—neither of us likes dancing much—and drink some of the punch. We hang out with my friend Cameron and his date.

I try to act like everything's okay, when it isn't. Her father's words keep repeating in my head, over and over. *You're going to drag my daughter down to your level, aren't you? If you truly care about her, you'll think twice about doing that.*

Eventually she stops asking me what's wrong.

I'm awarded the Prom King crown—no surprise there. And no big deal. One of the cheerleaders, a gorgeous blonde named Makayla, is crowned Prom Queen. I actually dated her once. Hell, I probably dated all the cheerleaders at least once before I met Annie.

As Prom King and Queen, we stand on the stage and accept all the cheers and camera flashes. Annie is standing front and center in the crowd, clapping and waving at me with a genuine smile on her face. She doesn't resent my popularity, and that makes her a far better person than me. If guys were trying to beat down her door, I'd lose my shit.

She is a far better person than I am, and a hell of a lot smarter. It never bothered either one of us before, but now the consequences are getting serious. Her future is at stake. And I don't ever want to be accused of holding her back.

She has to go to Harvard. I know this, and yet the idea scares the ever-living hell outta me. If she goes—*when* she goes—I'll lose her. I just know it. She won't mean for it to happen, but it will. She'll get caught up in her new life, and she'll make new friends—friends who are as smart as she is. She'll meet guys who have big futures ahead of them. And I'll fade into the background as I try to figure out what the hell I'm going to do with my life.

As I look down at her standing at the front of the crowd, her smile falters until it's gone altogether. It's the beginning of the end for us, and she knows it. She's known for a month now and hasn't said a word. That's just like her—not wanting to hurt my feelings.

When all the annoying pomp and circumstance is over, and Makayla and I have our stupid King and Queen dance, I go looking for my girl. It takes me a few minutes to find her seated alone at a little round table in the back corner of the ballroom.

I sit in the chair next to hers and look at her, trying not to appear as depressed as I feel. "It's okay," I tell her, reaching for her hand. "I know about Harvard. Your dad told me tonight when I came to pick you up." I take a deep breath and paste another fake-ass smile on my face. "Congratulations, Elliot. That's awesome. I'm so proud of you."

Her brown eyes fill with tears as she shakes her head. "I don't want to go anymore."

"You have to go, Elliot. This is a huge opportunity. You can't pass this up."

Her hand starts shaking. "I don't want to leave you, Jake."

I plaster on another fake smile. "Don't worry. We'll make it work. People have long-distance relationships all the time. It's not the end of the world. It's only four years. It'll be fine."

Tears spill out of her eyes, ruining her mascara. She doesn't believe me. "I don't want to go."

I can hear her father's words in my head. *Are you going to pull her down to your level?* Hell, no. I can't let that happen. I won't.

I'm getting good with the fake smiles now. "Don't worry, babe. You'll go, and it'll be fine. You'll see."

That was the first, and the last, time that I ever lied to her.

* * *

She went to Harvard, and I drifted aimlessly from part-time job to part-time job, totally lost without her. Every time she called or e-mailed me, I put on a fake smile and told her how great everything was back home. Our calls and e-mails became fewer and farther between as she got busy with her classes. She never came home for breaks—her parents always went to Massachusetts to see her.

I was slow to reply to her e-mails and texts. It was my fault. I know I pushed her away too many times. But I kept hearing her father's words in my head, and I didn't want to be the guy who ruined her life.

One day I ran into Annie's father downtown. He told me Annie was doing well in school. He said she'd decided she was too young to settle down, and that she thought she should start dating other guys. I drove up to my dad's cabin and got trashed with a bottle of whiskey.

A year later, after getting arrested the second time for drunk driving, I took the only option I had that would keep me out of jail. I followed in my older brothers' footsteps and joined the military. That was probably the best decision I ever made.

I spent a decade overseas fighting in Iraq and Afghanistan. Finally, here was something I was really good at. Fighting. Guns. Killing bad people. I worked my way into a special ops unit, where I thrived.

When I eventually left the military, I tried professional heavyweight boxing for a while. I had the body for it, the musculature, and the grit. I did well, won most of my matches. But something was missing. I missed home. I missed my family. So I returned to Chicago and joined my brother's fledgling private security company.

Annie was home, too, had been for a long time, and was married to some guy who worked in her father's accounting firm. Ted Patterson. The prick. Just the thought of him makes my blood boil.

I can't believe I lost her.

How the fuck did I let this happen?

~ 3

Annie, 2018

Gazing out the rear passenger window of my father's Mercedes-Benz, I watch the downtown Chicago office buildings pass by in a blur. The sidewalks are filled with pedestrians—tourists and locals—bustling about on their way to work or out shopping and sightseeing. My father's chauffeur weaves the vehicle effortlessly through hectic traffic as we head toward the McIntyre Security building. We have a meeting scheduled this morning with Shane McIntyre, CEO of the company. Shane is the eldest brother of the boy I once loved... and lost. Still love actually, because I never stopped. I rub at the stab of pain that hits me whenever I think of Jake. He left a void in my heart that can never be filled.

I swallow hard, fidgeting nervously in my seat.

"Don't worry, honey," my father says as he reaches over to pat my leg with a shaky hand. "It's going to be all right."

Absently, I rub my right pinkie. It aches, as it always does... ever since my husband—my *ex-husband* rather—snapped it in two because I dared to get between him and our young son. I put up with a lot of abuse from Ted, but when he started in on our son, Aiden, that was the final straw. That's when I filed for divorce.

My father sounds confident, but the tremor in his hand gives him away. He's scared. We all are. Ted is unpredictable, and we never know what he's going to do next, or where he'll show up. Just last week, despite a restraining order prohibiting him to have any unsupervised contact with Aiden, Ted tried to remove Aiden from his preschool class. Fortunately, the director of his school refused to let Ted into the building. Two days later, he barged into my parents' home, where Aiden and I have been living since the divorce, during supper, brandishing a handgun at the four of us. He wrapped his hand around my throat and squeezed hard enough to cut off my air. I still have bruises to show for it.

I reach into a side pocket of my purse and touch the edge of my phone case, just to reassure myself it's there. I'm fighting the urge to call my mother and check on Aiden. She took my son to a nearby hotel, just a mile from where we are now. No one outside our family knows where they are. Surely, they're safe. I can't help worrying, though, because Ted has an uncanny knack for showing up in places he shouldn't.

My poor, sweet baby. Aiden is so young and so confused. How do you explain to a five-year-old why his father hurts people? Why his father flies into a rage at the drop of a hat? Why a glass of spilled milk leads to a beating so severe the bruises last for weeks?

Sometimes I wish I'd never met Ted Patterson. I wish I'd never heard his name. But if I hadn't married him, then my precious son wouldn't exist, and I would never wish for that. Aiden is my life.

"They're perfectly safe, Annie," my father says, as if he can read my mind. "No one knows where your mother took Aiden. There's no way he can find them."

I'm not feeling as confident. Ted has a way of doing the impossible. He's proven that time and time again, finding us when we think he can't.

The vehicle stops at the curb in front of a towering office building on N. Michigan Avenue. The driver gets out of the car, looking smart in his freshly pressed uniform, and walks around the front of the vehicle to open the rear passenger door. My father steps out, then holds his hand out to me. I'm not sure which one of us is shaking more.

The prospect of seeing Shane McIntyre again scares me to death. I remember him from high school. He was a few years older than me, and even then he intimidated me. Now he's some bigshot CEO of a prestigious security company, and my father has scheduled a meeting with him this morning to arrange for private security for me and my son.

I glance up at the engraved name on the front of the building—THE MCINTYRE BUILDING. The building itself is impressive, the façade a mixture of stone, steel, and glass. But the company that Shane McIntyre has built, with its impeccable reputation, is even more impressive. My father could have gone to any number of security agencies in Chicago for help, but he insisted it had to be McIntyre Security, even though he knows full well that Jake McIntyre works here.

My father motions for me to precede him through the revolving glass doors into the building's main lobby, which is just as impressive as the exterior. The floors are perfectly polished marble, and the lobby is brightly lit with natural sunlight. Potted trees and a small water fountain add a sense of restfulness and tranquility to the wide-open space.

I follow my father to the reception desk, where he signs us in. When a guard hands me a visitor's badge, I pin it to the front of my blouse. My heart is pounding so hard I can barely pay attention. We follow a small group of people heading for the bank of elevators and step inside one of the waiting cars.

I wonder if Shane will even remember me. He's the oldest in a long line of McIntyre siblings, seven of them in all if my memory is correct. My impression of him in high school was that he was smart, kind, quiet, and very competent at whatever he did, whether it was sports or academics. The girls worshipped him, just as they worshipped all of his younger brothers, most especially Jake.

Jake... the boy who stole my heart in high school when he

stopped in a crowded hallway to help me pick up the textbooks that he'd accidently knocked out of my arms when we collided. We dated for almost three wonderful years before I left for college. After that, everything fell apart. He started dating another girl not long after I left Chicago. She got pregnant, and he married her before leaving to join the military.

I think back to high school, back to the good old days when we were together, and it feels like a lifetime ago. I miss him terribly. I miss his humor, his chivalrous nature. His playfulness. He never let me take myself too seriously.

In hindsight, I don't blame him for moving on. We were young, just eighteen, and he had wild oats to sow. I was halfway across the country at Harvard and rarely ever made it back to Chicago. It would have been selfish for me to expect him to wait four years for me.

One by one, the occupants of the elevator get off at various floors until my father and I are the only two left. We ride up to the twentieth floor, where the executive offices are located.

"Don't be nervous," my father says, as he opens the glass door that leads to the suite of executive offices. "I'll do all the talking."

An elderly woman with a cloud of short, curly white hair greets us. "You must be the Elliots," she says, smiling first at my father and then at me. "I'm Diane, Mr. McIntyre's executive assistant. If you'll follow me, I'll take you to the conference room."

We fall in step behind the petite woman as she leads us down a hallway to a closed door. She opens the door and ushers us inside.

"I'm afraid there's been an unavoidable change in plans," she says, smiling apologetically. "Mr. McIntyre sends his regrets. He's dealing with a family emergency and won't be able to attend the meeting today. His brother will take over."

My father frowns. "His brother? Which brother?"

"Jake McIntyre," the woman says. "Can I offer either of you something to drink? Water? Coffee? Tea?"

At the mention of Jake's name, the bottom falls out of my stomach, and I fear I might be sick. *Jake, here? No!* My pulse starts racing and all I want to do is run away. I can't see Jake! I can't face him.

"No, thank you," my father says, casting a worried gaze in my direction. He looks as shaken as I feel.

"Please make yourselves comfortable," the woman says, smiling pleasantly, completely unaware of the inner turmoil I'm experiencing. "Jake and his team will be with you in just a moment."

I collapse into one of the chairs at the table, shaking so badly I don't think I can stand. Just the mention of Jake's name sends my mind reeling. My stomach is in knots. I haven't seen him in... oh, my God, how many years has it been? I think back... fourteen?

As Diane quietly closes the door behind her, I stare at my hands lying clenched in my lap, my fingers twisting and knotting nervously. I stare at my crooked little finger—a constant reminder of my bad decisions and their consequences.

When the door opens again, I jump as four people enter the room single file, a young woman and three men. The last to enter is Jake. My eyes go right to him—I can't help it. And I can't stop staring. He's changed so much since high school he might as well be a stranger now. I hardly recognize him.

When I met Jake, he was big for his age even then, very muscular, and so handsome with his dark hair and obsidian eyes. But this man, dressed in all black, is nothing short of lethal. There's no other way to describe him. He has no soft edges. He's intense. He's intimidating.

And while I can't take my eyes off of him, he hasn't glanced my way once. He has to know it's me, so he's intentionally avoiding looking at me.

Jake takes a seat at the head of the table, and the other three individuals who came in with him sit across the table from me and Dad. The two men are about Jake's age—early thirties, I would guess—and the African-American woman is a little younger.

"Frank Elliot and his daughter, Annie Patterson," Jake says as he gestures to us.

I'm shocked by the change in his voice—it's deeper now, rougher, and so much more resonant. The sound of it sends a shiver down my spine.

He gestures to his three companions. "My team. Cameron Stewart, Killian Deveraux, and Charlotte Mercer—Charlie."

Cameron Stewart... I remember him from high school. He was one of Jake's best friends. Cameron nods at me, offering a friendly smile. He remembers me.

The young woman makes eye contact, too, displaying a charming set of dimples as she smiles warmly.

The other man—Killian—nods politely.

"Where's Shane?" my father says, glaring at Jake. He's clearly unhappy with the change in plans. "We were supposed to meet with Shane today, not you."

Jake gives my father a hard look. "Shane is dealing with a family emergency," he says in a tight voice. "He asked me to meet with you on his behalf. It couldn't be helped."

My father slams his fist on the table, making me jump. "I hardly think this is appropriate, Jake! I don't see how you can possibly be objective where my daughter is concerned."

"Dad, please." I lay my hand on the sleeve of my father's suit jacket. "You're not helping."

Jake finally makes eye contact with me, and it feels like all the air has been sucked out of the room. My chest tightens, and I'm finding it difficult to breathe. Our gazes lock, and we stare at each other. It's the first indication he's given that he even recognizes me.

How can he sit there so calmly when I'm absolutely reeling inside?

Jake shoots to his feet without warning and points to the door. "Everyone out, now! Everyone except for Annie."

4

Jake

I'm trying hard to keep my shit together and not stare at her like a raving maniac, but damn it! It's hard to be in the same room with her for the first time in so many years and not just want to fall down at her feet. To hell with my dignity because I don't have any where she's concerned.

I've craved this woman for *years*. I've chased her in my dreams, and she's always remained just out of reach. To be in the same room with her now—it's absolute torture. I want to reach out and grab her and never let her go. I want to haul her away somewhere safe, where no one can ever hurt her again. I've read the police reports. I've seen pictures of the bruises on her body and on the child's. Just give me five minutes alone with the ex-husband—that's all I need.

I watch as Cameron and Charlie file out of the conference room. Killian's got his eyes on the father, gauging his compliance. But the old man doesn't look like he plans to go anywhere.

"You've got to be kidding me," Frank says, scoffing with indignation. "I am not leaving this room!"

The years have not been kind to Annie's father. Frank Elliot looks frail, his complexion sallow. His expensive suit hangs on his frame, and there are dark shadows beneath his eyes. I'd say he's on the verge of a medical crisis, but that's not my concern right now. I'm not here for him. I'm here for *her*.

I nod to Killian.

"You heard the man," Killian says as he skirts the table and positions himself behind Frank Elliot's chair. "Everyone out. That includes you, Mr. Elliot."

Frank sputters and glares at me, then looks worriedly at his daughter.

Killian takes hold of Frank's arm. "If you'll come with me, sir."

"It's okay, Dad," Annie says. But she's not looking at her father. She's looking at *me*. "I'll be fine."

Muttering obscenities under his breath, Frank leaves with Killian. The door closes quietly behind them, leaving me alone with Annie.

She's no longer the teenage girl I once worshipped, obviously. She's matured into a woman now. But she looks so achingly familiar that it's difficult to believe so many years have passed. Her hair is still long, a silky shade of fine dark chocolate. Her big, brown eyes look the same, but now they have a wariness to them that wasn't there before. I'm sure her asshat of an ex-husband is to blame for that. I used to stare into those eyes, wanting to lose myself in their depths. God, I still do.

Her body has changed the most. She's filled out quite a bit since high school. She's got curves that weren't there before, curves I'm trying really hard to ignore. Still, she's Annie. My *Elliot*. I'd recognize her anywhere. Only now, she's no longer a girl. She's a woman. And she's stunning. I knew seeing her again for the first time would be difficult, but I didn't realize it would rip a fresh hole in my heart. *Damn.*

"Hello, Jake," she says, eyeing me with uncertainty.

Jesus, I can't do this. Just hearing her say my name...God! I can't pretend that seeing her again hasn't knocked my world off its fucking axis. I can't just sit here, acting civilized, while we discuss the weather as if our past never happened.

Time stops as I stand here, staring at her, hungrily devouring her with my eyes. Her eyes are locked on mine, just as intensely.

I walk around the table toward her, and she stands.

She's shaking. I don't blame her. I'm shaking in my damn boots.

For a moment, I just stand there, and we stare at each other. The room is still, silent, although there's a rushing in my ears. I reach out to her, moving slowly to give her a chance to back up or tell me no. When she doesn't, I cup her face with both my hands, threading my fingers into her hair. I'm so close now, she has to tilt her face up to meet my gaze.

Jesus, she looks as lost as I feel.

I think we've both been struck dumb by the shock of seeing each other again after so many years apart.

Her eyes fill with tears. "I thought I'd never see you again." Her voice is a broken whisper. "I—"

This is too much. She's single. I'm single. There's nothing standing between us. "For God's sake, Elliot, tell me I can kiss you."

Her eyes widen in surprise, as if that was the last thing she expected me to say. Tears spill over her bottom lids, streaming down her cheeks. "Yes," she breathes.

I pull her into my arms and hold her close, not sure which one of us is shaking more. Her lips tremble, and when I crush her mouth with mine, I taste the salt from her tears. There's no holding back. I devour her, drinking her in, stealing her breath as she gasps. Time hasn't just stopped—it has reversed, and we're right back where we started.

We don't say anything, but just stand there holding each other, our hearts pounding. I loosen my hold finally, afraid I'm hurting her. I pull back, breathless, and then I press my forehead against hers, like we used to do, and it's like a dam breaks, freeing years of pent-up emotions, both good and bad. She starts sobbing, loud heart-rending cries that tear me wide open, and I tighten my arms around her.

She wraps her arms around my waist, and we hold each other through the onslaught of pain and confusion and self-recrimination.

What the hell happened to us?

I've asked myself that a thousand times.

How did we let it happen?

Now that she's back in my arms, where she belongs, I don't see how I can ever let her go again.

My girl. My Elliot.

My own face is damp with tears as I pull back to look at her. Her lips are still trembling, and I kiss them again—just because I can. But more gently this time. Finally I force myself to stop. So much has happened. There's so much I don't know. And I sure as hell don't know if she even wants this now, wants me. She might not.

I press my lips to her forehead and close my eyes, letting the pain of uncertainty knife through me. "My God, Elliot," I breathe against her skin.

When her knees buckle, I catch her and ease her back down into her chair. Then I grab the chair next to hers and pull it close, so that we're sitting facing each other. I take her hands in mine. "I read the police reports. I saw the photographs."

I glance down at her hands, as if to reassure myself this is real. When I catch sight of her crooked little finger, something in me snaps. "I'm going to kill him, Elliot. I'm going to kill him with my bare hands."

"No, you can't!" she cries, squeezing my hands. "Jake, he's dangerous."

It's all I can do not to laugh. Her ex-husband, dangerous? She has no idea what I'm capable of. I eat guys like him for breakfast.

She pulls her hands free to wipe her damp cheeks. "We shouldn't have come here. I'm sorry, Jake. This isn't fair to you."

"Of course you should have come. If you need help, I'll be the one to help you."

Staring down at her hands in her lap, she shakes her head. "But you don't owe me anything. I got myself into this mess. It's entirely my fault. You shouldn't have to—"

I grab her hands, holding them still. "Stop! I am here because I want to be here. I didn't have to take this case. I could have bowed out easily if I'd wanted to."

A single fat tear courses down her pale cheek, and she shakes her head. "This isn't fair to you."

"Hey." I let go of one of her hands to brush away that tear with the pad of my thumb. God, I'd forgotten how soft her skin is. "I'll be the judge of what's fair to me, okay? Now, tell me about your ex."

Her expression crumples. "He's a monster, Jake. The things he's done... to me, to Aiden." She shudders. "I'm afraid to think what he's capable of."

The shadows in her eyes are telling, and part of me doesn't want to hear what's coming next. But in order to protect her, I have to know. "Tell me."

She looks away, unable to meet my gaze.

"Annie."

When she finally looks at me again, her expression guts me.

The quiet is broken by a ringing sound.

"That's my mom's ringtone," she says, frantically grabbing her purse off the table and reaching inside. "I'm sorry, but she wouldn't call if it wasn't urgent." She accepts the call. "Mom, what is it?"

As the blood drains from Annie's face, and horror sets in her eyes, I'm up and out of my chair, already in motion as I head for the door.

She's on her feet, looking stricken as she heads my way. "He's there! At their hotel!"

"Who? Patterson?"

"Yes! I don't know how he found them. Mom took Aiden to a local hotel. I didn't even know where she was taking him until after they got there. Ted shouldn't have been able to find them."

"He's there now?"

She nods. "I have to go! He's at their hotel door right now, demanding that she hand Aiden over to him."

"Where are they? Which hotel and room number?" As soon as she gives me the information, I pass it on to the rest of my team via a text message. Then I open the conference room door. Killian is standing just outside the door, on guard, and Cameron and Charlie are seated with Frank Elliot across the room.

"We have a situation," I tell Killian, keeping my voice low. "I sent you the details. Annie's mom and Aiden are hiding out in a nearby hotel. Patterson's there now, trying to grab the kid. I'll go ahead and intercept him. You bring Annie and her father."

I head for the elevator, leaving behind quite a bit of commotion and a lot of raised voices, namely Annie's.

She runs after me. "Jake, wait! I'm coming with you."

She clearly doesn't intend to be left behind, and I don't have time to argue with her. I hold the elevator for her, releasing the button when she's beside me.

Frank heads our way, too, but the elevator doors close before he reaches us. Annie's shaking so hard I'm afraid she might collapse. I know a full-blown panic attack when I see one.

"I don't know how he found them," she says, wrapping her arms around her torso, as if she's trying to hold herself together. "He keeps doing this! Finding us when he shouldn't be able to. I don't understand it."

"It's going to be all right," I tell her, pulling her close. We're just minutes away from that hotel, and I'm sure as hell not going to let anything happen to her kid. "Don't worry."

She leans into me, letting me support her. There's so much we need to talk about, but now's not the time. I've got to get Annie and her son to a safe house. Then we can talk.

We take the elevator down to the underground parking garage, and when the doors open, I take her hand and walk her to the front passenger door of my Tahoe. Annie's already buckled in her seat when I slide behind the wheel. I glance over at her. Even though she's clearly shaken, she's not cowering or backing down. She's like a mama bear gearing up to fight for her cub. *That's my girl.*

Just as I back out of the parking spot, I see Killian and Charlie shoot out of the elevator and race for their transportation. Cameron, I presume, is still upstairs running interference with Annie's father. Good. The more we can slow him down, the better. Coming face to face with Annie's bitch of a mother will be bad enough; I don't want to have to deal with both Elliot parents right now if I don't have to.

It's just a five-minute drive to the hotel where Annie's mother has Aiden stashed. I pull up to the front entrance and hand the keys to the valet, snatching the claim ticket out of his hand. Annie hops out of the vehicle and is already running for the revolving doors.

I follow her inside, and we make a dash for an available elevator. As the car heads up to the seventeenth floor, I reach inside my jacket and pull the hand gun from my chest holster, flicking off the safety. I sure as hell hope I won't have to use it—not with Annie and her kid around—but I'm prepared for anything.

Out of the corner of her eye, Annie watches me slip the gun back into its holster, but she doesn't say anything.

"If Patterson is still here, you stay back," I tell her just before we reach our designated floor. "Do you hear me? Just go back down to the lobby and wait at the front desk for Killian and Charlie to arrive. They're right behind us."

She nods as the elevator car doors open. I step out and glance down the hall. A man I presume to be Ted Patterson is banging his fist on a door, shouting. He's flanked by two hotel security guards who are clearly in over their heads.

"Please, sir!" one of the guards says. "I'm afraid I'll have to ask you to leave."

Ted's hands are empty, and I don't see any sign of a weapon, but that doesn't mean he's not hiding something in his pockets. I charge straight for him, one hand grabbing the back of his jacket collar and the other clamping around his neck. I pull him from the door and slam him face first into the wall.

"What the hell!" he yells. "Get your fucking hands off me! You can't manhandle me like this."

"You'd be surprised what I can do." I shove him harder, pressing the side of his face against the wall and holding it there with one hand while I frisk him with my other hand. I confiscate a switchblade from his back pocket.

Ted Patterson is a lightweight, about five-ten, one-hundred-forty-five pounds, with dirty-blond hair that looks a little too shaggy for an accountant. I guess I should say former accountant. My understanding is he's jobless now. He's way too pale, sickly pale, and there are purple shadows beneath his baggy eyelids. I'm pretty sure if I rolled up his sleeves and pant legs, I'd find needle tracks.

"Let go of me before I call the authorities," he demands, struggling to break free of my grasp.

"I am the authorities, asshole," I say. I haul him back, then slam him into the wall again, just for good measure. I know this guy's type. He's a bully. A bully and a coward who thinks if he makes enough noise, he can scare people into compliance. Well, that's not going to work with me.

"Did you call the cops?" I ask the security guards.

They nod in unison. "Yes, sir. They're on their way."

Annie runs past me to her mom's hotel door and knocks.

"Mom? We're here. Are you guys all right?"

"Annie, God damn it!" Ted yells, still trying to break free of my grasp. "Tell this moron to let me go."

The hotel door opens, and Annie slips inside the room, closing the door behind her.

"Annie!" Ted yells.

I cuff him upside the head. "Don't you dare talk to her. You do know what a restraining order is, don't you?"

"Fuck you, asshole!" Ted says, panting with exertion.

I plant the side of his face into the wall once more, just as the elevators open and two police officers walk out, accompanied by the rest of my team and Annie's father, who looks like he's on the verge of having a heart attack.

"Arrest this guy, will you?" I say to the officers, pulling Ted away from the wall and shoving him toward the cops' waiting arms. "For trespassing, disturbing the peace, and violating two restraining orders."

After the cops get official statements from me and the two hotel security guards, as well as Mrs. Elliot's contact info from Frank, they haul Patterson away.

I knock on the hotel door. "Annie? It's okay. He's gone."

Annie opens the door and peers out into the hallway to confirm that her ex is gone. Then she steps aside for me to enter. An ashen Mrs. Elliot stands in the center of the sitting room, wringing her hands nervously. Wow. The mother has changed so much I hardly recognize her. Her hair has gone completely gray, and her wrinkled face is pinched with disapproval.

When she sees me, her pinched expression turns into a scowl. "What is he doing here?"

"Mother, please!" Annie says. "He's here to help."

Ignoring the mother, I turn to Annie. "Where's the boy? Is he okay?"

"He's in the bedroom," she says, heading for a closed door inside the suite. She knocks softly. "Aiden? It's Mommy. I'm here. You can open the door now."

We hear a snick as Aiden unlocks the door and opens it a couple of inches, peering warily at us through the crack. When he sees me, he slinks back behind the door, out of sight.

"Aiden, sweetheart, it's okay," Annie says, gently pushing the door open. "Come here, baby."

A boy with spiky brown hair and big brown eyes peeks around the door, and as soon as Annie opens her arms to him, he darts out of the room and into her arms, clutching her desperately.

Damn, he's a cute kid. But of course he is. He looks nothing like his deadbeat father. With his dark hair and eyes, he takes after his mother. For a fleeting second, I feel a stab of pain in my chest as my brain sends me a mind-fuck. *Why couldn't he have been my kid?*

Annie leans down to kiss the top of the boy's head. "It's okay, sweetie," she murmurs, rubbing his back. "Daddy's gone. You're safe."

The boy pulls back and looks up at Annie with this incredibly earnest expression on his face. "What if he comes back?"

Shit. Not on my watch, he won't.

I must have made a sound, because Aiden clings to his mother, clutching her slacks tightly as he peers warily at me.

"Aiden, this is Mr. McIntyre," Annie says. "He's my friend. He's here to help us."

The kid looks at me doubtfully as he clings to Annie. I notice he's holding onto something a bit worn and tattered and green. Some kind of stuffed animal. Is that a dinosaur?

I give him what I hope is a friendly wave. "Hi, Aiden. Your dad was here?"

The child nods. "He banged on the door really loud and told Grandma to open the door. He said I had to go with him."

"Well, he was wrong. You don't have to go with him. You're safe now, okay? You and your mom both. I won't let your dad hurt either one of you."

Aiden looks skeptical.

I shift my gaze to Annie, who looks pale and unsteady. Now that the excitement is over, I'm afraid she might keel over. "Here's what we're going to do," I tell her, keeping my voice low and even, for both her benefit and the kid's. "You and Aiden are going to pack up your things, and I'm taking you both to a safe house."

Annie glances nervously at her mother. "We've been staying at my parents' house since the divorce was finalized. Everything we have is there."

"Fine. Let's go get your stuff. The sooner we get to where we're going, the better."

"Where are you taking them?" Mrs. Elliot says, scowling.

I ignore the mother and address Annie instead. "I'm taking you both to a place where Patterson can't touch you."

"Are you coming with us?" Annie asks.

"Yes. I'm not letting either one of you out of my sight until your ex is... neutralized."

"Neutralized?" Mrs. Elliot says. "What exactly does that mean?"

"That depends entirely on Patterson," I say, my eyes still on Annie. "Now, shall we go?" I hold my hand out to her. "The sooner we disappear, the better. I doubt the police will be able to detain him more than a few hours."

Looking far too brave for his age, Aiden glances up at me. "My dad always finds us, no matter where we hide."

"He won't find you this time, Aiden. I guarantee it."

Annie clutches her son's hand and lifts her chin. "We're ready."

"Let's go."

5

Annie

I ride with Aiden in the back seat of Jake's black SUV as he drives us to my parent's house. We're followed by two of Jake's colleagues in another SUV, and my mother drives herself in her Mercedes coupe. I'm not sure where my father is right now... probably in his own car.

Everything's happening so quickly, it's hard for me to keep up. I only just saw Jake for the first time in years, and yet it all feels so right again. My lips are still tingling from our kiss back in the conference room.

That kiss... I suppose it was crazy to kiss him like that, but when he asked, I couldn't say no. It was a dream come true, kissing him again. Feeling his lips on mine, his hands on my body. I could have melted. But the truth is, it was a foolish thing to do. I don't know anything about his life now. Is he married? Or does he have a girlfriend? I have absolutely no idea. I can't just go around kissing men I know nothing about.

Aiden is buckled into the seat next to mine, his favorite toy clutched tightly on his lap. His gaze is locked on the back of Jake's head, and I'm sure he's scared. Thanks to Ted, Aiden has grown wary of men in general, let alone someone as physically intimidating as Jake. Aiden looks at me with big, wide eyes, and I can tell he's got a million questions.

I reach over and pat his leg. "It's okay, honey. Everything's going to be fine."

Then I catch Jake's gaze in the rearview mirror. "We'll need to get Aiden's booster seat," I say. "It's in my car, which is parked at my parent's house."

Jake nods. "No problem. You can bring whatever you need. Clothes, toys for the boy. If you forget anything, we'll get it for you."

"Where are we going, exactly?"

"Somewhere safe," he says. "I can't say more than that right now."

Instead of worrying about his cryptic answers, I attempt to relax in my seat and give Aiden a reassuring smile. I trust Jake. Even though I haven't laid eyes on him in over a decade, I believe him when he says Ted won't be able to get to us. Jake has always exuded confidence, but it's even more palpable today.

I finally have a moment to look at Jake—really look at him. In some ways, he hasn't changed at all. He's still tall, dark, and handsome. He still gives me butterflies. Although now, he's clearly older, more mature. His face has lost any softness it might have had in high school. Now, it's all sharp planes and angles, strong jaw lines, and an aquiline nose that looks like it's been broken a time or two. Physically, he dominated high school sports, excelling at whatever he did. But now, his body looks like it has been carved from stone, all hard muscle and rough edges.

He's clearly not a boy any longer. He's all man now, and the impact he has on me is unsettling. Just looking at him now makes my insides quiver.

Jake pulls the SUV into my parents' driveway and parks near the bay of garages. Another SUV pulls up beside us, followed by mother's car. My father's Mercedes-Benz, bringing Cameron as well, brings up the rear. Everyone exits their respective vehicles so we can convene in the driveway.

Jake points in my direction. "Annie, go inside and collect your things. Lay everything you want to bring out on your bed. Charlie, help Aiden get his things. Bring them to Annie's room as soon as you're done."

Charlie approaches Aiden slowly, as if she's addressing a frightened animal, smiling at him as she holds out her hand. "Hi, Aiden. I'm Charlie. Can I help you pack your things?"

Aiden looks back at me, and I nod. "It's okay, sweetie. Why don't you take Charlie inside and show her your room."

"Yeah," Charlie says, holding out her hand. "Come show me your room."

Charlie takes Aiden inside the house, and as soon as they're out of hearing, my father steps forward, clearly not happy.

"Get their things?" my father says, scowling at Jake. "Why? They're not going anywhere."

"Yes, they are," Jake says. "They're coming with me to a safe house."

My father shakes his head adamantly. "Absolutely not! They'll stay right here with us where they'll be safe. Surely your people can guard the house."

Jake shakes his head. "I think this afternoon was a pretty good demonstration of why the status quo isn't good enough. Patterson is determined to get to your daughter and grandson. I'm taking them to a secured facility, where he can't do that. End of discussion."

My father's expression darkens. "Where exactly is this secure facility?"

Jake takes a menacing step toward my dad, towering over him more than a few inches. "That's classified information, Frank."

"Bullshit! You are not taking my daughter away—"

"Frank, you hired us to keep your daughter and grandson safe. Now you need to let us do our jobs."

"For how long?"

"Until Patterson is no longer a threat."

"What does that mean?"

Jake looks completely nonplussed. "Until he's either in jail or dead. Either works for me."

My mother gasps, her eyes wide, but she doesn't say anything more. Neither does my father.

"After you," Jake says, motioning me toward the house.

Killian and Cameron follow us inside, and we all head up the stairs to the bedrooms.

* * *

As Jake leans against the door jamb, watching me quietly, I stand in the center of my bedroom, feeling at a complete loss. It's hard for me to know what to pack when I don't know where we're going, or for how long. "What should I—"

"Bring whatever you want," he says.

"But I don't know where we're going, or for how long—"

"Just grab the basics for now. If you forget anything, I'll get it for you. You don't need to worry about a thing, Annie. And as for the duration, that's open-ended. Just grab what you want to bring and lay it out on the bed."

It's a little unnerving to root through my underwear drawers and my clothes closet while Jake is watching me like a hawk from the bedroom door. Hastily, I grab a couple pairs of jeans, a few tops, a sweater, and one dress. A pair of sneakers and a pair of boots. Then my undergarments, panties and bras, and a few nightgowns and PJ shorts.

I fold the clothing as neatly as possible and arrange the items in a couple of small stacks on my bed. I set my boots on the floor, then run into the bathroom to grab my toiletries. I also grab my laptop, my iPad, power cords and chargers, and the small stack of paperback books on my nightstand.

Just as I'm done collecting my things and have everything laid out on my bed, Aiden and Charlie enter my room. Charlie is holding a stack of Aiden's clothing, socks and underwear, and Aiden is juggling half a dozen stuffed animals and a red toy car in his arms. Charlie sets Aiden's clothing on the bed, then motions for Aiden to deposit his toys there as well.

"Is this everything?" Jake asks.

I nod hesitantly. "I'm sure we're forgetting something, but this will have to do for now."

"Have you got suitcases?" Jake says.

"Oh, right, of course." I pull two small, wheeled cases out of my closet, one for each of us, and my toiletries organizer.

I lay one of the suitcases on the bed and unzip it. But before I can start packing, Jake holds out his hand. "Wait."

Cameron and Killian walk into the room.

"Ready?" Killian says.

Jake points at our belongings on the bed. "Yeah. Go ahead."

Killian pulls a small device out of his jacket pocket, something about the size of a pack of playing cards. He pushes a button. Then small indicator lights along the top start blinking.

"What's that?" I say, watching Killian wave the device systematically over our belongings.

"It's a bug detector," Cameron says. "It detects tracking devices, listening devices, any and all bugs."

"What in the world are you doing?" my mother says from the open doorway.

"Checking for tracking devices," Killian says.

"What?" I say, utterly shocked.

Jake steps forward. "How else do you think he always knows where you are? He's bugging you."

6

Annie

I 'm practically holding my breath as Killian waves the device over my clothing and shoes, my laptop and iPad. Then he does the same thing with Aiden's clothes and toys. He scans the suitcases. He even waves the electronic device over Aiden's toy dinosaur, which Aiden is clutching tightly to his chest, and the sneakers on Aiden's feet.

"Well?" Jake says, when Killian finishes.

Killian switches off the device and slips it back into the pocket inside his jacket. "I found eight tracking devices in all. Both suitcases, the laptop, the iPad, both their sneakers, Annie's purse, and the dinosaur."

Jake nods, clearly not surprised.

I feel sick. "Ted's been bugging us?"

The idea that my ex-husband has been tracking our movements sickens me. It's no wonder he kept finding us when he shouldn't have. I sit at the foot of my bed as my mind reels with the implications. He's been watching us. Listening to us. I shudder, feeling sick and... violated. "How is that even possible?" I say. "Ted doesn't know how to do things like that."

Jake comes to stand in front of me, taking my hands in his. "He may not know how, but I suspect he's working with people who do. It explains a lot, like how he found Aiden at the hotel this afternoon." Jake nods at the stuffed Stegosaurus clutched in Aiden's arms. "The dinosaur is bugged. So are the kid's shoes."

"Oh, my God. Ted knows that's Aiden's favorite toy," I say. "Aiden takes it with him everywhere he goes."

Killian pulls out a small kit from his jacket pocket and opens it, selecting a tiny scalpel. He inspects each of the tampered items and removes the tracking devices, bagging them up as he goes.

Killian asks Aiden to remove his sneakers so he can remove the tracking device. The only remaining device is embedded in Aiden's favorite toy.

"Can I see that, son?" Killian says gently, holding his hand out for the stuffed animal.

Aiden shakes his head vehemently. "No! He's mine. You can't have him."

Killian sighs, tossing Jake a quick look before he transfers his gaze back to my son. "You can have him back, Aiden. I just need to remove the tracking device. It'll just take a second."

"But Stevie doesn't have a tracking device," Aiden argues. "He's a dinosaur."

"Stevie?" Killian says, grinning. He retrieves the electronic scanning device from his jacket pocket, switches it on, and waves it over the stuffed dinosaur. Immediately, tiny LED lights on the device begin to blink rapidly. "You see those lights, Aiden?"

Aiden's eyes narrow suspiciously. "Yes."

"That means there's a tracking device in your dinosaur. That's how your father is finding you when he shouldn't be able to."

"Oh." Aiden's eyes widen as he begins to process the information. His lips press into a flat line, and I can tell he's trying hard not to cry. "My dad can find Stevie?"

"Yes," Killian says.

"Even when Stevie's hiding?"

"Yes. But I can take the bug out, and then Stevie will be fine."

"He can still come with us?"

"Yes."

"But he'll have a hole in him. His stuffing might fall out."

My poor, brave sweet boy. I rest my hand on his back. "Sweetie, I can sew him up. His stuffing won't fall out, I promise." I glance up at Killian. "Right?"

Killian nods, biting back a grin. "Yes, ma'am," he says, in all seriousness. "Stevie will be fine. And then your dad won't be able to find you at the safe place where we're going."

Aiden's big brown eyes fill with tears as he hands his beloved dinosaur over to Killian. He watches closely as Killian examines the underside of the stuffed animal with gentle fingertips.

"Here it is." Killian makes a small cut in the toy's seam at the base of its tail. He slips a finger into the opening and scoops out a small metal disk. Then he hands Stevie back to Aiden. "There you go. Just a tiny cut. He'll be as good as new once your mom sews him up."

Aiden nods at Killian, in all sincerity. Then he looks at me. "I'll just hold him carefully until you can sew the hole."

"What do we do with the tracking devices?" my father says. He's standing out in the hall next to my mother, looking shell-shocked at the revelation that Ted's been tracking our movements.

Jake props his hands on his hips. "Absolutely nothing. We leave the devices here in Annie's room. It will buy us time as we leave the city. It will take Ted a day or two to realize what's happened, and we'll be long gone by then."

Charlie grabs the second suitcase and sets it on the bed, unzipping it. "Here, buddy. I'll help you pack."

While Charlie and Aiden pack his belongings, I pack my own.

"If you're not going to tell us where you're taking them, then how can we contact them?" my father asks Jake.

Jake shrugs. "Annie can contact you when we arrive. And we'll give you a secured number you can use to reach us in case of emergency. That's all I'm prepared to say right now."

"Now wait just a minute!" my father says. "You can't just—"

"Oh, yes, I can," Jake says.

"Dad, please," I say, when I can see that he's only getting more worked up. "We'll be fine. I'll contact you when we arrive at our destination."

Now that our belongings are packed and bug free—Killian checks everything over one more time to be sure—we head downstairs. The two suitcases go into the back of Jake's Tahoe. Aiden's booster seat has magically appeared in the back seat of the Tahoe, so I strap him into his seat.

Jake joins me at Aiden's door. The warm weight of his hand on my back is comforting. "You can sit up front with me, or ride in the back with your son," he says quietly. "Whichever you prefer."

"I need to sit with Aiden."

Jake nods, and his hand absently slides up to cup the back of my neck. The warm, intimate touch sends a shiver down my spine.

"Charlie will ride with us," he says. "Cameron and Killian will stay here in the city so they can monitor Ted's whereabouts."

After Aiden and I say good-bye to my parents, we're off, heading north out of the city.

While Aiden's busy inspecting the small slit in Stevie's underbelly, using his fingertip to poke some escaped stuffing back into the toy, I catch Jake's gaze in the rearview mirror. I can't imagine what he's feeling right now. Surely he's as thrown off guard as I am.

"You'll be comfortable where we're going," he says. "It has all the amenities you could wish for. And it's as secure as Fort Knox—no one gets in without permission."

I nod in gratitude. "Thank you."

And then he turns his eyes back to the road, and we drive in silence for the next half-hour.

"Kenilworth?" I say, when he exits the highway. I'm very familiar with this suburb north of the city. My parents have a summer home here, not far from Lake Michigan.

"Yes. My brother has an estate here."

Suddenly it dawns on me that we'll be living with Jake for the foreseeable future. I'm nervous. My mind races with all the what-ifs and the unknowns. It's been so many years. We aren't the same people we were back then. And yet, I feel the pull between us even now. Every so often I catch him watching me in the rearview mirror. His dark eyes lock onto me with an intensity that takes my breath away.

A shiver crawls down my spine, leaving in its wake a tingling awareness of the man seated in front. Anticipation unfurls in my belly at the thought of being alone with him again.

❧ 7

Annie

"Mom, can you sew him shut?" Aiden whispers, holding his stuffed dinosaur up to me so I can see the one-inch slit that Killian cut into its underbelly.

It's a neat little incision, right along the seam. It'll be no trouble to stitch up. *Thank you, Killian.* I give Aiden a reassuring smile. "Yes, sweetie. I can fix him. Piece of cake."

His shoulders slump in relief. Aiden nods, looking far too serious for a five-year-old. "Thanks," he whispers, his gaze darting to the two people sitting in the front seat.

Aiden hasn't been around many men in his life, other than my father and Ted, and I can't blame him for being cautious.

Charlie, who must be in her late twenties, seems an unlikely bodyguard. She's got a calm, gentle way about her, though, that puts everyone at ease. But Jake—there's nothing calm or easy about him.

I have to admit even I find Jake intimidating. He's changed so much since high school that he almost seems like a stranger now. I'm not afraid of him, but I will admit he makes me a little nervous. But I guess intimidating is exactly what we need right now. Ted would never stand a chance against Jake, or against any of these McIntyre Security employees.

I reach over and pat Aiden's leg, giving it a gentle squeeze. "Are you doing okay?"

He nods, saying nothing as he clutches Stevie to his chest. But his gaze continues to focus warily on Jake.

Half an hour into our drive, Jake turns the SUV onto a paved two-lane road that meanders through a heavily-wooded forest. There are no markings on the road, no signs, so I suspect we're on private property.

Aiden looks out his window at the towering canopy of trees high overhead. Then he turns to me, his eyes wide. "Where are we going?" he whispers.

I shrug. "To a safe place."

He nods again, reaching across the seat for my hand.

My throat tightens painfully, and I have to force myself to smile when what I really feel like doing is crying. No child should be afraid of his father.

"Do you think there are tigers here?" Aiden whispers.

I bite back a smile. "No, honey. I don't think there are any tigers here."

Up ahead, our way is blocked by a towering wrought-iron gate. Jake stops the vehicle and speaks on a radio to someone. When the gate opens, we proceed. A few minutes later, we leave the trees behind us as the landscape opens up to rolling pastures on both sides of the road. And then we stop at a second gate, passing through that one after Jake says something to someone over the radio.

"Mom, look!" Aiden cries as he points to the right side of the road. "Horses!"

I'm surprised to see a small herd of horses grazing on a rise. On the left side of the road is a small lake with a floating wooden dock and several rowboats and canoes, not to mention a collection of ducks and geese paddling on the water.

"Can we ride horses?" Aiden says. "And go boating?"

"I don't know, honey. Let's just wait and see."

Charlie shifts in her seat to face us. "Would you like to ride horses, Aiden? I'll take you riding if it's okay with your mom."

Aiden looks at me with such a hopeful expression on his face. "Can I, Mommy? Please?"

I brush my hand over Aiden's hair, happy to see him so enthusiastic about something. "Sure."

"Wow..." Aiden says when the house finally comes into sight.

Jake follows the curving drive to the front entrance of a sprawling wooden lodge. "Here we are," he says, turning in his seat to face us. "This will be your home for the foreseeable future."

"How long are we staying?" Aiden says, clearly intrigued by the idea.

Charlie opens her door and hops out of the vehicle. Then she leans back in to address Aiden. "As long as it takes to make sure you and your mom are safe."

The front door opens and out walks a woman with a long silver braid hanging over her shoulder, dressed in a pair of riding trousers tucked into a pair of boots.

She smiles as she jogs down the steps and opens my door. "Welcome! You must be Annie." She glances past me at Aiden. "And you must be Aiden. I'm so glad you're here."

"We saw horses!" Aiden says, unbuckling himself from his booster seat and climbing over me to jump out of the vehicle on my side. "Are they yours?"

The woman nods. "They are. Would you like to see them sometime?"

"Yes! Charlie said she'd take me riding."

Charlie gives the woman a hug. "Hi, Elly."

"Hello, dear," the older woman says. "I'm so glad you came."

Charlie shrugs. "When Jake said he needed me here, I could hardly say no."

Jake walks around the front of the vehicle and wraps the older woman in a bear hug. "Elly, let me introduce you." He turns to face me as I climb out of the SUV. "This is Annie and her son, Aiden."

Elly shakes my hand, her grip strong and comforting. "Welcome, dear. I'm the housekeeper."

Jake laughs. "Don't let her fool you, Annie. She runs this place, top to bottom."

A tall, slender man with a silver buzz cut, dressed in dirty coveralls and equally dirty work boots, walks into view. He extends his hand to Jake, and the two men shake heartily. Then the older gentleman turns a curious gaze to me and Aiden.

"This is Elly's husband, George," Jake says. "He manages the grounds."

"Welcome, Annie," George says in a gruff voice as he offers me his hand. His steely-blue gaze transfers to Aiden, who slips behind me, clutching my thighs and half-hidden from view. "And you must be Aiden," the man says, nodding decisively. "Pleased to meet you, son."

Aiden moves further behind me, completely out of sight, and I can feel his hands grasping the back waistband of my jeans.

I smile apologetically. "I'm sorry. Aiden's a bit shy." That's not entirely true. Aiden isn't shy, exactly—he's just afraid of men in general. Like a puppy who's been kicked too many times, he's learned to be cautious. But once he gets to know someone, he comes out of his shell pretty quickly.

George gives me an understanding nod. "Not a problem, miss. We're happy to have you here."

Jake has been busy pulling suitcases out of the back of the Tahoe, setting them on the ground in front of the steps. There are four suitcases in all. Mine, Aiden's, and two others I don't recognize. I look at Jake.

"Mine and Charlie's," he says. "We're staying here with you."

My heart skips a beat. I remember Jake saying he'd be staying here with us, but Charlie too? For a moment, I wonder if... surely they're not involved with each other. He wouldn't have kissed me in the conference room if he was involved with someone? Right? "You're both staying here?"

He nods. "I asked Charlie to stay with us because I thought you might appreciate having another woman around. Plus, she can help you keep an eye on Aiden. I thought a female bodyguard might make things easier for him."

"Come on, Aiden," Charlie says, holding her hand out to him. "Let's take your suitcase upstairs to your room."

Aiden comes out from behind me and takes Charlie's hand.

"Why don't you two take our guests upstairs and help them settle in," Elly says, "while I get started on some lunch. You must be getting hungry." She cocks her head as she peers down at Aiden. "Are you hungry, honey?"

Aiden nods as he sidles closer to Charlie. I can tell she's already won him over.

"Well, then," Elly says, "I'll get right on lunch. What would you like, Aiden?"

But the cat seems to have his tongue now, and he presses closer to Charlie.

"Sweetie, can you answer Elly?" I say.

"I dunno," Aiden says, clutching Stevie to his chest.

Elly grins at him. "What do you like to eat?"

Aiden shrugs. "I like peanut butter and jelly sandwiches and cookies."

Elly nods, biting back a grin. "I make really good peanut butter and jelly sandwiches. And I can probably rustle up a chocolate chip cookie or two. Do you like strawberry or grape jam?"

"Straw-ba-rerry!"

"That's my favorite, too," she says. Then she looks at me. "And for you, Mom?"

"Anything is fine, really. I don't want to be any trouble."

"Don't be silly," she says. "How about sandwiches for lunch? Perhaps a turkey club?"

"That sounds wonderful, thank you. Can I help in the kitchen?"

"Goodness, no. You and Aiden go upstairs and get settled in. When you're ready to eat, Jake will bring you downstairs. It's so pretty out today, why don't you have lunch on the deck?"

"Thank you."

Jake and Charlie gather up all the suitcases and carry them inside. Aiden and I follow them through the big wooden doors into a spacious foyer that is brightly lit, thanks to large windows high overhead. The floor is smoothly polished wood, and there are three hallways leading off in different directions.

"Whoa," Aiden says, craning his head up to look at the grand curving staircase and the second floor gallery. "This is the biggest house I've ever seen! It's even bigger than Grandma's house."

"Aiden, hush," I say, grabbing his hand.

Elly chuckles as she heads down a central hallway leading to the rear of the house, leaving us to follow Jake and Charlie up the stairs. At the top of the stairs, we turn left.

"This is your room," Jake says, pausing in front of an open door. "Yours and Aiden's. I figured you would want to keep Aiden with you."

Relieved, I give him a grateful smile. "Yes, thank you."

Charlie walks into the room and sets our two suitcases on the floor at the foot of a king-sized bed.

"My suite is right across the hall from yours," Jake says, pointing at a door opposite ours. "And Charlie will be sleeping in the suite next to yours. We'll both be close by in the night if you need anything. Just call for either one of us; we'll hear you."

I nod, clutching Aiden's hand in mine. "Thanks."

"I'll give you a few minutes to settle in," he says. "When you're ready to go down for lunch, come get me. I'll be in my room. After lunch, I'll take you both on a tour of the place."

"Can we see the horses?" Aiden asks, peering from behind me at Jake.

Jake smiles. "Sure, you can see the horses. And the pool, and the lake, and the boats."

"There's a movie theater downstairs and an arcade," Charlie says, grinning down at Aiden. "Do you like to play pinball and video games?"

Aiden's eyes grow huge in his small face as he stares in awe at Charlie. "Yes!" Then he glances up at me. "Can I, Mommy?"

I lay my hand on his head and ruffle his short, spiky hair. "Sure, you can. If it's okay with Mr. McIntyre and Miz...." I look at Charlie. "I'm sorry, I didn't catch your last name."

"It's Mercer," she says. "But you can call me Charlie."

"Thank you, both," I murmur to Jake and Charlie, as I steer Aiden into our room. "We should unpack. We'll see you in a bit."

Once we're alone, I close the door behind us and lean against it as I blow out a nervous breath. This whole day has been surreal. First seeing Jake again, then Ted trying to take Aiden from my mother. And now this place! This place is unreal.

With Stevie tucked safely beneath his arm, Aiden wanders across the room and peers through an open doorway. "It's a bathroom," he says, disappearing inside.

While Aiden's exploring the bathroom, I lay our two suitcases on the bed and start unpacking. The walk-in closet is spacious, and there's a dresser for the rest of our things. The bed is easily big enough for four people, which means it's more than big enough for the two of us to share. Aiden has a habit of moving around a lot at night, and on the few occasions we've shared a bed, I usually end up with his feet digging into my back.

Two large windows on the back wall look out over the backyard, which slopes gently down to the shoreline, with Lake Michigan expanding beyond as far as the eye can see. From here, I can see a dock with several boats moored in place. "This place is unbelievable."

"What's unbelievable?" Aiden says, popping up beside me like a little ninja.

"This house."

"I know! There's a swimming pool in the bathroom."

I laugh. "A pool? I hardly think there's a swimming pool in the bathroom, honey."

"No, really, there is!" He grabs my hand and hauls me across the room and into the bathroom. "See!" he says, pointing. "I told you."

"Honey, that's a sunken bathtub."

"It looks like a swimming pool. Can I take a bath in it tonight?"

"Sure." I ruffle his hair. "Why don't you take a potty break now, and then we'll meet up with Mr. McIntyre and Ms. Mercer for lunch."

"She said to call her Charlie, Mom," Aiden says, disappearing into the bathroom. A moment later, he reappears, holding out his dinosaur. "Can you sew Stevie now?"

"Sure, honey." I retrieve a mini sewing kit from my purse and quickly stitch the dinosaur's small incision closed. Then, before I forget, I make a quick call to my parents to let them know we've arrived safely.

❧ 8

Jake

After Annie closed the door to her suite, and Charlie disappeared into her own room to unpack. I stood in the hallway like an idiot, staring at Annie's door, itching to break it down and sweep her up into my arms and carry her off. But I can't. She's got a traumatized kid in there, for one thing. But I don't even know if she'd want that. Yes, she let me kiss her back in the conference room, but that doesn't mean she's ready to pick up where we left off.

I'm not going to start making assumptions where she's concerned and risk fucking this up. Not when I might have a real

chance with her. We're both single, and I sure as hell didn't imagine the heat in that kiss we shared this morning.

Hell, I don't know what I'm doing. I've dreamed of having a
chance like this for so long. And now that it's here, I'm—*shit!* I
don't know what I'm doing, and I can't stop second-guessing
myself.

I thought I could handle this. I thought I could compartmen-
talize my feelings for Annie... treat her like she was just another
client. But I can't. I can't even take my damn eyes off of her. Every
moment I'm around her is nothing short of torture.

I pick up my suitcase and carry it into my suite, leaving the
door open in case Annie needs me for something. All she'd have
to do is call my name or snap her fingers, and I'd be there. I'm
whipped. No point in denying it. I'm glad my siblings aren't here
to witness this. They'd never let me live it down. I tease them for
being lovestruck whenever I get the chance, and everyone knows
paybacks are hell.

I flip on the light and toss my suitcase onto the bed and start
unpacking. Once everything is put away, I'm restless. I sit at the
foot of my bed and wait for Annie to come get me.

When my brother Shane asked me if I could handle this, I told
him I could. Now, I'm not so sure. I can keep her safe, sure. That's
the easy part. That asshole Patterson can't touch her, or Aiden,
here at Kenilworth. But can I keep a handle on my emotions? The
last thing I want to do is chase her off, or overwhelm her. She's
had enough drama in her life already. I don't want to add to it.

I guess, in hindsight, I probably overstepped my bounds earlier when I kissed her back at McIntyre Security. I shouldn't have done that. Not until I know where I stand with her.

If she gave me the slightest indication that she still wanted me, I'd be all over her. I tossed my pride out the window years ago when she left for college. In the beginning, we talked or texted almost daily. I missed her something awful, and I was desperate for her to come home for a visit. I thought for sure she'd come home for Christmas break, but she didn't.

I waited and waited for her to come back for a visit, and when she didn't, I was so disappointed. And then her dad told me why— because she'd met someone else, and she wanted to spend her school breaks with him, and she was afraid to tell me. The news gutted me. And then she stopped answering my calls—letting me go to voicemail—and she was slow to return text messages. Gradually the bottom fell out of my world.

I feel like I've been living in limbo ever since, waiting. But waiting for what? For this day? For another chance? For her to be back in my world?

Hell, I have to remind myself over and over again that just because she's divorced from that asshat doesn't mean she wants *me*. But God, I want it to be true. I'd give anything for the right to pull her into my arms and keep her there.

So much for me being the tough guy. Ha. I'm a complete fraud.

When I saw her again for the first time, back at the McIntyre Security building, it was like the years we've been apart just evaporated. There she was, standing right in front of me, looking so familiar and so beautiful it hurt. All I had to do was reach out and touch her again.

Fuck!

I don't know what it is about this girl—hell, woman now—but when I look at her, my knees go weak and I feel like I've been punched in the gut. I can't explain it—the instant I look at her, I feel like I'm where I'm supposed to be. I'm *home*.

She's still the quintessential girl next door, with her sweet face and gentle smile, those big brown eyes, her hair the color of fine whiskey. Right now, with her hair up in a ponytail, she looks so much like the girl I fell in love with in high school. She's a little rounder now, her body more filled out with age and time, but she's still so achingly familiar.

I was crazy about her from the moment we met during our first year of high school. We ran into each other in the hallway—literally. Running late for study hall, I came storming around a corner just as she was walking out of the library. I plowed right into her, knocking a stack of books right out of her arms. She would have hit the ground, too, if I hadn't scooped her up into my arms. I'll never forget the expression on her face as she stared up at me, her eyes wide with a combination of shock and wonder.

From the beginning, there was something about her that drew me like a moth to a flame. I guess opposites do attract, because we couldn't have been more different. I was the big tough jock, all brawn and little brain. She was the quiet, nerdy girl who actually liked school.

I set her on her feet, giving her a moment to regain her balance. Once I was sure she wasn't going to plant herself on her ass, I bent down and picked up her books. "Sorry," I said, handing them to her.

She gazed up at me with her big doe eyes, and my body immediately went on red alert, heating up in a very inconvenient way. Her cheeks turned the cutest shade of pink as she stared at me, practically gawking.

I knew perfectly well the effect I had on girls. Girls had been fawning all over me since my growth spurt in middle school, when I shot up over the heads of all the other boys and most of the teachers. The popular girls, the cheerleaders, the easy girls... they all followed me with their eyes when I walked down the hall, whispering to each other, blushing, laughing nervously. Hell, I'd already dated half of the cheerleaders my first year of high school before football season was even over for the year.

"It's all right," the bookworm said. "Thanks."

It became imperative that I find out her name. Before I could ask her, though, she turned away and started down the hallway toward the cafeteria. I realized she must have study hall this period, too. I didn't remember ever seeing her in there before. But hey, it was a big, crowded room with over a hundred kids in there.

I followed her into the cafeteria and waited to see where she'd sit. Once she made her choice, I picked a seat a couple of tables away that gave me a clear line of sight to her. I watched her open her math book and take out a sheet of paper and a mechanical pencil, and then get to work solving equations and scribbling down the answers *like a boss.*

Damn, she was amazing. Pretty _and_ smart.

When the bell rang, I waited until she'd collected her things and was walking out of the cafeteria before I followed her out.

I caught up to her in the hallway and walked beside her. She gazed up at me nervously a few times, her brow furrowing as if she was trying to figure me out. She was taller than most of the girls, the top of her head coming up to my chin, and reed thin. Sort of gawky looking, and definitely lacking in the curves department. But hell, I didn't care. She was amazing.

"We're in the same study hall," I said.

She nodded. "It would seem so."

"What's your next class?"

"Biology."

"Oh. I'm headed that way. I'll walk with you."

"Oh. Okay."

That was a lie, of course. I was supposed to be going to English class, which was in the opposite direction, but she didn't know that. "Do you mind?"

She shrugged. "I guess not."

"Great. I'm Jake."

I saw a hint of a smile play on her lips, as if she knew damn well what my name was, but she suppressed it handily. "I'm Annie."

As I sit here now, remembering, I find myself smiling for the first time in a long time. For years, I've tried not to think of her, because it hurt too damn much. But now, seeing her again, catching sight of the fleeting smiles on her face, it doesn't hurt quite so much.

She's back.

She's *here*.

And damned if I won't do everything in my power to win her back. I'm not the same clueless kid I was in high school. This time, I have a hell of a lot to offer her. Security, for one thing— both financial and physical. I'm not hurting for money, not by a long shot. In addition to my hefty salary at McIntyre Security, I also own property as well as stock in the company. And in terms of physical security, I've got that covered.

I look up when I hear a hesitant knock on my open door, my heart in my throat. There she is, looking so much like that brainy girl I walked to biology class. "Everything okay with your room?" I ask her, trying to play it cool.

Nervously, she tucks a strand of lose hair behind her perfect little shell of an ear and nods. "It's perfect. Thank you."

"Where's Aiden?"

"In our room, playing with Stevie—his dinosaur." Cautiously, she glances back toward her room before turning to face me. She hesitates for a moment, as if debating with herself, and then she steps inside my room. "Can we talk?"

9

Jake

Of course." I get up and shut the door behind her. She's not here to talk about the weather, so I guess we're going to need some privacy.

We stand there for the longest time, just staring into each other's eyes, and I swear she's feeling the same thing I am. *Please, God, let her feel the same.*

She starts to talk, gesturing nervously. "Back in the conference room, when you kissed me—"

"Yeah?" This is it. She's either going to make my day or crush me.

She looks away, so uncertain it breaks my heart. "I'm not sure... what that meant."

I catch her hand and bring it to my chest, pressing it directly over my heart which is slamming against my ribs. With my other hand, I reach out to cup her cheek.

She closes her eyes and leans into my touch with an audible sigh.

I take a deep breath and let it out slowly, forcing myself to remain calm when I'm feeling anything but calm on the inside. "Elliot, I'll be honest. I don't fully understand what happened to us... back then. All I know is that I *never* stopped loving you. Not for a second. I'll love you until the day I die."

When she opens her eyes, they're glittering with tears, and I feel my own throat tighten with emotion.

I lift her hand to my mouth and kiss the back of it, just like I used to do, marveling at the softness of her skin and breathing in her familiar scent. "Look, I don't blame you for wanting to date other guys in college. You were so young, and you had your whole life ahead of you. I totally get it—" I stop mid-sentence when I see the look of utter shock and confusion on her face. She's staring at me like I just told her the Earth is flat.

She shakes her head. "What are you talking about? I never wanted to date other guys in college. I never wanted to date anyone other than *you*." She looks absolutely thunderstruck.

Her father's words replay in my head. All the times he told me she wanted to date other guys. That she'd decided she was too young to settle down. Finally, that she'd moved on. *Jesus Christ, he played me.* And like an idiot, I fell for it. *Damn, we have a lot to talk about.*

"If it wasn't that," I say, "then why did you stop taking my calls?"

"What do you mean, why did I stop?" She breaks off, looking... furious. Resentful.

"It's not a hard question, Elliot."

Her expression tightens in anger. "Because... you—you know why! I *knew*, Jake! I knew about the girl. My dad told me."

My stomach sinks. It looks like I wasn't the only one who got played. "What girl? What did your dad tell you?"

"He told me all about your girlfriend. My parents told me they saw you with a girl, and that she was obviously pregnant. And soon after, you left to join the military."

My vision goes red, and I want to strike out at something... preferably Frank Elliot's head. I pull away from Annie and start pacing, charged up with so much frustration and anger I can't see straight. *Jesus Christ, they played us!* Her fucking parents played us both! And like a couple of naïve kids, we fell for it.

"Don't you see what they did?" I say, gritting my teeth so hard I'm afraid they'll crack. "Your parents lied to us, to both of us! Your dad told me you wanted to date other guys at school. And your parents told you I got some girl pregnant? Well, that's rich, because I never fucking had sex with *anyone* after you left Chicago! Well, not for a few years at least. God damn it! They played us, Elliot. Your parents played us!"

I'm so angry right now, so fucking wound up, I have to hit something. I turn and punch my fist right through the wall, putting a nice big hole in the plaster. *Shit!*

Startled, Annie flinches and draws back from me, and immediately I regret losing it like that in front of her. She's just divorced a violent, abusive asshole. The last thing she needs to see is me punching holes in the wall. "Shit, I'm sorry, but you have to know I would *never* hurt you."

She grabs my hand and inspects my knuckles, frowning at the split skin and the blood. "Oh, my God, your hand!"

I glance down at the damage and shrug. It's not the first time I've punched a hole through a wall, and it certainly won't be the last. "It's nothing."

"It's *not* nothing," she says, clutching my fist to her chest. "You're bleeding!"

She pulls me by the hand into the bathroom and turns on the faucet, holding my fist under cold running water. "Do you have a first aid kit?" she says, frantically opening and closing drawers as she searches for supplies. "Bandages? Antibiotic ointment?"

Unable to help myself, I start laughing. After everything we've been through, and after all the years we were separated, she's worried about a few bloody knuckles?

When she comes up empty-handed, she plants her hands on her hips and glares at me. "Why are you laughing? This isn't the least bit funny."

"Oh, yes it is." I shut the faucet off and grab a hand towel to blot the water and residual blood from my injured hand. The look on her face is both priceless and so damn familiar, it makes my chest ache. "Baby, come here."

"Don't you dare 'baby' me," she says, clearly annoyed. "I'm serious."

I bite back a grin, liking this new feistier side of her. She never talked to me like that before. "I'm sorry, Elliot. Come here, please." I hold out my arms, and she studies me as if debating her next action. And then, to my relief, she walks toward me, looking kind of flummoxed.

When she's within reach, I lift her up and sit her down on the bathroom counter. "I'm laughing because... well, it's either laugh or cry, and frankly I don't want to break down like a big baby in front of you. I have my reputation to think about."

I step between her knees and get as close to her as I can. It's not close enough, far from it, but at least it's a start. We have to walk before we can run.

I thread my fingers into her hair, loving the silky feel of the strands. Leaning my forehead against hers, I close my eyes and just breathe, savoring the moment. *She's here, in my arms.* That's what matters now. I'll deal with the rest of it later. After a few moments, I pull back and look down at her.

Her eyes are red, glittering with tears as reality starts to sink in. "I can't believe my parents lied to us."

My anger dissipates when I hear the sorrow in her voice. "I know. I'm sorry."

"How could they do that? They knew what you meant to me!"

I brush my thumb along her bottom lip, which is pink and plump and so damn luscious. I *need* to kiss her.

"I'm going to kiss you now," I say, giving her plenty of time to object. I wait for a reaction because the last thing I want to do is overstep my bounds. Mesmerized, I watch as the tears in her eyes collect into pools until suddenly they're spilling over her lids. Her face screws up in pain, and she looks away. "I can't believe they did that. This is all my fault."

"Hey." I turn her face back to me. "No, it's not your fault. This is on them, not you."

"Yes, it is my fault! I should have talked to you about it. If I had, we would have figured out what they were doing. Instead, I was hurt and afraid, and I buried myself in schoolwork and hid at school to block out the pain."

"Then it's as much my fault as yours. I should have gone after you, confronted you. If I had, everything would have turned out differently. We were both young and insecure, easily manipulated. But that's old history, Elliot. We're here now, you and me, together, and that's what matters. Now, about that kiss..."

She grins at me through her tears. And then, to my surprise, she reaches up and skims her fingers over my beard. "I like this. Your beard."

She proceeds to explore my face with gentle fingertips, as if learning me all over again. The pleasure of her touch is so exquisite I close my eyes and let it wash over me. She traces the crooked bridge of my nose. She traces the shape of my eyebrows and my brow. Then her fingers slide through my short hair and up into the longer bit on top, which she grips firmly, as if tethering me to her.

Her touch hits me like a blow, and I groan loudly. "Elliot."

"You're the same," she murmurs, "and yet so different."

She releases my hair and slides her hands down past my shoulders to my upper arms. "Your arms are freaking huge." She slides her cool fingers up beneath the short sleeves of my T-shirt and skims them over my biceps, sending a jolt of electricity down my spine, straight to my dick, which instantly begins to stiffen.

I laugh. "Are you trying to torture me?"

"I don't think I could ever get enough of touching you." Then her hands slide up to cup my face. "Jacob McIntyre."

She says my name like it's an oath. I grasp her waist and squeeze gently. "Yeah?"

Her voice is soft, almost wistful, as if she's dreaming. "You have no idea how I've longed for you."

"Oh, I think I do. I never stopped chasing you in my dreams."

We lost so much. But we've also been given another chance. A chance I'm not going to waste. I cradle her face in my hands and gaze down into big luminous pools of brown. "I love you, Annie Elliot. I've always loved you. I never stopped. And this time, I'm not letting you go. We're not kids this time. We don't have to worry about people interfering in our lives. If you want me, then you have me, from now until the end of eternity, just like we planned."

When I slide my hands from her waist up her torso, letting my thumbs brush against the plump sides of her breasts, she shivers. And when she opens her mouth on a gasp, I take advantage of the situation and press mine to hers, using my lips to coax hers apart.

I drink in the sounds she makes, reveling in the knowledge

that she's really here in my arms. In my world again. And damn it, I'm not going to lose her this time.

The kiss quickly turns heated, and we devour each other, our lips and tongues working feverishly to get reacquainted. The sounds she makes, those sweet, feminine whimpers, make me weak in the knees.

"Mommy!"

We both freeze, then break apart at the frantic voice coming from across the hall.

"Oh, my God! Aiden!" She jumps down from the countertop and scurries out of the bathroom. "I'm coming, sweetie!"

Aiden.

Jesus, there's a kid. It's not just the two of us now. Surely that's going to complicate things.

And then it dawns on me. *That's my kid now, too.*

Damn. I'm going to be a step-father.

* * *

I head out into the hallway to see what all the fuss is about. Aiden is sobbing his eyes out, poor kid, clinging to Annie for dear life, and Annie's trying to comfort him.

"I couldn't find you," Aiden cries, his face tucked against Annie's belly. He's got that dinosaur clutched in one arm and his other arm around his mom.

"Sweetheart, I'm sorry," she says, wincing apologetically. "I was talking to Mr. McIntyre. I was right across the hall the whole time." She points at my room. "Right in there."

"But I couldn't find you," he cries, sniffling against her top.

"Hey, Aiden," I say, in what I hope is a friendly voice. I know jack shit about kids, but I guess I'd better start learning as I fully intend to become an integral part of this kid's life. "Are you hungry? I'll bet lunch is ready. Do you want to go downstairs and find out?"

Aiden peers cautiously at me and nods.

"Aiden, you should answer Mr. McIntyre," Annie says. "It's not polite to—"

"No, it's okay," I say, crouching down beside Aiden. I wink at him. "We don't stand on ceremony around here. Whatever he's comfortable with is fine."

Charlie's door opens, and she strolls out dressed in ripped jeans and a superhero T-shirt.

As Aiden gets a look at Charlie's shirt, his eyes widen. "You like the Avengers? Me too! Who's your favorite?"

She winks at Annie. "I kind of have a thing for Thor."

"Cool!" Aiden says. "Mine's Ironman!" And then he extends his arms into the air and makes "whooshing" sounds as if he's flying.

Charlie nods in appreciation. "Good choice, dude. I approve."

I can tell by the smile on Annie's face that Charlie just hit one out of the park with the kid. I make a mental note to get myself an Ironman T-shirt as soon as possible, because scoring points with the kid is probably a surefire way to score points with the mom. I think a couple of dinosaur T-shirts wouldn't be out of line either.

"Who's ready for lunch?" I say, motioning toward the stairs.

"I am!" Aiden says, jumping up and down like a pogo stick, his recent trauma forgotten.

Annie smiles up at me, grateful for the distraction.

Charlie holds out her hand to the boy. "Come on, Aiden. Let's go see what Elly made us for lunch."

Aiden looks back at his mom, and then cautiously at me. He's so obviously torn between wanting to trust, and possibly have fun in the process, and fearing some kind of repercussion.

"Go ahead," I tell him, nodding toward the stairs. "Charlie doesn't bite."

Aiden glances up at Annie, who smiles gently and nods. "You can go with Charlie. It's okay."

Aiden lays his hand in Charlie's, and the two of them set off toward the stairs. I watch Annie as she watches her son walk away, a bittersweet smile on her face. She obviously loves her son dearly, and I'm glad the kid has such a great mom. Too bad his dad is a prick.

"Shall we?" I say to Annie, offering her my hand.

She grins bashfully as she takes it, and we head down the hallway after the others.

Walking with her gives me such a sense of déjà vu. We never missed an opportunity to walk together in the hallways at school. I study her out of the corner of my eye, taking in all the physical changes to her body and appreciating her new curves. Her hips are wider than they used to be, her butt more rounded, which is a huge plus. She's definitely filled out in adulthood. Motherhood likely had something to do with that.

Charlie and Aiden have pulled ahead of us and are already halfway down the stairs when Annie and I reach the second floor landing. She pauses for a moment and looks up at me. "Your friend Charlie is really good with Aiden. I can't thank you enough for asking her to come. He could really use a friend."

"I figured Aiden would feel safer with a female bodyguard than with a male. But don't let her easy-going ways fool you—she won't let anything happen to Aiden. Charlie is a mean, ass-kicking machine when the occasion calls for it."

She laughs. "I'm glad to hear that."

I walk her backward until she meets the wall and use my arms to cage her in. I lean close, pressing my body to hers, reveling in the feel of her breasts cushioned against my chest. I would so love to pick up where we left off in my room. I lean down and brush my nose against hers, then hover my lips above hers.

Her sweet lips curve into a playful grin, giving me a glimpse of the old Elliot. "Well, what are you waiting for?" she whispers.

"I'm waiting for you to tell me I can kiss you."

"Since when did you ever wait for an invitation?"

"Since I started worrying about fucking this up."

She smiles sadly, pressing her hands to the sides of my face. Her thumbs brush over my bottom lip, making me shudder. "You have nothing to worry about, Jake. Just kiss me."

"That's all I needed to know." I lower my mouth to hers, taking my sweet time so I can savor the anticipation.

She meets me halfway, lifting her mouth to mine, and when

our lips touch, it's electric. She gasps, and I groan, and we give in to years of pent-up longing. I press into her, one arm going around her waist and the other hand cradling the back of her head. I can't get enough. I'll never get enough.

"Mommy! Are you coming?"

Annie breaks our kiss, breathing hard, and I step back to give her some space. *Slow down, man. Don't rush her.*

"We should go downstairs," she says, ducking past me to get to the stairs. "They're waiting for us."

I follow her at a more sedate pace, hoping to give my erection time to settle down before I join the others.

✎ 10

Annie

I practically race through the foyer to the back of the house where 1 can hear Aiden and Charlie talking. My heart is racing, and I have to shake myself out of a sexual stupor. I lose my head when I'm around Jake. It's like my brain goes on hiatus, and my ovaries explode.

He was always a big kid in school—the hotshot, high school quarterback—but now he has a man's body, all hard planes and rough edges. He's lost what little softness he had back in his teenage years. His physique now is hard and unrelenting, and ridiculously sexy. How am I supposed to think clearly when I'm around him? It's impossible.

Upstairs just now, I was overcome by a wave of sexual heat so intense it left me hot and aching in a place that hasn't felt want or need in a very long time.

I simply can't imagine what it would be like to have all that masculine intensity directed at me. We're both adults, and we're both single, so really there's nothing keeping us apart. But when I hear Aiden's voice, I realize that's not exactly true. I have Aiden to think about now. I can't jump into bed with a man just because I want to.

"There's a little swimming pool in our bathroom!" Aiden is telling Charlie when I join them in the great room. He's gazing up at her with a beaming smile. Charlie obviously puts him at ease, and I'm grateful to her for that. He needs all the friends he can get. "Mommy said I can take a bath in it tonight."

"There's a real swimming pool downstairs, Aiden," Jake says, as he walks into the room a few seconds behind me. "I'm sure Charlie will take you swimming if you ask her."

Aiden eyes Jake. "A *real* pool?"

"Yep."

My son looks more than a little skeptical. "Downstairs? You mean, like *in* the house?"

"Yes. It's *in* the house. It's indoors so we can use it all year around. If we want to go swimming outside when it's nice, we swim in the pond or in Lake Michigan."

Aiden shakes his head and laughs. "There's no pool in the house. You're just foolin' with me."

Charlie laughs. "He's right, Aiden. There is a pool downstairs. I'll show you after lunch."

"But I don't know how to swim."

"Do you want me to teach you?" she says. "Every kid needs to know how to swim."

"Yeah! If my mom says it's okay."

Charlie glances at me. "Is it okay if I teach Aiden how to swim?"

I nod. "That would be wonderful."

The great room is impressive, with its soaring ceilings. The massive wooden beams overhead and the two-story stone hearth give the place the feeling of a ski lodge. The room is divided into several cozy seating areas, and there's a bar in the back corner near the sliding glass doors leading out onto a deck.

Elly comes through a side door carrying a tray of food. "The weather is so nice today, I thought you might want to eat outside."

Charlie opens the door for Elly, and then she and Aiden follow Elly outside.

I stop at the door, watching Elly arrange Aiden's plate and glass of milk on one of numerous bistro tables arranged on the deck. Jake comes up behind me and lays his hands on my shoulders, squeezing gently. The feel of his hands on me makes me shiver. I really want to sink back against him.

"I have to think about Aiden," I say, as reality hits me. "I can't just—we can't—he might not understand."

"I know. Trust me, I want what's best for him, too."

"It's just that… it would be hard for him to understand, you know. He has enough to deal with right now, with the divorce, with his father, and with us moving in with my parents."

"I know." Jake gently pushes me through the door and out onto the deck. "Come on."

Instead of heading toward the table Aiden and Charlie are sharing, Jake steers me to a table for two in the back corner of the deck. "Let's sit here so we can talk," he says, pulling out a chair for me. Then he takes the chair next to mine.

Elly was certainly right. It's a beautiful summer day. It's pleasantly warm, but not too hot, and we're saved by a light breeze. The lake view is superb. There are plenty of boat enthusiasts taking advantage of the nice weather. There's a veritable parade of sailboats and yachts making their way up and down the coastline.

I watch Aiden digging in to his peanut butter and jelly sandwich with gusto. It looks like he has carrot sticks on his plate, too, with some kind of dip, and a bowl of fresh-cut fruit.

Elly returns shortly with lunches for the grown-ups, turkey club sandwiches with potato chips and fresh fruit. "What would you like to drink?" she asks me.

"Water would be great, thank you."

"And for you, honey?" she asks Jake.

"I'll have a Coke."

"Coming right up." Elly looks at me again. "How about pasta for supper? I was thinking Fettucine Alfredo with garlic bread and roasted veggies. And a cheesecake with strawberry topping for dessert. Does that sound good?"

"That sounds delicious," I say. "But please, don't go to any trouble on our account. I can help—"

"Thank you for the offer, dear, but it's not necessary." She pats my shoulder. "It's always a pleasure to have guests to cook for. George and I end up eating the same old sandwiches night after night in the kitchen. Having guests gives me an excuse to make something special and serve dinner on the nice china in the dining room."

Once she's back inside the house, Jake turns his chair slightly to face mine. "We need to talk, Annie. I have questions."

My pulse starts racing. "Okay. What do you want to know?"

"Let's start with the easy stuff. I need to know what your schedules look like. In other words, what are you going to be missing for the foreseeable future? Work? School? Any other commitments?"

"Well, Aiden goes to a year-around pre-school. And I recently cut back to working part time at my father's company. I'm just helping out on odd projects right now, so he can easily reassign my work."

"Anything else?"

"No. Not really. We've been keeping a low profile since the divorce. Other than going to Aiden's school and my part-time job, we generally don't leave my parents' house."

Jake frowns. "I'd prefer it if Aiden didn't go to school right now. Ted already tried to grab him there once. Can you homeschool him for a while?"

"Sure. That's no problem."

"Good. I don't want him going back until Patterson is contained. We'll keep him here at home with us."

I nod, trying not to be distracted by how much I liked hearing him say *we* and *home* and *us*.

"So, there's nothing else on your calendar?" he says. "No meetings, doctor appointments, anything like that in the near future?"

"Nothing."

He grins. "Okay. Now we get to the hard part. I need to know
about your ex-husband."

And here it is... the elephant in the room. *My marriage.* My
ex-husband who turned out to be a big mistake. I laugh bitterly.
"You weren't kidding. This is definitely the hard part. It's not easy
for me to talk about Ted."

He reaches for my hand, bringing it to lie on his rock-hard
thigh. He covers my hand with his, and I can feel his muscles
bunching and flexing underneath my palm. A rush of heat settles
deep in my core, and my sex tightens.

Jake strokes the back of my hand with warm, gentle fingers,
and it feels so good I just want to close my eyes and think about
nothing else.

"I'm sorry, Annie, but I need to know." There's no censure in
his tone. No recrimination. Just quiet acceptance.

Not ready to face him, I look away with a sigh. "When I came
back to Chicago after graduating college, you were long gone. My
father told me you'd married and joined the military. I started
working right away for my father's accounting firm. That's where
I met Ted. He was a junior partner already at the age of twen-
ty-eight. He had a bright career ahead of him. My parents invited
him over for dinner a lot. I think they wanted us to get together."

I pause, taking a moment to stare out over the water, watching sailboats and yachts skim over the water as if they had no cares in the world. Knowing what I know now, that my parents deceived me, I feel anger simmering beneath my skin. How could they have done this to us? I know they never approved of Jake, but still—how could they go that far?

Jake squeezes my hand. "He must have been good to you in the beginning, or you wouldn't have married him."

I nod. "He was. He was polite and funny. He was very much a gentleman in the old-fashioned kind of way, opening doors for me, that sort of thing." *But he never made my heart race the way you did with just a look.*

"What happened?"

"I'm not sure," I say. "We were pretty happy in the beginning— or at least I thought we were. Life was peaceful enough."

"Did you love him?" This he asks hesitantly, as if he's not sure he wants to know the answer.

I shake my head and finally glance at him. "Like a friend, maybe."

It's hard to watch the sadness and anger warring in his expression. I'm not exactly sure who the anger is directed at. Me? Or at my parents? If they know what's good for them, they'll steer clear of Jake for the foreseeable future.

He starts rubbing the back of my hand, as if to soften his words. "If you didn't love him, why did you marry him?"

"I was lonely and hurting so badly. I felt lost without you. I needed someone...to fill the void. If it couldn't be you, I didn't really care much who it was."

Elly brings our drinks out, and I pull my hand out from beneath his, resting mine in my lap. "Thanks, Elly," I say, giving her a smile.

Once she leaves, I take a long sip of my chilled water and let the iciness numb my tight throat.

Taking a deep breath, I figure I might as well get this over with. "As I said, things seemed okay in the beginning. A few years into the marriage, I told him I wanted to start a family. He agreed, and we started trying, but we didn't have much luck. We tried for several years without success, and I'd just about given up hope when out of the blue, I found myself pregnant. I was elated. Ted wasn't. He grew more and more distant, never showing any interest in the pregnancy. Then, after Aiden was born, things quickly got worse. He almost seemed to resent Aiden. Ted became angry so easily. He would fly into a rage at the slightest provocation. And over time, it just got worse."

I swallow hard against the painful lump in my throat. "Maybe it's my fault for marrying someone I didn't really love. I *liked* him. I *cared* about him. But I didn't *love* him." And then I look Jake in the eye. "I knew I'd never love anyone the way I loved you. I figured what I felt for Ted was enough. Apparently, it wasn't. I think Ted suspected as much, and over time, it started to eat at him. When Aiden was about a year old, Ted accused me of having had an affair. Because Aiden didn't look anything like him, Ted decided that Aiden wasn't his. Ted's a blond, you know, and Aiden has brown hair."

"Just like his mom," Jake says. "Aiden clearly takes after you.

Who did Ted think Aiden's father was?"

I meet Jake's gaze, facing my pain head on. "You."

Jake looks dumbfounded. "*Me?*" He lets out a harsh breath. "Jesus. I wasn't even in Chicago at the time."

"It didn't matter. That's when I learned about his drug use. He'd been using heroin for a while with some friends. The drug use escalated, and soon it was painfully obvious that he was addicted."

Jake pinches the bridge of his nose and shakes his head. "When did he start hurting you?"

"After he started using drugs. First, it was little things. He'd get mad at me over silly stuff, like his dinner getting cold, or he didn't like what I made. Gradually, it got worse. I think the older Aiden got, the worse Ted got. As you said, Aiden takes after me. Ted would make off-handed comments about Aiden looking like his *dad*. And of course, in his mind, that wasn't him."

Our conversation is cut short when Aiden hops down from his chair and runs to our table. "I'm done, Mommy! Can I go down to the beach with Charlie? She said she'd take me to look for shells!"

"I don't know, sweetie," I say, hesitating. I glance at Jake. "Aiden doesn't know how to swim." It makes me nervous when he's around water.

Charlie rises from her seat and joins us. "Don't worry, Annie," she says, laying her hands on Aiden's shoulders. "I've got this."

Jake nods. "He'll be fine."

"Okay." I reach for Aiden's hand. "You do what Charlie says, all right? And be careful not to get Stevie wet."

"Thanks! I won't." Aiden takes Charlie's hand and drags her

across the deck to the steps leading down to the lawn.

"Aiden needs to learn how to swim," Jake says as he watches the two of them race down the path to the beach. "There's a lot of water around here. It's a safety issue."

I nod. "I just never got around to enrolling him in lessons."

"Charlie and I will teach him."

We watch as Charlie and Aiden reach the private beach and sit down on a fallen log to remove their shoes and socks and roll up their pant legs. It looks like Charlie is successful in talking Aiden into leaving Stevie behind, perched on the log, as they go wading through the water.

Charlie has a tight hold on Aiden's hand as he stomps through the cold Lake Michigan surf. A surge of water washes up on the shore, halfway up Aiden's shins, and he squeals with delight.

"Charlie's a godsend," I say.

She's got a killer fit body, but then I guess that would be a requirement for a bodyguard. She's beautiful, with her lovely brown skin and big dark eyes, and her ready smile. Her hair is pulled up onto the top of her head, the short strands curling tightly. I would imagine Charlie has men dropping at her feet wherever she goes.

I glance at Jake, who's watching them with an indulgent smile. "You and Charlie seem pretty close."

Jake laughs as Aiden jumps in the incoming rush of water. "Yeah, we are. She's been part of my team for a couple of years now."

"You two aren't—I mean, you've never..." I stop mid-sentence, embarrassed when he turns incredulous eyes on me.

"Are you asking me if Charlie and I have ever been involved?" My face heats up. "I guess so. I mean, she's very attractive."

"Yes, she's very attractive." He's clearly trying not to laugh. "But no, we've never been involved. *Never.*" His expression sobers. "Annie, I can't say I've been a monk since high school, but I've never been with Charlie. I've never been with any of my co-workers. I don't mix business with pleasure."

"What am I then? Surely I'm a little bit of both."

He reaches for my hand and kisses the back of it. "You are an exception."

Jake's smile falls, his expression suddenly turning solemn. "Back to our discussion."

"What else do you want to know?"

"In order for my guys to figure him out and find a suitable resolution to this situation, we need to know everything. Who were these friends of his? Where does he get the drugs? Who is his supplier?"

‿ 11

Annie

J ake fixes his gaze out over the lake, staring at something in the distance. I answer his questions, sharing what little I know about Ted's drug use and who he got the drugs from. He never said much about it to me. Jake clenches his jaws, his cheek muscles tightening and releasing. He closes his eyes for a moment, inhaling a deep breath and blowing it out hard through tight lips.

By the time he looks at me again, his emotions are once more under control. "Jesus, Elliot, if I'd known any of this, I would have done something about it. I swear. But I had no idea."

"I know you didn't. Our paths never crossed. There's no way you could have known. Honestly, I was shocked when my father told me he'd talked to Shane about hiring private security."

Jake sits quietly, saying nothing—just waiting for me to continue.

"I've hurt so many people, Jake. First you, and then Ted."

"You are not responsible for Ted's actions. There's no excuse for a man to hurt a woman. You aren't to blame for his actions. If he knew you were in love with someone else, and yet he married you anyway, then it's as much his own fault as anyone's."

I've carried this guilt inside me for years. It's been a constant source of pain, of shame. Of self-loathing.

Jake's lips flatten. "Did your parents know how things were between you two?"

"No. Not for a long time. I tried to keep it all to myself. But when Ted started in on Aiden, I couldn't keep it a secret any longer."

Jake lets out a pained groan as he runs his fingers through his hair. He stands abruptly, brushing a hand over his beard and mouth. He looks toward the shoreline, where Aiden is happily digging in the sand with a stick while Charlie watches over him, the two of them chatting companionably.

"You have no idea—" Jake says. Then he stops himself and sits back down, all business once more. "I don't understand how anyone could hurt a child. Tell me about the divorce."

"He was using pretty heavily by that time. He'd stay out late and come home high several nights a week. He started hanging out with some pretty awful people—I think they were the ones who were supplying him with drugs. I told him it had to stop, or I'd leave him."

"What did he say to that?"

"He broke my right arm and said that if I threatened to leave him again, it would be my neck the next time." Absently, I rub my right forearm.

Jake rises abruptly from his seat once more. "I'm going inside to grab a cold drink. Can I get you anything?"

"No, I'm fine. Thanks."

I watch Jake's retreating back as he disappears inside the house. I don't blame him for needing a moment. He's clearly upset by the things I'm telling him, and I appreciate that he's trying hard to keep his cool.

A few moments later he returns to the table and opens another soft drink. Funny, I expected him to grab a beer. I remember his fondness for stealing beers from his dad's stash when we were in high school.

He catches me eyeing his choice of beverage. "I don't drink alcohol anymore. I got into trouble with it and had to give it up."

"Trouble?"

"I never wrecked or hurt anyone, but I did get pulled over by the cops a couple times. After my second DUI, the judge gave me a choice: either go to jail or join the military. I opted for the military—the Marines. It was the best thing I ever did. They kicked my ass and put me back together again."

He jumps right back into painful territory. "Eventually, Ted lost his job?"

"Yes. The drug use got so bad that he was missing a lot of work. His manager fired him, and things quickly got worse. The money soon ran out, and Ted went into debt with his supplier. That's when he started selling, trying to pay off his debt with his dealer. He got more and more angry, and he'd fly into a rage at the slightest thing. He'd get mad at me for no reason. If Aiden knocked something over or dropped something, Ted would rail at him."

Jake shakes his head in disbelief. "He hurt Aiden."

"Yes. He'd kick him, knock him down. He whipped him viciously once with a belt." I shudder at the painful memories. "When I'd get between Ted and Aiden, Ted would go berserk." I hold up my right hand, staring at the crooked little finger. "He broke my pinkie for getting between them. When I told my parents, they moved us out of our apartment and into their home. I filed for divorce shortly after. Ted wanted us to come back, but I told him no. Over my dead body would I let him hurt Aiden again."

Jake downs the rest of his soft drink in one long swallow and stands. "Patterson will never hurt you or Aiden again. I guarantee it."

I can practically feel the nervous energy radiating from him.

"How about that tour?" he says, abruptly changing the subject. His entire demeanor changes, as if he's trying to shake off painful feelings. "For the sake of my own credibility, I need to show Aiden there is indeed a pool downstairs."

I stand, grateful this conversation is over—at least for now.

"That sounds like a great idea."

Jake whistles, catching Charlie's attention. He gives her a hand signal. While Charlie is rounding up Aiden, his shoes and socks, Stevie, and his collection of beach souvenirs, I gather up our plates and carry them inside.

"Oh, my goodness, you didn't have to do that," Elly says when she sees me enter the kitchen with a stack of plates in my hands. She wipes her wet hands on a dishtowel. "I'll clean up, honey. You just relax and enjoy yourself."

"Thank you, but I want to help out, really. I wouldn't feel right if I didn't."

She meets me halfway, taking the dishes from me. "That's very sweet of you. Thank you."

I do want to be useful, but the truth is I need a moment to collect myself. Telling Jake about my history with Ted was difficult, but seeing his raw reactions was even more painful. It clearly hurt Jake to hear these things.

Elly sets the plates on the counter near the sink. "Did you get enough to eat? Did Aiden?"

"Yes, thank you. Lunch was delicious."

Elly's warm smile seems perfectly genuine, and I wonder if she knows about my history with Jake. I suspect she doesn't, because if she did, she probably wouldn't be quite so welcoming. I'm sure his entire family resents me for what happened, or at least they'd resent my parents if they knew the whole truth. I certainly wouldn't blame them.

"Annie?" Jake's standing in the kitchen doorway. "Are you

ready for the tour?"

Elly shoos me toward the door. "Go have fun. I'll see you at supper. We'll have a big family meal in the dining room."

❧ 12

Jake

Seeing Shane's estate through Aiden's eyes gives me a whole new appreciation for the place. I've grown accustomed to it, and I guess I'd lost sight of how *awesome* it is—Aiden's word.

They'd already seen the great room and the kitchen, so I show them the dining room and the library. That's about it for interesting highlights on the first floor. The north wing is just a bunch of meeting rooms for clients, *boring* according to Aiden, and we skip the south wing, which is where the on-site security staff live and work.

But the lower level—that's where the fun is. We head down the stairs, and I show Aiden the arcade, the theater, the work-out room, and of course the pool.

He stands in front of the double glass doors and stares at the Olympic-sized swimming pool. "Wow!" Then he looks up at me, his eyes wide. "How did you get a swimming pool inside the house?"

I laugh. When I reach out to him, intending to ruffle his hair, he flinches, drawing away from me and slipping behind Annie.

Annie gives me an apologetic smile as she reaches back to re-assure her son. "I'm sorry," she says to me. "He—"

"No, it's okay. I understand." *Shit.*

"Hey, Aiden," Charlie says, opening the pool room door, letting out a waft of warm, humid air heavily scented with chlorine. "Let's check out the pool."

Aiden follows Charlie through the doors. Clearly, he's not afraid of *her*. Just *me*.

"I'm sorry about that," Annie says, once the doors close behind them. "He's a little skittish around men."

My jaw clenches as I ponder how one goes about making friends with a traumatized five-year-old. "Don't worry, it's fine. I certainly don't blame Aiden." No, it's the father I blame.

I open the door and motion for Annie to precede me into the pool room. Aiden's laughter echoes through the cavernous room as he and Charlie wade barefoot in just a few inches of water at the zero-entry end of the pool. They've already discarded their socks and shoes and rolled up their jeans.

Aiden's practically bouncing with excitement as he scoops up water and sends it airborne. "Mommy, can I get in the pool? Charlie said she'd teach me how to swim!"

"That sounds great, but, sweetie, we didn't bring our swimsuits."

"Not a problem," I say. "Shane keeps the locker rooms stocked with new swim gear in every size and style imaginable for visiting guests. Aiden can help himself. So can you, if you'd like to get in the water, too."

"Yay!" Aiden cries, having decided the question has been settled. He grabs Charlie's hand and jumps up and down.

While Charlie takes the kid to the boys' locker room, presumably to help him pick out a pair of swim trunks, I step in front of Annie and cup her face with my hands. "Swim with me." We used to love swimming together in the neighborhood pool. In the summers, we'd spend hours goofing around in the water.

When she bites her lip, looking torn, I brush my thumb across it, freeing it from torment. "What's wrong, Elliot?"

She's distracted when Aiden comes tearing out of the boys' locker room wearing a pair of blue and neon green boys' board shorts. She smiles as she watches him set Stevie and a beach towel on a lounge chair at a safe distance from the water.

A moment later, when Charlie exits the women's locker room wearing a form-fitting, Navy blue one-piece swimsuit, Annie frowns.

"Hey," I say, catching her attention. "What's wrong? You used to love swimming."

She sighs. "I'm not eighteen anymore, you know."

"What's that supposed to mean?"

She looks at me with exasperation, as if I'm an idiot for not getting her meaning.

"Spell it out, babe. I'm not following."

"It's just that I'm not the svelte young girl you remember. In case you haven't noticed, I've put on a few pounds since then."

I bark out a laugh, earning myself a scowl. "Oh, yeah, I've noticed."

She flashes me an angry look. "Oh, thanks for pointing that out."

"Are you talking about these curves?" I run my hands down her sides, over her waist and hips, then I slide them around so I can cup her round ass in my hands. "You mean this bodacious ass?"

She shoves my hands away. "Jake, stop! It's not just the weight." She lowers her voice. "I have stretch marks, from pregnancy."

I feel a momentary pang of jealousy when she mentions her pregnancy. It should have been me who got her pregnant. *Fuck.*

Despite the flash of pain, though, I can't help smiling at her obvious discomfort, which is completely misplaced. I lean closer and whisper in her ear. "I've noticed the changes to your body, and I damn well like them. In fact, I love them. There's more for me to love, more for me to grasp." I lean close and lower my voice. "When I look at you, Elliot, I get hard. How do you think I'm going to manage hiding an erection in a pair of swim trunks?"

She pushes me back playfully, her frown morphing into a reluctant grin. "Oh, stop it."

I reach for her hips. "I'm dead serious."

"Are you coming, Mommy?" Aiden calls from the shallow end of the pool, where he's wading in a foot of water under the watchful eye of Charlie.

She sighs. "Yes, I'm coming." Then she looks up at me. "Behave yourself. My son is watching."

"Yes, ma'am." I give her a little salute, and then I take her hand and lead her to the locker rooms. I nudge her toward the door to the women's. "Pick out a suit and get changed. I'll meet you in the pool."

Reluctantly, Annie walks into the women's locker room, and I head into the men's to my personal locker, where I keep a pair of board shorts. I quickly strip down naked and pull on a pair of black swim trunks. Glancing down, I skim my eyes over the black tattooed letters and numbers taking up residence on the left side of my torso. It's too soon for Annie to see this, so I pull on a dark gray swim shirt to hide the tattoo. I'm going to look pretty foolish wearing a swim shirt at an indoor pool, but I'm not ready for her to see this. I know she'll see it eventually—sooner rather than later, I hope—but not right this minute.

When I come back out, Aiden and Charlie are splashing each other. There's no sign of Annie.

"She hasn't come out yet?" I say to Charlie.

Charlie shakes her head. "Nope."

So I wait. And I wait. And just when I think she might have gotten cold feet and changed her mind about swimming, the door to the women's locker room opens and Annie pokes her head out.

"It's about time, Elliot," I say, trying to make light of her hesitation. I hold my hand out to her, motioning her forward. "I was about to send a search-and-rescue team after you."

She laughs nervously, and then she takes a deep breath and walks out wearing a floral one-piece swimsuit with a fitted top and a flouncy skirt. She picked the busiest damn suit in there, but it does nothing to camouflage her generous curves. *Dear God.* It's a good thing my board shorts are baggy enough to camouflage my growing hard-on, or I'd be displaying a lot more than I should in front of an audience.

I swallow, my throat suddenly gone dry. What I wouldn't give to peel that swimsuit off her, slowly, exposing inch after inch of her delectable body. *Damn.*

I need to get in the pool before I embarrass her and myself. I motion for her to follow me as I wade into the water. Aiden splashes me, and I splash him back. Then I execute a shallow dive and swim underwater the entire length of the pool before surfacing at the deep end, beneath the diving boards. When I turn to face the others, treading in deep water, Annie's just wading into the shallow end.

Aiden's excited to see his mom in the pool, and he's kicking up water and splashing her. She squeals and runs from the splashes, but I think it's mostly for Aiden's sake. Annie's a great swimmer, and she was always a good sport. She never minded getting splashed or dunked.

As soon as she's waist deep in the water, Annie dives below the surface and swims toward me, eventually coming up beside me with a gasp. She pushes her wet hair out of her face.

"Wanna race?" I ask her, remembering how we used to challenge each other in the water. Who could stay underwater the longest? Who could swim the fastest? Dive the deepest? We were so competitive.

"I'm so out of shape," she says, breathing hard. "I haven't swum in so long, I barely remember how."

"It's like riding a bike. You never forget."

I heave myself out of the pool and climb the ladder to the high dive. Aiden stops what he's doing to watch me. I'm not above showing off a little for the kid—and maybe for the mom, too—so I line myself up to do a backflip off the high dive. When I surface, Aiden's out of the pool and racing along the edge toward us in the deep end.

"Walk, Aiden!" Annie says.

The kid slows to a fast walk, his wide eyes locked on me. "Can you teach me to do that?"

I swim to the side of the pool and look up at him. "You have to learn how to swim first."

Aiden nods eagerly. "I will! I promise. Can I come in there with you guys?"

"Sure," I say, holding my hands out to him. "Jump in, pal."

Aiden looks less than sure about this. He gives his mom a beseeching look, as if he's not sure if he wants her to say yes, or no. "Can I, Mommy?"

"Yes. Just be careful."

Aiden holds out his arms and leans over the water.

I move a little closer to him, holding out my hands. "Come on, buddy. Jump." I can tell he really wants to, but he's scared. "It's okay, Aiden. I'll catch you. I promise."

Aiden glances at Annie, who nods. "It's okay, honey. Jake will catch you."

The kid takes a deep breath, then launches himself in my direction. I snatch him out of the air right before he hits the water. He squeals, then clings to me like a frightened little monkey, his arms tight around my neck.

I secure him with an arm around his waist, and I use my free arm to tread water. "It's okay, pal. Relax. I've got you."

"Did you see me, Mommy?" he says. "I did it!"

"Yes, you did," Annie says. "Good job, honey."

"Come on, let's swim back to the shallow end." I tow Aiden back to the other end of the pool and hand him over to Charlie. "Do me a favor and teach him to swim, will ya?"

She grins. "I will."

I swim back to Annie, who's watching me with a smile on her face.

"What's that for?" I ask her.

"What's what?"

"That smile."

She shrugs. "Nothing. It's just that you're really good with kids."

"He's a great kid." I move in a bit closer, treading water less than an arm's length from her. "You must be very proud of him."

"I am. Aiden is without a doubt the best thing I've ever done.

Despite everything he's been through, everything he's seen, he's a good boy with a kind and loving heart. That's all a mother can ask for."

I drift closer to Annie, and she backs up until she's got herself pinned in the corner. As I glide in closer, letting my body drift against hers, her eyes widen and her cheeks flush a pretty shade of pink. I'm pretty sure the blush is because my erection is nudging her belly.

"Jake..."

"Hmm?"

She glances nervously over my shoulder at Aiden.

"Don't worry," I tell her. "He's not paying us any attention."

Aiden is quite happily preoccupied with his first official swimming lesson. *Thank you, Charlie.*

When Annie turns her gaze back to mine, her eyes are filled with a myriad of emotions. Uncertainty, arousal.

I dip my head and kiss the spot where her shoulder meets her neck. "Put your hands on me, Elliot. Hold on."

Annie lets go of the wall and slides her arms around my neck, which brings her body more fully against mine. I hook one of her legs with my arm and wrap it around me. Her other leg follows on its own accord, and when I feel her core pressing against my belly, I shudder.

"You're killing me, Elliot," I choke out. My throat is squeezed tight, and my heart is pounding. Her sweet spot is barely inches away from where I want it to be, and all I can think about is sinking inside her. I could lose my shorts in the pool and slide that little scrap of fabric between her legs to the side, uncovering her, and then slide in. No one would even know.

Damn, I've never felt so desperate.

ও 13

Jake

Annie smiles, but it's bittersweet. Sweet that we're together again, quite unexpectedly, but there's also an undeniable sense of bitterness for the time we've lost.

Her voice drops to a whisper. "Jake." She keeps glancing nervously over my shoulder at her son. "He'll be confused. He won't understand."

I brush back her wet hair. "We'll take it slowly, I promise. He's your son, and that makes him important to me." I wince at the sharp stab of pain I feel. I don't resent her for having a child—I would never think that. It just... hurts that he isn't mine.

"I'm so sorry." Her eyes fill with tears.

I lean in for a quick kiss. "Shh. It's okay. Water under the bridge, right?"

She nods, but I can feel her limbs shaking. We both know the truth. The damage can't ever be undone.

I cup the back of her neck. "I'm not going to lose you again," I tell her, and yes, it sounds like a vow. Because it is.

She nods. "Me too."

I glance behind me and see Aiden and Charlie laying on their bellies in the shallow water, facing away from us. Charlie demonstrates basic arm strokes for Aiden, who copies her movements. Taking advantage of the moment, I cup the back of Annie's head and bring her toward me for a kiss. Our lips cling, gently moving in tandem, and it's a slow, languid kiss. When I release her, she's breathless, her face flushed and her eyes bright.

Her position has shifted, and now my erection is pressing insistently against the soft place between her legs, causing me sheer agony. "You're going to be the death of me," I say, laughing.

She smiles. "I could say the same about you."

All I can think about is getting her alone in my room, in my bed. Or anywhere, really. I'll settle for the locker room. I just need to be inside her again. I need to bury myself in her and reclaim what's mine. "When can I have you again, because you're killing me, babe."

"I don't know." She frowns. "I need time to tell Aiden about you. About us."

We break apart guiltily when we hear Aiden running down the

side of the pool toward us. "Mommy, I did it! I'm learning how to swim." He stands at the side of the pool, bouncing eagerly. "Can I jump in again?"

I hold my hands out to him, jumping at the chance to score more points with the kid. "Sure, buddy. Hop in."

Aiden doesn't need a second invitation. He throws his arms wide and launches himself into the air. I catch him before he hits the water to keep his head from going under. He laughs as he wraps his arms and legs around me, while I tread water, keeping us afloat.

"Can I jump off the diving board?" he asks me, looking hopeful.

"You think you're ready for that?"

Aiden nods.

"Okay." I take him to the edge of the pool and lift him out. "Walk to the diving board and climb up."

He hustles to the board and climbs the ladder. Once he's at the end of the board, he pinches his nose closed. "Here I come, Jake! Catch me!"

He bounces a few times, as if trying to work up the nerve to jump. But he just stands there, staring down at me. Treading water below him, I wait, wondering if he's actually going to go through with it. The wait stretches out, with Aiden staring at the water. I'm sure it looks like quite a drop from his perspective.

"It's okay, honey," Annie says. "You can do it. Jake will catch you."

Aiden looks at me, clearly torn. Then he shakes his head. "I can't."

I move right beneath the end of the diving board and reach up with both hands. "Sit down on the board and let me catch you."

Aiden sits and dangles his legs over the edge.

"Come on, buddy, I've got you."

Gingerly, he lets himself slide over the end of the board and fall the short distance into my hands.

"I did it, Mommy!" he crows, clearly proud of himself. "I jumped off the board."

After letting Aiden have a few more pseudo-jumps off the board, we call it a day and head to the locker rooms to dry off and change back into our clothes. Annie lets me take Aiden into the men's room with me, while she and Charlie go into the women's.

After I help him dry off and put his clothes on, Aiden wanders around the locker room, going on and on about the diving board and wanting to learn to swim, giving me a chance to dry off and get dressed.

"Can we go swimming again tomorrow?" he asks as we hang up our wet suits to dry.

With hair the same shade of dark chocolate as his mom's, and those big brown eyes, he reminds me so much of Annie that it makes my chest hurt. He's part of her. *How can I not love him too?* They're a package deal. If she's going to be mine, which she damn well is, then he's mine too.

"Sure. We can swim every day if you want."

"I do!" He beams at me. "I can't wait to learn how to swim by myself. Can I jump off the board all by myself then?"

I smile at him, reaching out impulsively to ruffle his tousled wet hair. This time, he doesn't flinch. He doesn't even blink. The realization that he's starting to trust me makes my chest swell with an unfamiliar emotion. "You bet."

"I like it here," he says as we're sitting side by side on a bench, putting on our socks and sneakers. "I'm glad we came."

"So am I, pal."

* * *

After swimming, I take Annie and Aiden outside and show them around the grounds. Of course the first thing Aiden wants to do is visit the barn, so we head that way. Aiden runs ahead with Charlie, eager to see the horses. Annie and I follow at a more sedate pace, falling behind the others.

I hold my hand out to her, and after a moment of indecision, she takes it.

"I'm sorry," she says, squeezing my hand. "If it was just me, I wouldn't hesitate. But it's not just me. I have to think about Aiden."

"I get it. I do. And it's okay. We'll move at his pace."

She frowns. "I need to talk to him, try to explain."

I nod, then bend over and lift her into a fireman's hold over my shoulder and march down the path toward the barn.

Annie squeals good-naturedly. "Oh, my goodness, Jake! Put me down!"

Laughing, Aiden comes running back to join us. "Can I have a turn?"

I let Annie slide down to the ground, then swing Aiden up so that he's sitting on my shoulders.

Towering above us, he's holding on to me with one hand, and clutching his dinosaur with the other. "Mommy! Look how high I am!"

"I see that," she says, reaching up to take Stevie from him, so he can hold on with both hands.

Annie smiles at me, and I wink at her. I can do this dad thing. I know I can.

"All right, let's go see some horses," I say, and we start down the path toward the barn.

The trail is a little rocky in places.

"Don't let me fall, Jake," Aiden says, tightening his grasp on my head.

I've got a tight grip on his legs. He's going nowhere. "Don't worry, buddy. I've got you."

Aiden and I lead the way, with the girls following behind us, chatting and laughing at something. Probably at us.

When we reach the corral, I sit Aiden on the top rung of the fence, holding him securely by the waist. He grips my arms tightly as he gains his balance.

The horses are in the corral, and one of them—a friendly gelding—comes over to check us out. Aiden shies away from the inquisitive horse, leaning back against me.

"It's okay, Aiden." I tighten my grip on the boy. "He won't hurt you."

The gelding sniffs Aiden's sneakers and his jeans before lifting his big boxy head to nuzzle the boy's hand.

"He's looking for a snack," I say. "Next time, we'll bring some treats for the horses. Would you like that?"

"Okay." Aiden sounds rather hesitant as he continues to lean away from the horse, pressing back into me. "I want down now."

I set Aiden on the grass beside me, and he slips his hand in mine. Then he reaches for Annie's hand, and the three of us stand at the fence holding hands.

Charlie, who's standing on my other side, nudges me with her elbow. "Good job, dad."

This kid is going to be the death of me. I feel a surge of intense emotion, followed by a sharp spike of anger directed at his father. The thought that anyone would hurt this innocent little boy makes me want to break something with my bare hands. The idea that his own father would hurt him—*fuck!*

I catch Annie's gaze, and I can tell she's feeling it too—this connection among the three of us.

The three of us.

As in, we're a family now.

And just like that, Aiden's mine. It doesn't matter that I didn't father him. I don't care that he's not mine by blood. He's mine now, and I'll protect him with everything I've got.

Aiden releases our hands so he can pluck tall grasses from the ground and feed them through the fence to the horse.

Annie's face wavers in front of me, and I find myself blinking away tears. When I look back at her, I see I'm not the only one with damp eyes. She leans toward me, meeting me halfway, and we share a quiet kiss.

Family.

Yeah, we're on the same page.

✐ 14

Annie

After our visit to the barn, we're all more than ready for dinner when Elly summons us by ringing the dinner bell. We head back to the house, entering through the front doors.

"I'm taking Aiden upstairs to clean up before supper," I say, taking my son by his grubby little hand and leading him to the stairs.

"I'll come with you," Jake says, following us up.

When we reach our room, I open the door and usher Aiden inside. "Use the potty and wash your hands really well."

Aiden runs off to the bathroom, and when I start to follow him, Jake grabs my hand and pulls me back out into the hallway. "What—"

"Come with me," he says, opening his door and pulling me into his room.

"Aiden will wonder where I am."

Jake closes the door partway, then presses me up against the wall, grinning at me. "I figure we've got three minutes before he yells for you."

And then his mouth is on mine, hungry and fierce, and my head spins. He groans, the sound low and rough, and I lose myself in him. His hands are everywhere, on my face, on my shoulders before skimming down my arms. He links his fingers with mine and raises our hands, holding them to the wall above my head.

My heart pounds as liquid heat pools at my core, making me hot and achy. The rush of need I feel takes my breath away.

He releases one of my hands so he can press his palm to my breast, squeezing me gently, brushing his thumb across my nipple, which puckers so quickly it hurts. I gasp.

He kisses his way up my throat to my ear. "God, I want you. Being this close to you and not being able to have you is driving me insane."

His mouth returns to mine, and he coaxes my lips apart so he can slip his tongue inside. His hands slide down to my waist, and he pulls me flush against him so that his erection is prodding my belly.

"Do you feel that?" he says. "Do you feel what you do to me?" He pulls back to make eye contact. "The waiting is killing me. Do you want me, Elliot? God, please say yes. I don't know how much longer I can wait."

I lift my hand to his face, cupping his cheek and brushing my thumb over his lower lip. He groans and kisses my thumb, then pins me with his gaze. "Say you want me."

"Yes, I want you."

With an exasperated sigh, he presses his forehead to mine. "I'll figure out something. We desperately need some alone time. We have a lot to make up for."

"Mommy, I'm done! Where are you?"

Jake releases me, stepping back with a chuckle. "And... grown-up time is over." He opens the door to his suite. "She's in here, buddy."

Aiden walks into Jake's room, Stevie clutched under his arm. I'm still standing against the wall, trying to get my bearings. My body's still reeling with endorphins, aroused and flushed with need.

Aiden glances around for me. "Oh, there you are, Mommy."

"Hi, sweetie," I say. "Ready for dinner?"

"Yeah. I'm starving."

* * *

Elly has gone all out and arranged a fabulous spread on the dining room table. There's a big platter of Fettucine Alfredo, a basket of warm garlic bread, salad, and roasted veggies. There's milk for Aiden, a pitcher of ice water, and a bottle of red wine. The table is set for six—the four of us, plus Elly and George.

The table is covered with a fine burgundy tablecloth and white china plates trimmed in gold, fancy silver utensils, and elegant crystal stemware. The centerpiece is a glass vase holding a lovely bouquet of wildflowers.

I smile at our hostess as I take my seat. "Elly, this is wonderful. Thank you."

"Oh, it's nothing," she says. "I love it when there's lots of family here at the house." She winks at her husband. "It gets old with just the two of us eating in the kitchen."

"Don't let her fool you, Annie," George says when I hand him the bread basket. "She always goes all out, whether she's feeding twenty people or just the two of us."

George has cleaned up after working outside all day and changed out of his dusty coveralls into a pair of jeans and a red-and-white plaid shirt. His face is weathered and wrinkled from spending so much time outdoors, but the twinkle in his blue eyes as he smiles across the table at his wife makes him look far younger than his actual age.

Everyone digs into their meals, clearly enjoying the food and drink. I indulge in a glass of wine, hoping it might help settle my nerves.

Aiden chatters on and on about his swimming lessons earlier in the afternoon and the horses we visited. "I hope I can ride one," he says, his gaze darting back and forth between Jake and Charlie.

"Do you think I can?"

I can't remember the last time Aiden was so talkative and so excited about anything. Coming here has been really good for him. He's opening up more than I've ever seen him do. He reaches for his glass of milk but in his exuberance, he miscalculates, knocking it over, sending milk spilling across the table.

As George picks up the basket of bread, saving it just in the nick of time, Elly shoots to her feet and grabs a stack of cloth napkins from the buffet and lays it over the spreading puddle of milk.

"I'm sorry!" Aiden cries, jumping up from his seat. He slips behind his chair, gripping the wooden frame tightly, his wide gaze darting wildly from me to Jake and back again.

I reach for him. "Aiden, sweetheart—"

Jake rises slowly, motioning for me to stay still. "Let me." His expression softens when he looks at Aiden. "Hey, pal, it's okay."

Panicked, Aiden backs away from the table until his back hits the wall. "I'm sorry, Jake! I didn't mean to! It was an accident!"

My heart is in my throat as Jake walks around the table toward Aiden, who moves away, sliding along the wall until he finds himself backed into the corner, trapped between the wall and the china cupboard.

Jake reaches for him. "Aiden, it's all right."

Aiden cringes as he presses back into the corner, trying to put as much distance between himself and Jake as he can.

The fear on Aiden's face breaks my heart. *My poor baby.*

Jake sighs, scrubbing a hand over his beard. Then he drops down onto his knees, almost at Aiden's level now. "Aiden, it's okay. You don't have to be afraid. No one's going to hurt you, I promise."

I glance around the table. Elly has tears in her eyes, and the compassion on George's face is unmistakable. I find myself wiping tears from my own face, too. Even Charlie appears shaken.

Aiden finally brings himself to look Jake in the eye. "I didn't mean to do it," he says, his voice barely audible.

"I know you didn't." Jake slowly reaches out to lay his hand on Aiden's shoulder and give it a gentle squeeze. "Did someone hurt you before? For spilling something?"

Aiden nods.

"Was it your dad?"

Aiden looks clearly conflicted, as if he's afraid to tell the truth.

"It's okay, honey," I tell him. "You can tell him."

Aiden looks warily at Jake. "Yes."

Jake reaches out to wipe the wetness from Aiden's cheeks. "I won't ever let your dad hurt you again. Do you hear me? I won't let *anyone* hurt you."

Aiden is visibly shaking now as his body struggles to process the adrenalin coursing through him.

Jake opens his arms. "Come here, buddy."

Aiden stares at Jake for a moment, looking so painfully uncertain, as if he fears it's a trap. As soon as Aiden takes a hesitant step forward, Jake pulls him close, one hand cradling the back of his head as the other hand rubs his back. "It's okay, pal."

Aiden wraps his arms around Jake's neck, holding him tightly.

After a long, quiet moment, Jake releases Aiden and stands,

holding out his hand. "Come back to the table and finish your dinner before it gets cold, okay?"

Aiden allows himself to be led back to his seat. Elly pours him a fresh glass of milk, and everyone returns to their seats and resumes eating.

Aiden looks at me out of the corner of his eye and offers a shy smile.

"It's all right, sweetheart," I say, stroking the back of his head. "Finish your dinner."

15

Annie

After dinner, I volunteer to help Elly clean up in the kitchen. Jake and Charlie take Aiden downstairs to the arcade to play video games. After that, the three of them are going to watch Aiden's favorite Disney movie, *Cars*, on the big screen in the theater.

I'm happy that Jake is taking so much interest in Aiden, and I'm grateful for the respite this evening. I figure I'll have three whole hours to myself.

After finishing in the kitchen, I head up to my room and take a long hot bath in the sunken tub, relaxing in the luxurious jets of hot water. After my bath, I take the opportunity to shave my legs and underarms because... well, just in case... and brush my teeth and floss.

Jake made it pretty clear earlier, when he had me pinned to the wall in his room, that he wants us to be together. Knowing how determined and resourceful he is, I imagine he'll find a way to make it happen fairly soon. So I want to be ready.

The thought of having sex with Jake again both thrills and terrifies me. I'm thrilled because I love him, and of course I want to be with him. I never thought we'd be given another chance, and I don't want to squander it. I want him. I want to spend the rest of my life with him, assuming he feels the same way.

But I'm also terrified. When we were together in high school, we were both essentially still kids. Jake's all man now, and I have no doubt he'll be an aggressive, unapologetic lover. I don't know if I'm ready for that. Ted was satisfied with quick sex, no foreplay. It was plain old missionary style. But Jake doesn't strike me as the kind of man who's going to be satisfied with that.

I read a lot of romance books, and while I don't think Jake's going to want to tie me up or chain me to the bed, I don't think he'll be satisfied with a quickie in the dark. He's going to want to look and touch... and probably taste... and oh, my God. The thought of his mouth... his tongue... *there*. I don't know if I'm ready for that.

Just the thought of getting naked with him scares me to death. As I told him, I'm not the same girl he remembers. My body has matured, and time and childbirth has taken its toll. I have stretch marks on my breasts and belly and thighs. And there's a lovely cesarean section scar stretching across my lower belly that's impossible to miss.

I'm not vain, or at least I hope I'm not. But I don't want him to compare the *me* I am today with the girl he once knew and find the current *me* lacking. Or a disappointment.

Just the thought of being naked with him again makes me queasy. I saw glimpses of his body in the pool today. His muscular thighs are like tree trunks. And his arms... well, they're ridiculous. Arm porn, pure and simple. His biceps and triceps are huge, well defined, and rock hard. And those thick, ropy veins... not to mention the tattoos. *Good grief!* And that's just what I've seen with his clothes *on*. I can't imagine what he looks like naked.

After my impromptu spa treatment, I dress in a pair of comfy PJ shorts and a white cami and curl up on an armchair with one of the books I brought from home. I'd lowered the lights, and I'm so cozy I could melt into a puddle and stay like this forever.

I've been reading for about half an hour, struggling to focus on the words in front of me, when I hear a quiet knock. "Come in."

Elly opens the door and pops her head inside. "Would you like some tea? I brought you a pot of hot water and a cup. I've got an assortment of teas if you're interested."

"I'd love a cup. Thank you."

Elly pushes a small serving cart into my room and parks it beside my chair. There's a little stainless-steel pot of steaming water sitting on a trivet, a cup and saucer, and a basket of assorted tea bags. She rifles through the collection. "There's chamomile and peppermint. Lemon balm, passionflower, and here's a basic green tea. Do any of these sound good? Or, if you'd prefer coffee, I can bring you a cup of that instead."

"This is perfect, Elly, thank you." I select the peppermint tea thinking maybe it will help calm my nerves.

"May I sit?" She eyes the other armchair. "Just for a minute?"

"Of course! Please do."

Elly sits, turning in her seat to face me. "I know it's none of my business, but I just wanted you to know." She pauses, looking conflicted. "I've known Jake for several years, and he's never brought anyone here before. Not even during family parties or holiday get-togethers. *Never.* I've never even known him to be dating anyone. Since you arrived, it's like he's a different person. I've never seen him so relaxed and happy. I just thought you'd like to know."

"We have a history," I tell her, wondering how much she knows.

She smiles. "I've heard bits and pieces over the years. I know you and he were sweethearts in high school."

"We were."

"You don't have to explain. It's none of my business. I just want you both to be happy."

Suddenly, I want to tell Elly everything. In the little time I've known her, she's been kinder and more supportive to me than my own mother has ever been. My mother... who judges me constantly, always finding fault with me. My own mother, who others refer to as *the dragon lady*, and with good reason. Even Aiden's afraid of her. "Right after high school, I left to go to Harvard."

Elly's eyes widen. "That's impressive."

I shrug. "While I was gone, my parents interfered in our lives, telling me one thing, and telling Jake another. They lied to both of us, and in the end, their lies drove us apart. With hindsight, we shouldn't have let that happen, but we were both young and insecure, and it was easy for us to believe the tales they told."

"I'm so sorry." She frowns. "You're divorced now, right? And I take it that your marriage wasn't a pleasant one, based on poor Aiden's reaction at the dinner table tonight when he spilled his milk."

I nod. "My husband was abusive, both physically and emotionally. That's why Aiden and I are here under protective custody."

Elly smiles. "You're in very good hands, believe me. Nothing gets past Jake." She stands. "I'll leave you alone to enjoy your tea. If you need anything, you can call me on the house phone, there by your bed. Just dial 2 for the kitchen. Leave a message if I don't pick up when you call. Anything you need... just let me know."

"Thank you."

Elly quietly lets herself out, and I sip my tea, trying to get back into my book, but it's impossible. My mind keeps wandering to Jake. I was hoping the tea would settle the butterflies in my stomach, but so far that doesn't seem to be the case. If anything, the later it gets, the more nervous I feel.

I'm warm and comfortable, and before I know it, my eyelids are so heavy I can't keep them open. I close my book and lay it on my lap, then lean my head back and close my eyes. Just for a few minutes...

The next thing I know, I feel a pair of lips pressed to my forehead. Then I hear a male sigh combined with a quiet groan.

I open my eyes and find the room darkened. Jake is looming over my chair, gazing at me intently.

"Where's Aiden?" I glance around the room, realizing it's late. I must have dozed off.

Jake nods toward the bed. "He fell asleep during the movie, so I carried him up here to bed."

"Thank you. I was going to give him a bath tonight, but I guess that will have to wait until morning."

Jake reaches down to skim his index finger along the scooped neck of my cami top. "You smell really good."

I chuckle. "I had a rose-scented bubble bath tonight, and Elly pampered me with peppermint tea."

He leans closer and runs his nose down the side of my face to my throat, where he places a lingering kiss. "It's not roses or peppermint tea I smell. It's *you*." He presses his lips to my throat and growls quietly. "Your skin is an aphrodisiac."

He sets my book on the floor and pulls me to my feet, wrapping me in his arms and resting his chin on the top of my head. When he speaks, his rough voice makes my belly quiver. "Please don't make me sleep alone tonight."

His simple request makes my chest ache. "Jake, we can't." My throat tightens painfully. I hate saying no to him, but I have to think of my son. "I need to explain things to Aiden."

He sighs, then he presses his lips to my temple. "It's just been so long, Elliot."

I slip my arms around his waist and hold him tight, letting my hands slide up beneath his T-shirt and stroke his taut, bare skin. "I know. Believe me, I know."

With another quiet growl, Jake scoops me up into his arms and carries me to the bed, laying me down. Aiden is tucked in on the far side of the bed, fast asleep.

Jake crawls into bed with me. "Let me lie with you for a little while. I just want to hold you. I'll be gone long before Aiden wakes up, I swear."

How can I say no? I turn on my side, facing Aiden so I'll know if he awakes, and Jake molds himself to my backside, tucking his arm around my waist and pulling me against his body. We both ignore the huge erection pressing into my back.

He nuzzles the back of my head, his mouth slipping down to kiss my neck, making me shiver. "Go back to sleep," he murmurs. "I won't stay long, I promise."

Of course, I'm wide awake now and falling asleep seems almost impossible. Having Jake in bed with me, even with the two of us fully clothed, makes it impossible for me to relax. His warm fingers slip beneath my top and splay possessively over my abdomen, while he lays his forehead against the back of my head.

Suddenly, I'm overwhelmed with sadness for everything we've lost. I imagine him being alone all those years, hurting, and it breaks my heart. My eyes sting as tears begin to form. One sob escapes me, followed by another, and I have to press my face into a pillow to muffle the sound so I don't wake my son. The last thing he needs to see is his mother crying.

My heart cracks wide open, breaking into several jagged pieces, the sharp edges stabbing me from the inside.

"Shh." Jake presses his lips to the back of my head. "God, please don't cry."

But I can't help it. It's too late. The dam has ruptured. That protective wall that has been shielding my heart for all these years has finally crumbled, and I can't hold back the surge of pain. I feel completely lost, swept away by a rush of emotion that's pulling me down into a deep well of sadness and loss.

I sob into my pillow, grieving for the pain and loneliness we've both endured all these years.

He kisses my bare shoulder. "I'm sorry, Elliot. Jesus, I'm sorry. I shouldn't have let you go. I should have pushed. I should have fought for you. If I had, none of this would have happened."

"It... wasn't... your... fault." It's a struggle for me to speak between wracking sobs. "Not your fault. Mine—"

"No! Shh." He tightens his hold on me. "Baby, please."

I cry as quietly as I can manage into my pillow, afraid of waking my son, but fortunately Aiden is out cold, undoubtedly exhausted after a busy day.

Jake holds me tightly, comforting me—comforting both of us. I can feel his body shaking too.

16

Annie

I must have fallen asleep crying in his arms, because the next thing I know, there's sunlight streaming through the partially open drapes, and Aiden is sitting up in bed, looking well rested and refreshed. He's playing quietly with Stevie and his car.

I reach up to stroke his hair. "Good morning, sweetie. Did you sleep well?"

"Yes. Can I have another swimming lesson today? Jake said when I know how to swim, I can jump off the diving board by myself."

I smile as I stretch my limbs. The idea of another day spent with Jake fills me with anticipation. I close my eyes and remember him holding me in the night while I cried ugly tears. I feel so much better this morning, as if my crying jag last night released a lot of deeply harbored pain.

There's a quiet knock on our door.

"I'll get it!" Aiden says, jumping off the bed and running for the door.

Aiden opens the door wide and Jake walks into the room, dressed in jeans and an Ironman T-shirt.

"Oh, wow!" Aiden says when he sees Jake's shirt. "Can I wear my Captain America shirt, Mom?"

"Sure." I smile sleepily at Jake. How in the world did he manage to get that T-shirt overnight?

As Aiden runs into our enormous walk-in closet to find his Captain America T-shirt, Jake comes and sits on the side of my bed.

He brushes back my messy hair. "Good morning. Did you sleep well?"

"Good morning. Yes, I did."

He glances at the closet, making sure Aiden hasn't made a reappearance yet. When he sees the coast is clear, he leans down to kiss me. It's a gentle, reverent kiss that sets the butterflies loose in my belly again. "You look beautiful."

"I'm a mess. My eyes are probably puffy after last night."

He shakes his head. "Puffy eyes or not, you are the most beautiful woman I've ever seen."

I grab Aiden's pillow and hit him with it, laughing. "Never

admit a woman's eyes are puffy."

He snatches the pillow from me and tosses it aside. Then he makes a grab for my waist, tickling me mercilessly, making me squeal.

Aiden runs back into the bedroom and jumps on the bed. He frowns at Jake. "What are you doing to my mom?"

"I'm tickling her."

I'm laughing so hard I can barely speak. "Jake, stop! You're going to make me wet the bed!"

"That's all part of my evil plan." And then he makes his best attempt at an evil laugh, winking at Aiden. "Muah-ha-ha-ha."

Aiden decides to join in the fun, tickling me too.

"Hey," I gasp. "Two against one is not fair!"

"For God's sake," Charlie says from the open doorway. "You guys are making enough noise to wake the dead."

"We're tickling my mom!" Aiden cries.

Charlie shakes her head. "Yeah, I can see that. You people are nuts."

"Don't just stand there, Charlie!" I say, gasping with laughter. "Help me!"

Charlie comes to my defense, grabbing Aiden off the bed and throwing him over her shoulder. "Come on, pal. Breakfast is waiting, and I'm starving." Then, in a voice clearly directed at the grown-ups in the room, she says, "I'm taking the young man downstairs for a *very slow and thorough* breakfast. And then we'll take a walk out to the barn to see the horses. We'll be gone for *two hours* at least, so make them count."

Jake stops tickling me, and we both lie there on the bed, breathless, as Charlie's parting words sink in.

"That's my girl," he says, rolling up onto an elbow so he can loom over me. "She makes a great wingman."

"Did she just imply—"

"Yes, she did. Now, can I have my wicked way with you? We have two hours of grown-up alone time. Let's make them count."

"*Right now?* Are you serious?"

"I'm dead serious. Now's our chance."

It's morning, and my room is brightly lit with sunshine. There's no hiding in a brightly-lit room.

"What's wrong, Elliot?" Jake frowns. "You don't want to?"

"No, it's not that. I do! It's just that—"

"What?"

"I thought we'd do this at night time, you know. When it's not so bright."

Jake barks out a laugh as he pulls me out of bed. "You're coming with me. My room. My bed. Now."

"Wait! I need to brush my teeth first." *And pee.*

He gives me a look. "Make it quick. You have two minutes before I strip you bare and take you where you're standing."

I run for the bathroom and brush my teeth and hair, doing the best I can with my disheveled hair. My eyes are indeed puffy from last night's crying jag, but there's no help for that right now. Then I take a quick pee, rushing as quickly as I can because I'm pretty sure Jake was serious about the two-minute warning.

Just as I'm washing my hands at the sink, I hear a brisk knock on the bathroom door. *Crap!* "Yes?"

The door opens and Jake waltzes in, meeting my gaze in the bathroom mirror. "Time's up. You're coming with me, and for the next two hours, you're mine. Brace yourself, because I'm going to make up for lost time."

And then he sweeps me up into his arms and carries me out of my room, across the hall to his, slamming the door shut behind us. He reaches back to lock the door. "I'm not taking any chances."

$\mathcal{e}^{\mathcal{I}}$ **17**

Annie

J ake carries me across the hall to his room and dumps me
gently and unceremoniously in the middle of his big, unmade
bed.

"What time did you go back to your own room?" I ask him.

He crawls onto the bed like a panther, moving slowly and with
intent. "I left right after you fell asleep. It was too torturous to lie
there and not be able to touch you the way I wanted, so I came
back in here to suffer in silence. But I didn't sleep well."

I'm not surprised. The pillows and bedding are all jumbled
up, arranged helter-skelter, as if he spent the night tossing and

turning.

I can't help noticing that the drapes are wide open, letting in a whole lot of early morning sunlight. "Jake—wait."

He freezes. "What?"

"Can you close the drapes?"

"Why?"

"Because they're letting in an awful lot of light."

He grins. "Maybe I like the light."

I make a face. "How about a little less light?"

He climbs out of bed and pulls the drapes mostly closed, leaving just a sliver of light coming through. The room is cast in semi-twilight now. It's certainly not as dark as I would like it to be, but I can manage.

Standing at the foot of the bed, he whips his T-shirt over his head and tosses it to the floor.

"How did you get an Ironman T-shirt here so fast?"

"Killian. He delivered it early this morning. I told him I needed it ASAP to score points with Aiden."

It makes me smile knowing that Jake would go to such trouble just to make Aiden happy. That single gesture is more meaningful than anything Ted ever did for Aiden. "Well, you succeeded."

Jake unzips his jeans and shoves them down, along with his black boxer briefs, dropping them to the floor. He's certainly not bashful as he stands there naked, with his hands on his hips. Does he even know how magnificent he is?

My stomach flips, and I feel dizzy. When he starts to climb onto the bed, I notice a large black tattoo on the left side of his torso. "What's that?"

His smile fades, and he lowers his arms to his sides, clearly in an attempt to hide the tattoo. His reaction is unexpected, and so unlike him.

I scoot down to the foot of the bed to stand in front of him and get a better look. My mind starts racing with all sorts of possibilities. What could he possibly want to hide from me?

But he's not cooperating, which makes me even more intrigued. I have to physically move his arm aside. "Show me, Jake."

I have to turn my head to read the sideways text. It's a date in bold, black ink. *March 5, 2005*

The day we had planned to marry.

Stunned, I glance up at him. "When did you get this?"

He shrugs. "Maybe a couple years after you left for college."

Our date. The date we celebrated every year. The day we had planned on getting married. He marked his body with it for all time. And as far as he knew at that time, we'd never be together again. My God, he held onto that date.

Pain slices through me. "I don't deserve you." I practically choke on the words, and then I turn and head for the door.

"No! No no no!" He grabs me around the waist and brings me back to the bed, tossing me onto the mattress and following me down, crouching over me on all fours, reminding me once more of a dark panther on the prowl.

He grasps my jaw and makes me look at him. "I love you." His dark eyes are burning with emotion. "You're mine! You were always supposed to be mine. The important question is, am I still *yours?*"

My eyes flood with tears that spill over, running down my cheeks. I reach up and cup his beautiful face. "Yes."

"Say it, Elliot! I need to hear you say it."

"You're *mine.*"

He lowers his forehead to mine. "That's all that matters. Everything else is water under the bridge. We'll deal with your ex. We'll deal with your parents. We're together again, and that's all that matters."

And then he lowers his mouth to mine, giving me the sweetest kiss, lightly brushing his lips against mine, as if reacquainting me with his touch.

"God, I want you," he says. "You have no idea."

Oh, I think I do. Already my body is heating up, softening, growing wet. "I want you, too." I reach up and thread my fingers through his hair, stroking him, tugging firmly the way he likes it.

He groans. Then his lips grow more insistent, little by little coaxing mine apart. His tongue slips inside and strokes mine, and the heat grows and grows until he finally crushes my mouth with his, eating at me hungrily. He slips a hand beneath my cami and covers one of my breasts, teasing the nipple with a brush of his thumb. I cry out from the unexpected pleasure, as sensation streaks from my breast to my sex, as if the two places are directly connected by a million nerve endings.

Jake pushes my top up, exposing both breasts, and leans down to draw a nipple into his mouth, tonguing it and suckling while his hand plumps and shapes the mound.

"We gotta get this off," he says, sitting back on his heels. He reaches for the hem of my top and pulls it off me, tossing it aside. Then he stares at me, his gaze hot.

It's all I can do not to cover myself with my hands. But I'm thirty-one now, no longer a teenager. So I force myself to lie still and let him look his fill.

He reaches out, cupping one breast with his big hand. "Jesus." And then he lowers his mouth and reverently kisses my nipple. "Did you breastfeed Aiden?"

His question takes me by surprise. "Yes."

At my answer, his gaze darkens, and a muscle in his cheek starts twitching. "I wish I could have seen that."

Jake leans down and kisses a path down my throat, past my clavicle and down the center of my chest. He lavishes attention on one breast, and then the other, suckling on my nipples until they pucker up into tight little buds. With each draw of his mouth, with each suckle, I feel a corresponding tug between my legs, making me wetter and wetter until I'm aching with need.

"Now the rest of it," he says, reaching for the waistband of my PJ shorts. He pulls them, and my panties, down my hips, so slowly as if wanting to draw this out. My belly is quivering with nerves as the cool air brushes over my abdomen, and eventually my mound.

I'm grateful now for my little mini-spa treatment last night. At least my legs are silky smooth. And while I could never be brave enough to wax, I did a little bit of trimming just to tame things down. I had an inkling this would happen soon.

Jake whips my clothing off my legs, and then he nudges my thighs apart, spreading them wide enough to accommodate the incredible breadth of his shoulders.

From his vantage point, he can't miss the scar from my c-section. He pauses, studying it. Then he traces it with his fingertip, so gently it tickles. "You had a c-section."

"Yes."

He frowns. "It must have hurt."

"A little."

"I wish I'd been there, to help you."

Then his fingertip moves downward, over my mound, through the curls. I gasp when he pries the lips of my sex open, exposing all of me in my glory.

When his tongue flicks my clitoris, I throw my head back with a shocked cry. "Jake! A little warning would be nice."

"Elliot, in case you haven't noticed, I'm going down on you." He laughs, and I feel the vibration in my core.

My thighs are shaking, and I'm overwhelmed by the pleasure of his mouth on me. I don't remember oral sex being this amazing. He licks and suckles at my clitoris, setting off sparks of sensation rippling through me, before moving down, his hot tongue blazing a trail to my opening. He tongues me, lapping at my wetness with a heart-felt groan. He teases my opening with a fingertip, circling and rimming the sensitive flesh. Then his thick finger sinks inside me, so slowly, an inch at a time.

I gasp at the intrusion, at the sudden feeling of fullness. It's been such a long time for me and, honestly, Ted was never this attentive.

Jake's finger sinks deep, and then he withdraws it to the tip before sliding it in again, much easier this time. His finger slides through my slick channel, and then he starts stroking me from the inside. His mouth returns to my clitoris, and between his finger and his mouth, I think I'm in danger of losing my mind.

I writhe on the bed, squirming and thrashing, and he easily holds me pinned to the mattress. The pleasure intensifies, leaving me breathless.

"Jake!" His name is no more than a gasp.

And then my body detonates as an orgasm lights up my nerve endings, sending intense pleasure rolling throughout my body.

Jake looms over me, looking very pleased with himself. He grabs the sheet and runs it across his face and beard. But even so, when he kisses me, I still taste myself on his lips.

Reaching across me, he opens the top drawer of his nightstand and grabs a condom packet. Then he shucks off his boxer briefs, rips open the packet with his teeth, and lies on his back beside me so he can roll the condom onto his sizeable erection.

Dear God. His erection is just as big and imposing as the rest of his body. My belly clenches tightly in anticipation of having him inside me.

"You okay?" he asks me, as he rolls up onto his side, facing me.

I nod, not really sure if I'm okay or not.

He leans closer and kisses me, then moves to kneel between my legs. "Let's start easy, okay?" he says, moving closer. He guides his erection to my opening. "Missionary style. But eventually, I want to take you every way humanly possible."

I'm not sure when *eventually* is, and I'm not sure what ways he considers possible. My sex life has been pretty limited. When Jake and I were young, we didn't really move beyond the basics. And Ted, well not then either. I have a feeling I'm due for an education.

When Jake presses the head of his erection to my opening, I gasp, grasping his thighs, nervously holding on. He leans forward, letting his weight and gravity do the work. My body is more than primed, soft and slippery thanks to my orgasm, but it's still an effort for him to work himself inside. I know he's being careful, and I appreciate that, but sometimes a more direct approach is needed.

"You won't hurt me," I say, tugging him closer.

He grits his teeth and thrusts harder, still careful. At first, my body resists the intrusion, but then it gives way and he sinks inside me, filling me so thoroughly it takes my breath away.

We both gasp with a mix of pleasure and astonishment that we're together like this again. He pauses for a moment, giving me a chance to get used to him.

I look up into his eyes, which are glittering with intense emotion. "I dreamed of you so many times," I admit, sharing one of my deepest and darkest secrets with him. "I always felt guilty about it, because it seemed so disloyal. But that was the only time I felt truly happy, when I was with you."

"You're killing me, sweetheart," he says, groaning as he withdraws to the tip, then sinks back in.

I'm overwhelmed by the size and strength of him as he moves

over me, thrusting slowly at first, letting me get used to him again. So tempted by the sight of his body, I skim my hands across his shoulders and down his arms. His muscles are so well defined, his arms powerful. I trace the path of a prominent vein running down his forearm, and he shivers at my touch. He's holding his weight on his hands, one on each side of me, levered above me, and I grasp his forearms.

He's moving faster now, his length tunneling through my slick channel. He's like a machine, all that strength and power contained and controlled. When I brush my thumb against one of his nipples, he cries out sharply, gritting his teeth.

I want to touch and taste every inch of him, like he did with me. I lean up and press my lips to his sternum, then lick his hot, salty skin.

"Jesus, Elliot!" He shudders in my arms, and with a hoarse shout, he comes in a hot fury. Even with the condom in place, I can feel the throbbing pulse of his erection as he comes. He bucks inside me, grunting and gasping with each pulse. He tenses, arching his back, his neck muscles straining as he lifts his head and groans out his pleasure.

When the pulses stop, he rolls us to our sides, facing each other. We're still joined together, and he's still partly erect.

Jake brushes back my bangs and leans closer to kiss me. "I love you. I've always loved you. I never stopped, even when I thought there was no hope. And you are my reward for never giving up."

My eyes prickle as tears form. "I carried you in my heart at all times, and I never once forgot you." I lean closer and kiss him gently. "I love you, too."

"I want a life with you," he says. "I want a family with you. I want a do-over."

I nod, my throat tightening with emotion. "I want that too."

"I want babies with you. And Aiden. He's mine now."

That makes me smile, because above all, Aiden deserves to have a father who adores him. Jake's already shown him more kindness and affection in the past two days than Ted ever did.

"I know you're worried about Aiden and what he'll think of me. *Of us.* But I don't think he'll have a problem with me becoming part of your family. I don't think you need to worry."

"I'll need to figure out how to explain it to him."

"Let me," he says. "This is man's business. Let us men handle it."

I laugh. "Man's business?"

"Yes." Jake gently pulls out of me, his erection beginning to soften. "Give me a few minutes, and I can do this again. I'm not that old."

"I'd like that." And it's true. Even though I'm already a bit sore from how he stretched me, I'd love nothing more than to feel him inside me again.

Jake's phone rings, startling us both. He reaches for it and checks the caller ID and frowns. "It's Security." He presses a button. "Yes?" Then his face morphs into a pleased smile. "Tell them we'll be down in a bit."

Jake ends the call and looks at me, a bashful smile on his handsome face. "It looks like our round two will have to wait. We have company."

"Who?"

"My parents got wind of the fact that you're here. They want to see you."

"Your parents?"

"Yes. Relax. They just want to see you. And they want to meet Aiden. Shane must have told them you were here."

I sit up, nervously trying to restore order to my hair. "I have to take a shower! And get dressed! Oh, my God, your parents?"

Jake sits up, laughing as I scramble madly out of bed. "Shower with me," he says. "And then we'll get dressed and go down to meet them. Don't worry. Elly will entertain them until we come down."

$\backsim$ 18

Jake

I coax Annie into the shower with me, and we take turns soaping each other with eager hands. I want to take her right here, under the spray of hot water, but she's a nervous wreck now knowing that my parents are here. Unlike Annie's parents, who always disapproved of me, my parents adored Annie, and they always hoped we'd marry. I have no doubt they'll be happy to see her again. And as for Aiden—my mom will go nuts over him. As a former kindergarten teacher, she loves kids, and I have absolutely no doubt she'll love Aiden.

Once we've washed everything we can, at least twice, we turn off the water and dry off. Annie slips back into her PJs and runs across the hall to her own room to dress. I towel myself dry and pull on a pair of jeans and my Ironman T-shirt—gotta score points with the kid.

When I'm dressed, I knock on Annie's door.

"Come in," she calls.

I enter her room and find her in the closet, fretting over what to wear.

"I didn't bring many clothes with me," she says, as she picks through her meager wardrobe. "And only one dress." She holds it up to show me. "Do you think this is acceptable?"

"Honey, you can wear whatever you like. They're here to see you, not your clothes. Just throw on some jeans and a top, and you'll be fine. Hell, wear your pajamas if you want to. My folks won't care."

She sighs. "I can't believe they're here."

I walk up behind her, slipping my arms around her waist and resting my chin on her shoulder. "Trust me. They'll be happy to see you, and they'll go nuts over Aiden. My brother Shane and his wife just had a baby a few days ago, so my parents are in grand-parent mode. Aiden will give them someone else to spoil."

She turns to look back at me. "Do you think they will? Accept him, I mean."

"Of course, they will." I kiss her throat, feeling her pulse beating wildly beneath my lips. My hands slide down her sides to her hips, and I squeeze them. "You make me so damn hard, Elliot." I press against her back side, my erection hitting the small of her back. I push closer and groan. "You owe me a round two later. We didn't get our full two hours."

Now that we're living under the same roof, I know I'm not going to be able to get enough of her. I'd really like for her to move into my room and share my bed. Aiden can have this room to himself. But I'm getting a little bit ahead of myself. *Baby steps.* I don't want to push either of them too fast.

There's a brisk knock on Annie's door, and I leave her to get dressed while I answer it.

"Change in plans," Charlie says, grinning at me. "Your folks are here."

"So I heard. We had to cut playtime short. Annie's getting dressed, and then we'll be down. Where's Aiden?"

"Where do you think? With your mom. I think she's in love."

I laugh. "Not surprised."

Charlie pulls me out into the hallway and shuts the door to Annie's room. "Okay, dish, big guy," she says, facing me with her arms crossed over her chest. "What's going on?"

"Isn't it kind of obvious?"

"You still love her, don't you?"

"What do you think? I've got another chance with her, and I'm taking it."

She nods. "Yeah, I figured as much. You can't keep your eyes off of her. And your eyes just about popped out of your head when she walked out of the women's locker room in a swimsuit yesterday."

I chuckle. "Let's just say Annie's filled out a lot since high school. She's got some wicked curves. *Damn*."

"So, is this thing between you two serious?"

Charlie looks skeptical, but I can't say I blame her. In the couple years she's been with the company, she's never seen me date anyone. I look at her, deadpan. "As a heart attack."

She grins. "Like put-a-ring-on-it, serious?"

"Yes. Hey, thanks for running interference with Aiden this morning. I owe you."

She brushes off my thanks. "It's no trouble. I like the kid. He's cute and so damn funny." She pauses, eyeing me. "Wow, so this means you're about to become a step-dad?"

"Yep."

"Your parents are going to freak. Especially your mom. She'll love having *two* grandkids to spoil. First Shane's baby, and now Aiden."

The door to Annie's room opens, and she walks out dressed in a pair of jeans and a peach-colored top. Her hair is up in a ponytail, freshly brushed, and she looks amazing.

"I'm ready," she says to me. Then she smiles at Charlie. "Hi, Charlie. Where's Aiden?"

"He's downstairs with Bridget and Calum. I think Jake's mom is in love." Charlie snags Annie's hand. "Come downstairs and meet the fam."

Annie sighs. "I don't know if I'm ready for this."

I take her hand and lead her toward the stairs. "Yes, you are."

* * *

We find my parents in the great room, seated on a sofa with Aiden between them. He's introducing them to Stevie.

I walk into the room, pulling Annie along with me. "Hey, guys. I'm glad you're here. You remember Annie Elliot."

My mom shoots to her feet and opens her arms wide. "Annie! It's so good to see you again."

They meet each other halfway, and my mother pulls Annie into an embrace. "Hello, darling," Mom says. "How are you?"

"I'm doing well."

"I'm so sorry about the trouble you've been having. Shane called us. He thought you might like to see some friendly faces. You remember Shane, don't you?"

"I do. I heard he and his wife just had a baby."

"Yes. Oh, my God, yes. He's so adorable. Luke. He was born six weeks early, but he's doing well."

Mom gives me one of her looks. "Why don't you get your father a cold drink at the bar? Take Aiden with you. I'll bet he'd like some chocolate milk, wouldn't you, honey?"

Aiden pops up. "Can I, Jake? Please?" he says, looking at me for permission.

The fact that he looked to *me* and not to his mother hits me like a punch to the gut. Jumping on another opportunity to score some points, I hold my hand out to him. I'm not above spoiling the kid. "Sure, pal, come on. I think we can rustle up some chocolate milk for you."

Aiden takes my hand without hesitation, his little fingers wrapping around mine. *Dear God, this kid.*

Annie gives me a knowing grin as we three guys head across the room to the bar. Apparently, we guys aren't wanted right now. Mom wants to talk to Annie in private.

While the two ladies sit together on the sofa, talking, I lift Aiden up and sit him on a barstool. My dad takes the seat next to him, and I walk behind the bar to play bartender. Even though I don't drink alcohol anymore, I often play bartender. I guess it's my way of challenging my resolve to stay away from the stuff.

It's early in the day, so Dad opts for a cola. I pour a glass of chocolate milk for Aiden, and one for myself while I'm at it. I might as well go for as many points as I can. Aiden's eyes grow wide when he sees I'm drinking what he's drinking.

"Cheers," the kid says, lifting his glass toward mine.

I raise my glass and tap it lightly against his, and he giggles as we take our first sips.

With one eye on Dad and Aiden, I keep tabs on Annie and Mom. They're having a pretty intense conversation, and at one point, I see Annie wipe her cheeks. Is she crying? Mom pulls her in for another hug, rubbing her back, and I relax a bit. Annie's in good hands. Mom will take care of her.

Elly comes into the great room, along with her husband. Dad goes to join George, probably so they can talk sports, and Elly joins Annie and Mom on the sofa.

Nobody's paying me and Aiden any mind, so I take advantage of the opportunity to start cashing in on some of my points. I know Annie's worried about what Aiden will think about us being together. I figure we might as well get it out in the open and move on.

"Do you know what boyfriends and girlfriends are?" I ask Aiden, trying hard to keep a straight face.

He nods. "Sure. It's when a boy and a girl like each other. They hold hands and stuff."

Close enough. "Right. So, I want to be your mom's boyfriend. Is that okay with you?"

His little brow furrows as he processes my question. "You like my mom?"

"Yeah."

"And you want to hold her hand and stuff?"

"Yeah. I'd really like that. Is it okay with you?"

Aiden shrugs. "I guess so. You won't hurt her, will you?"

His question hits me hard. "No, Aiden. I won't ever hurt her. Or you. You can count on that."

"Okay, then. Go ahead. Does she want to be your girlfriend?"

"She does. Go ahead, you can ask her."

"Hey, Mommy!" Aiden yells across the room, turning heads. "Do you want to be Jake's girlfriend?"

Annie blushes. "Yes, honey. I do."

"Okay," he says after turning back to me. "If it's okay with her, I guess it's okay with me."

"Thanks, pal." I lift my hand for a high-five, and he smacks his little palm against mine.

"You're welcome," he says, with the utmost sincerity as he takes another drink of his milk.

19

Jake

George and Dad end up grilling burgers out on the deck. Annie, Aiden, and I go down to the shoreline and do a little exploring while the food is cooking. We walk down to the private dock and look at the boats moored there.

Before long, Dad's whistle signals us to come eat. We're going to sit out on the deck and have a picnic eating burgers and potato salad and watermelon.

Aiden insists that I sit by him at lunch. Annie and my mom share the table with us.

"How are Beth and the baby?" I ask Mom, when she tells us she spoke to Shane that morning.

"The baby is doing well. He'll likely remain in the neonatal in-tensive care unit for a couple of weeks, but his doctor says he's out of danger and that he'll be just fine. His lungs just need a lit-tle more time to catch up. Beth, on the other hand, is struggling a bit. To be honest, at this point I think Shane's more worried about Beth than he is about the baby."

I give Annie the condensed version of how my brother's wife ended up going into premature labor in the attic of a convenience store during an armed robbery.

"How horrible!" she says. "Thank goodness they're all right."

"It was pretty stressful at the time. But Beth is a trooper, and my youngest sister—Lia—was instrumental in helping her get through it."

My parents stay for the rest of the afternoon. While we're sit-ting and talking in the great room, Charlie takes Aiden downstairs for another swimming lesson. I think Annie and I will both feel a lot better once the kid learns how to handle himself in water.

I'm glad my parents stopped by. Annie seemed to enjoy talking to them, especially to my mom. My parents don't blame Annie for what happened between us. I wish I could say the same thing about her parents. I do hold a grudge against them, and I'll make damn sure they know it when I see them next.

* * *

My parents head back to the city late afternoon so they'll have time to stop by the Children's Hospital to see Beth and Shane and the baby before it gets late. After dinner, Annie and I take Aiden outside to play, letting him run around and burn up some energy.

"Can we go see the horses?" he asks, bouncing with excitement.

"Sure, why not?" I say. "Let's go ask Elly for some apple slices."

"Yay!" Aiden says.

We head to the kitchen, where we find Elly relaxing at the table with a cup of tea.

"Elly, can we have apples for the horses?" Aiden asks.

"Sure, you can," she says. She cuts several apples into wedges and puts the pieces into a baggie for Aiden to carry.

We head back outside, and Aiden takes Annie's hand. Then he looks up at me. "Can you hold Stevie and my apples?"

I'm surprised, but honored, by the request. When I take the items from him, he reaches for my other hand, and the three of us walk hand-in-hand down the path to the barn, Aiden in the middle. Something tells me Aiden's going to be just fine with me in the picture. I suspect he's hungry for a real father figure.

"Swing me!" he says, dropping his weight and hanging from our hands.

When Annie and I lift him in the air and swing him between us, he squeals with delight. Looking over Aiden's head, Annie smiles at me.

When we reach the corral, I lift Aiden up to sit on the top fence rail, my hands securely gripping his waist to keep him from toppling forward. A couple of the Quarter horses stop by out of curiosity, chuffing and nuzzling Aiden's hands and pockets as they search for snacks.

"Here you go, buddy," I say, handing him the bag of apple slices. I show him how to hold his hand and offer the treat to the horse.

Aiden laughs nervously as the horse's lips nuzzle his palm as it takes the piece of apple. "I did it!"

Annie and I supervise carefully as Aiden feeds each of the horses. She moves closer to me and slides her arm around my waist, leaning her head against my shoulder. While Aiden giggles over the horses nuzzling his palm, I stand here wallowing in emotions. If this is a taste of what it means to have a family, I'm all in.

I lean over and kiss the top of Annie's head, and she tightens her arm around my waist. I'm pretty sure she's feeling it too.

* * *

Bedtime for the little guy is eight o'clock. When we get back to the house, Annie takes Aiden upstairs for a bath. I go with them, sitting on the side of the tub watching as Annie helps him bathe and washes his hair.

Aiden's exhausted from his busy day, and he can hardly keep his eyes open.

"I can't believe I didn't think to bring bath toys," Annie says, frowning.

While she's helping Aiden get out of the tub and dry off, I send a text message to the guys.

Somebody bring me bath toys for the kid—dinosaurs and cars would be good. Also, bring a dozen pale pink roses. Really nice ones.

I've never forgotten Annie's favorite flower.

Aiden gets his PJs on, brushes his teeth, then climbs into bed with Stevie and his car. Annie sits beside him in bed and reads a couple of books to him, one about dinosaurs and another one about talking race cars.

As I watch them together, I feel an uncomfortable ache starting deep in my chest. How in the fuck could Patterson have screwed up so badly that he lost his family? What the hell was the guy thinking? If I'd been in his shoes, I would have bent over backwards to make them happy, not *hurt* them. And how in the hell could anyone hurt an innocent little kid? *Jesus!*

I hate to admit it, but I'm jealous of that asshat ex-husband of hers. The more I think about him, the more I resent him. The more I want to choke the life out of him. Patterson is Aiden's father, but the man doesn't deserve this kid. Shit, the guy never deserved Annie, either, and he was her husband for more years than I care to admit. That ache quickly turns into a burning lump of coal, and it's searing me from the inside. All I can think about is getting that cretin behind bars, where he belongs.

My hands start shaking as I grow increasingly irritated and restless. I need to strike out and hit something. I climb off the bed while they're in the middle of a storybook. "I need to go make some calls." And then I hustle out of their room and across the hall to mine.

Needing to do *something*, I pick up my phone and call Cameron. "What's the status on Patterson?"

"We've been tailing him twenty-four-seven since yesterday. Killian's on duty now. Nothing new yet, at least not anything we didn't already know. Patterson's working for a manufacturing firm on the south side now. He's got a rented room in a highly questionable neighborhood. We've filmed him meeting with his dealer, and we got him making a deal, exchanging cash for drugs. We've got a recording of him buying, but not selling. Not yet. We'll keep watching him, though. He was awfully chummy with the dealer, so we think the intel we've got on him is good. Don't worry. It's just a matter of time before we nail him."

"I want him behind bars, Cameron. Get me the evidence I need to do that."

"We can get him on possession and use right now, but I think you had something a little bigger in mind."

"Yes. I want enough to put him away for a long time. Get me the evidence. Irrefutable, iron-clad evidence. Then we'll go the police."

"Got it. So, how's it going with the mom and kid? Are they settling in okay?"

"They're fine."

Cameron snickers. "You just need bath toys and pale pink roses, right?"

I laugh. "Don't judge. Just get me the stuff. I'd come into town to get it myself, but I don't want to leave them here alone."

"Why not? They're perfectly safe there."

"I know. I just don't want to leave them."

"Wow." Cameron chuckles. "You've got it bad, don't you?"

"You could say that."

I abruptly end my call with Cameron when I hear a quiet knock on my door. Sure enough, when I open the door, Annie is standing there with a hesitant smile on her face.

"Everything okay?" she says, coming in when I step aside.

"Sure."

She closes the door behind her. "You left so suddenly, I wasn't sure."

"I'm fine. Is Aiden asleep?"

"Yes. He was so tired tonight."

I go sit at the end of the bed, and Annie comes to stand between my legs, reaching out to run her fingers through my hair.

With a groan, I close my eyes and lean into her touch. "God, that feels good."

"It was great seeing your parents." She runs her nails over my scalp, making me shiver. "Your mom was really sweet. I told her what my parents did, how they played us against each other. She said she doesn't blame me for what happened. I was afraid she might."

"It's not your fault, babe." I wrap my arms around her waist and pull her close. Then I lean forward to rest my forehead between her breasts and inhale deeply. Her warm, feminine scent makes me crazy, and I'm instantly hard. It's too bad there are so many clothes between us.

All I can think about is how much I want to lie down with her, skin to skin, heartbeat to heartbeat. Hell, we don't even have to have sex, although that would be really nice. I just want to be with her. "Sleep with me tonight, here in my bed."

She hesitates. "If Aiden wakes up alone in the night, in a strange place, he'll be scared."

"Then let me sleep with you in your room. No sex, I promise. Totally G-rated. I want to sleep with you in my arms. If we're going to be a family, the three of us, then he needs to get used to the idea of me sharing a bed with you."

"You're right." She smiles and leans forward to kiss me. "As long as it's G-rated."

The feel of her soft lips against mine does a lot to soothe the burning ache in my chest. I wrap my arms around her waist and pull her down with me onto the mattress, so that she's lying on top of me. My dick is hard as a pike, but it's happy because it's nestled between her soft thighs.

I kiss her, coaxing her mouth open so I can taste and tease her tongue. "I want you, Elliot. Right here, right now." I slide my hands down to her ass, grasping her butt cheeks and pressing her softness against me. "How about it? Then we'll go sleep in your bed."

She smiles against my lips. "That sounds wonderful."

"Mommy! Where are you? Where did you go?"

"Oops." She slides off me, and when I sit up with a frustrated groan, she kisses me. "I'll stay with him until he falls asleep. Then I'll come back so we can pick up where we left off. Deal?"

"Deal."

She rushes back to her room, leaving me alone with my

thoughts and an increasing sense of frustration and resentment and no easy outlet for releasing it. I just can't shake the thought that Patterson was her husband... for years. He held her, he touched her, *he fucked her.*

Restless, I get up and start pacing, trying to push these toxic thoughts out of my head before I lose my mind. But the harder I try not to think of Patterson, the more he's front and center in my brain. *God damn it!*

I'm pacing the room like a caged animal, wounded and wanting to strike out at something, anything. This isn't good. I need to get my head on straight before Annie comes back. *I need a distraction.*

I change into sweats and leave my room. Annie's door is closed, and when I listen for a moment, I can hear her quietly reading to Aiden. Sounds like it'll be a while until he's sound asleep.

The house is dark and quiet as I walk downstairs to the lower level. I head for the fitness room, where I can burn off some steam before I see Annie again. I head into the locker room and change into boxing shorts and wrap my hands with tape. I'm not in the mood for gloves. I'm in the mood to do some damage.

As soon as I plant myself in front of a punching bag, my hands and feet fall easily into a familiar and comfortable rhythm as I punch and jab at the bag, throwing in a few kicks as well. It would be nice if I had someone to spar with, but I don't want to bother Charlie just because I need a diversion. So I work the bag hard, channeling all my frustration and jealousy into physical exertion, until my knuckles hurt and the tape is stained with blood. At least the physical pain distracts my brain from thinking about other things. I'd rather deal with physical pain over emotional any day.

I don't blame Annie for any of this. She was as much a victim of her meddling and overbearing parents as I was. But I do blame her parents for interfering in our lives, and I hate Patterson's guts. He may have had good intentions in the beginning, I don't know, but in the end, he betrayed Annie in the worst way possible. Any man who abuses a woman or a child deserves what he gets.

I slam my fists into the bag, sending it rocking on its chain. Over and over, I beat the bag, wishing it was Patterson's face. My shoulders are aching, as are my arms. My knuckles sting, and the bag is slippery with blood. But I don't care. This is my therapy. This is what I need to process what I'm feeling.

My muscles burn with exertion, but I keep at it, embracing the physical pain. That I know how to handle.

☙ 20

Annie

After I read him two more bedtime stories, Aiden finally falls asleep, clutching his dinosaur to his chest. Normally, he sleeps pretty soundly, but I think being in a strange place and meeting so many new people has him a bit hyped up.

I lie beside my son and watch him sleep for a few moments, wanting to memorize his sweet little face. I gently brush my fingers through his spiky hair and admire his long eye lashes and that cute little nose. He's my baby. He's brought me nothing but joy from the moment he was born. It was Aiden who gave me the courage to leave an abusive husband. There was no way on Earth

I'd stand by and let Ted hurt Aiden again.

Once I'm certain he's deeply asleep, I climb gingerly out of bed and practically tiptoe to the bathroom to brush my hair and teeth. I set up the nanny cam so I can monitor Aiden remotely, and then I let myself out of the room.

By the time I step in front of Jake's door, the butterflies in my belly are going crazy. I knock lightly, but there's no answer. I try again, a little bit harder this time. Still no answer. I try the door knob and find it unlocked, so I open it and step inside. "Jake?"

A quick search of his suite confirms what I already suspected. He's not here. That's odd, because I said I'd come back. I find his jeans lying on the floor at the foot of his bed. Where could he have gone?

I check the nanny cam app to make sure Aiden's still asleep. Then I head down to the kitchen to look for Jake, thinking maybe he'd gone downstairs looking for a snack. I find someone standing in front of the open fridge, but it's not Jake. "Hi, Charlie."

She pulls a bottle of beer out of the fridge and holds the door open. "Hey, Annie. You want something?"

"No. Thank you. I'm looking for Jake. I thought he'd be in his room, but he's not. I thought maybe he came in here."

Charlie closes the fridge and opens her bottle. "Try the fitness room downstairs. When he's restless, he works out. Beating something up tends to calm him down."

"He's restless?"

She nods. "As hell."

"Why?"

Charlie rolls her eyes at me. "You're kidding, right? He's been restless since the moment he laid eyes on you."

"Oh. Well, I'm sure this is difficult for him. It is for me."

She leans against the fridge. "Can I ask you something?"

"Sure."

"I know it's none of my business, but... what exactly is the history between you two?"

"How much has he told you?"

"Just that you guys dated in high school. But it's got to be more than that. I've never seen him mooning over anyone before."

Her terminology makes me smile. "We were together in high school. And yes, it was a lot more than that. We loved each other—we still do. We had plans to marry after we graduated high school."

"Obviously that didn't happen. So?"

"No, it didn't. My parents—it's a long story. I went away to college, and we never saw each other again, not until yesterday. I believed he was married—which as it turns out wasn't true—so I got married."

"Wow." Charlie is silent for a moment as she sips her beer. I can tell she's debating whether or not to dig for more information. "Since I've known him, he's pretty much been a loner," she finally says. "He's never dated anyone that I knew of. I never understood that, given how hot he is."

I laugh. "You think he's hot?"

Charlie grins. "Hello, girl! I'm not blind." She looks at me out of the corner of her eye. "Go downstairs. You'll probably find him beating on a punching bag."

"Thanks, Charlie."

I retrace my steps back to the foyer and take the stairs down to the lower level. It's dark down here, but I can see a faint light coming through the viewing pane outside the work-out room. I stand at the window, peering inside the dimly lit room. There's just a tiny bit of light coming from the locker rooms in the rear.

It takes me a minute for my eyes to adjust to the darkness, but I finally spot Jake standing in front of a punching bag, just as Charlie predicted. I watch him, mesmerized by his strength and coordination as he delivers blow after blow to the bag, sending it rocking on the chain it's suspended from.

He's wearing a pair of black shorts and that's it. Even his feet are bare, and when he pivots and kicks the bag with the edge of his foot, I cringe. That's got to hurt. Those bags are hard.

He pummels the bag relentlessly, his fists slamming into it, sending it reeling.

Suddenly, he stops, catching the bag and stopping its momentum as it swings back toward him. He turns to look right at me, his chest heaving, his face dark and sweaty from exertion.

I walk inside. "I went back to your room, but you were gone. Charlie said you'd probably be down here." I don't know why I'm practically whispering, as there's no one else down here but us.

I don't know what to make of the expression on his face. Just an hour ago, he wanted me to meet him in his room. Now, he looks agitated, angry. "What's wrong?"

"Nothing," he says, wincing. His jaws shut tightly, and he turns away from me, heading for the locker room. "I need to shower."

I run after him. "Jake, wait!"

He stops dead in his tracks, his chest heaving as he draws in air. "What?"

It's a little disconcerting to see him practically naked. I'm still not used to seeing his body like this, a far cry from what it was when he was eighteen. Now, he's a monster of a man. He doesn't even have to try to be intimidating. He just is.

I lay my hand on his chest, shocked by how hot his skin is to the touch. "I know something's bothering you."

He opens his mouth as if to speak, but then he shuts it. He's looking everywhere but at me. "You should go to bed, Annie. It's getting late."

"Just an hour ago, you were trying to sweet talk me into having sex, and now you're shutting me out. What happened after I left your room?"

He squeezes his eyes shut and grimaces, obviously upset about something.

"Jake." I slide my hand down his arm to his wrist. Glancing down, I see that the material wrapped around his hands is bloody. "Talk to me."

"I can't!" he hisses, pulling his hand free. "Not right now. It's not a good time. Please, just go to bed."

Clearly he's hurting. Charlie's comment about him being restless comes back to me. "You can talk to me, you know. You always talked to me before."

"That was *before!*"

He makes a fist and slams it into the wall, leaving a blood-stained hole.

"Jake!" I grab his hand and hold it to my chest, mostly to prevent a repeat. He's going to break his knuckles if he keeps that up.

His face screws up in pain, and he pulls away from me, staggering back to lean against the wall.

My throat tightens painfully, and my eyes tear up. I can't bear to see him hurting like this. "Jake, please. Talk to me."

"I'm so fucking sick with jealousy!" he yells. "I can't get it out of my head!"

"Jealousy?"

"Yes! I'm fucking jealous of your ex-husband. That motherfucker was *married* to you. He made a *baby* with you! He had everything with you, when I had *nothing!*"

Jake throws his head back against the wall with a loud thud, his face twisted in agony. I'm stunned by his reaction. He's been holding this inside all this time? Never letting it out, never letting me see how much he was hurting. *Dear God, I did this to him.*

I don't even realize that tears are streaming down my face until he looks at me and his expression softens instantly.

"Ah, shit, baby. Don't cry." He reaches for me with blood-stained hands.

When he realizes he's still got the bloody wraps on his hands, he tears at them. The skin over his knuckles is torn and bleeding, and his knuckles are already swelling. Still, he pulls me into his arms, pressing his lips to my forehead as he speaks. "Jesus, Elliot, don't cry. It's not your fault. I just can't stop thinking about him with you. It's driving me crazy!"

"It is my fault. I married him."

"No. It's not. I don't blame you."

He's a sweaty, bloody mess, but I don't care. He's hurting, and it's my fault. I pull his head down to mine and kiss him, both our lips trembling as they come together in a rush. He tightens his arms around me, holding me close as he closes his mouth over mine. He seems almost desperate, his mouth eating at me, his lips crushing mine. Our teeth knock together, and I taste blood, but I don't care, and he doesn't back down. This is necessary, this reclaiming of each other.

"You are *mine*," he grounds out against my lips. "You've always been mine."

"Yes." My heart breaks at the pain in his voice, and I think I'd give almost anything to move the clock back in time and change history. But I can't because that would mean never having had Aiden.

"You're both mine," he says, his mouth gentling.

My heart swells with love for this man until it hurts. I don't know what I ever did to deserve his loyalty and his affection, but I'm grateful for it. It's not too late for us. We can get back what we lost and move forward, together, as a family.

Jake pulls back to study me. "Did I hurt you?"

"No." I reach up, staring into his dark, glittering eyes and brush his hair back. "Come," I say, linking my elbow with his and leading him into the locker room. "Is there a first aid kit in here?"

"In the bathroom," he says, pointing at an open door across

the room.

I lead him into the bathroom and steer him to the counter. "Sit here." Then I search through the cabinet drawers for a first aid kit. After locating a clean hand towel and wetting it, I dab gently at the blood on his hands.

Neither one of us talks while I administer first aid, first cleaning his hands, then carefully blotting them dry before applying an antibiotic ointment and bandages. When I'm done, I move to stand in front of him, between his knees, and take his battered hands carefully in mine.

I meet his gaze, swallowing hard against the lump in my throat. "I'm so sorry."

He looks away as his eyes fill with fresh tears.

I lift one of his hands to my lips and kiss it. "I would do anything to take this pain from you, but I can't change what happened. I'm sorry, and I love you."

He's struggling not to cry, and it breaks my heart to see this strong man brought to his knees. He closes his eyes and squeezes my hands. "I should have fought harder," he says. "I should have gone to you. If I had, we would have realized we'd been lied to." He shakes his head. "I don't know why I didn't."

"Because you were still just a kid. We both were. And we didn't know how much power we had back then. It's just as much my fault. I could have insisted on coming home to confront you about this supposed girlfriend you'd gotten pregnant."

He laughs bitterly. "That's so ironic, considering there hasn't been anyone since you. Sure, I had the odd one-night stand. I'm no monk. But I never *dated* anyone—never cared enough about anyone to make it official."

We're both silent for a moment, as the implications of his words float in the air between us. He stayed true to me. I married the first man who came along when I thought I'd lost Jake. I feel sick with shame. "I wasn't as strong as you," I say, my words breaking apart.

"No, don't. Listen to me." He gets right in my face. "I don't blame you. Do you understand that? I. Don't. Blame. You."

Jake slides off the counter and pulls me into his arms. "I need a shower. I'm a hot mess."

I laugh, turning my face to kiss his sternum. "You are a hot mess, all right. But you're *my* hot mess."

"I'll be anything you want me to be, as long as I'm *yours*." He bends down to touch his nose to mine. "Elliot?"

"Yes?"

His breath is shaky when he says, "Please grab on tight and don't ever let me go. No matter what happens. Promise me."

I wrap my arms around his waist, my heart aching. "I promise."

↶ 21

Jake

I take the fastest shower ever known to man, just to rid myself of all the sweat and blood so I can touch Annie. Then I pull on my sweats and swing Annie up into my arms.

She squeals. "Put me down before you hurt yourself!"

I laugh as I carry her out the door and down the hall. "I'm not taking any chances of losing track of you before I get you back into my bed."

"Jake, I'm serious," she says, laughing. "I'm too heavy. Put me down."

"Oh, come on. How much do you weigh? One forty?"

She hesitates. "Close. One forty-five."

"I can bench press three of you, babe, so don't worry."

When we reach the foyer, she tries to shimmy out of my arms, but I hold onto her and begin to climb the stairs, taking two at a time.

"Oh, now you're just showing off," she says, laughing.

She's right. I am. I need to show off a little after that sissy crying fit downstairs. *Not my greatest moment.* I can be sensitive, but for a grown man to bawl his eyes out in front of his woman is a bit embarrassing. Thank God the guys didn't see that. Or Charlie. They'd never let me live it down.

Once we're safely in my room, I nudge the door closed with my shoulder. Only then do I set her on her feet. She pulls out her phone and checks the nanny cam app—showing me the screen. Aiden is sound asleep.

"This is going to take some getting used to," I say.

"What is?"

"Having a kid. I'm not complaining, mind you, but I've never had to worry about a kid waking up and walking in on me having sex."

She laughs. "Get used to it, pal. We're a package deal. If you want me, you have to want him too."

"Oh, believe me, I do! It's actually kind of cool. Shane has a son now, and so do I." I know there's a stupid grin on my face. I can tell by her pleased expression.

Smiling at me, she steps closer and wraps her arms around my waist. "I love you, Jacob."

My heart contracts at the sound of those words. Words I thought I'd never hear from her again. "I love you, too, Elliot. For now and for always."

I lean down and nuzzle the side of her neck, right below her ear, and place a series of open-mouth kisses there. The scent of her skin really is an aphrodisiac for me. I so desperately want to suck on her skin and leave my mark behind, but she might not appreciate being covered in hickeys tomorrow. My body responds instantly, growing hard and hot and impatient. While she's distracted by my kisses, I pick her up and sit her on my dresser.

She grins. "What are you up to now?"

"I'm making up for lost time. I want to take you on every possible surface, starting with this dresser. Then we'll move to the bed and try a few other positions. But first I want to strip you bare and taste every inch of your delectable body."

I take hold of the hem of her top and pull it up and off her, dropping it at my feet. She's left in a pretty pink bra and pink PJ bottoms.

My gaze is locked on her cleavage. Unable to help myself, I cup her breasts, weighing them in my palms. They're substantial and heavy, much more so than when we were kids. I press a kiss between the soft mounds and breathe in her warm scent.

My dick twitches in my sweats, lengthening and hardening, straining.

Her nipples tighten into little pebbles, and I can see the little points pressing against the sheer fabric of her bra. I brush one of the tips with my thumb, and the sound she makes goes straight to my dick. Her cheeks flush a pretty pink. She wants this, just as much as I do. When I gaze into her eyes, her pupils are dilated, glittering with arousal... and something else. Is she self-conscious?

Holding her gaze captive, I reach behind her and unhook her bra, letting the silky fabric slide into her lap. I can't stop staring at her bare breasts... plump, creamy flesh topped with luscious pink nipples. *Dear God.* I'm so hard it hurts.

22

Annie

Jake's expression darkens with hunger. He dips his head to take one of my nipples into his mouth, gently suckling, making the stiff peak even tighter. His hands clutch at my waist, squeezing and kneading my flesh, as he continues to worship my breasts. He doesn't seem to mind the faint, silvery stretch marks left behind as reminders of my pregnancy.

After paying thorough attention to one breast, and then to the other, he trails kisses down the center of my chest to the waistband of my PJ bottoms. His beard tickles my skin, teasing my nerve endings until I'm shivering from head to toe.

As he tongues my bellybutton, rimming it gently, he works my PJ shorts over my hips and pulls them off. Then he dips down between my legs and presses his nose to the wet gusset of my panties, inhaling deeply. He lifts his dark gaze up to meet mine, and he watches me intently, gauging my reaction.

"Spread your legs," he says, his voice a low growl.

When I do as he asks, he lowers his mouth to the soft skin of my inner thighs and he sucks hard, hard enough to leave a mark.

He's marking me.

Then he raises up and slips a hand into my panties, his fingers skimming through my pubic hair, until finally a finger sinks deep between my folds and strokes my clitoris. He growls—a sound I'm quickly becoming very familiar with.

As his finger teases my clit, my sex clenches hotly, and I can feel myself growing warm and wet with desire. The butterflies are going berserk in my belly.

Growing impatient, he takes hold of the waistband of my panties and tugs, working them down my legs and dropping them unceremoniously on the floor. Then he grabs my knees, raising them to force my thighs wide, exposing my sex to his hot gaze and even hotter mouth. Tipped off balance, I throw my hands back on the dresser to catch myself.

He covers my sex with his mouth, showing no mercy. He's voracious, licking and sucking my wet flesh. He slides his arms beneath my knees, raising and spreading my legs wider. There's no hiding from him. This is raw and wild, something I've only read about in romance novels, but never experienced before. My heart is pounding, my chest heaving, as he pushes me closer and closer to an orgasm.

I spare one hand to stroke his hair, running my fingers through the thick, dark strands, petting him, trying to tame this beast. He releases one of my legs to free up a hand so he can slide a thick finger inside my opening. His finger curls upward, stroking a tender spot deep inside me. That wicked finger, combined with his equally wicked tongue, drives my arousal higher and higher until I'm gasping, poised right on the verge of coming. The pleasure is intense, unrelenting, and so exquisite it's almost unbearable.

My body explodes in a blinding wave of pleasure that starts in my core and sweeps through my body, a firestorm singeing my overstimulated nerve endings. Unable to hold it in, I cry out shamelessly.

He suckles my clit gently as the pleasure rolls through me, keeping me on the edge of pleasure, prolonging the sensations until I collapse.

Jake shoves his sweats down his long legs and kicks them off. Then he pulls me to him, wrapping my legs around his waist, and carries me to the bed, laying me down gently. He kisses me, then reaches over me to pull a condom packet from the top drawer of his nightstand.

He stands beside the bed in all his naked glory, and oh, my God, is that man glorious. His body is a living work of art—there's no other way to describe it. His chest looks like it was carved from stone. His abdomen has more ridges than I can count.

His erection, which is in perfect proportion to the rest of his massive body, defies gravity as it rises into the air. I watch, mesmerized, as he rolls on a condom. Then he leans over me, caging me in with his arms. "Okay?"

I nod, feeling my face heat up.

Gently, he turns me over and pulls me up onto my hands and knees. He stands at the foot of the bed behind me, his hands settling on my hips, gripping them hard as he holds me in place. When I feel his lips graze my lower back, pressing lightly, my heart breaks. This man is so full of love, and so tender in spite of his great strength, it's humbling to be the recipient of his affection. I realize how lucky we are to have rediscovered each other.

I feel his fingers between my legs, gently touching me, opening me. Then I feel the blunt head of his erection pressing into my wetness, careful, yet unrelenting. Slowly, he pushes inside, just an inch at a time. My arms are shaking, so I lower my face to a pillow, clutching it. The feeling of fullness as he sinks deeper inside me makes me gasp.

He takes his time, rocking slowly in and out of me, a little deeper each time, giving my body a chance to get used to him. Once he's fully seated, his thighs pressing against mine, he starts to move. He reaches for my clit, teasing it, stroking it lightly, just enough to keep me on edge.

He thrusts in and out, slowly at first, letting the length of his erection drag along my insides. The friction and the heat are incredible, and already I feel my body ramping up for another explosion. I groan, pressing my face into the pillow.

I feel his body heat sinking into me as he leans over me, covering my back with his chest. His hands grip my hips, holding me firmly in place as he thrusts, while his lips pepper gentle kisses along my sensitive spine, making me shiver from head to toe.

Without warning, a second orgasm hits me unprepared. I cry out hoarsely and collapse onto the mattress. He follows me down, pinning me to the bed as he thrusts into me, harder and faster now. He holds his weight on his arms, allowing me to breathe. Then he rolls us to our sides, still inside me, and thrusts from behind.

His arm snakes around my waist, holding me to him as he thrusts into me. One of his legs slides between mine, raising my leg to give him better access.

My mind is reeling, and I'm overwhelmed with sensation. Ripples of pleasure continue to course through my body, setting off little fireworks throughout.

With a final powerful thrust and a deep grunt, he comes, bucking wildly into me, over and over. I can feel his erection shuddering inside me, pulse after pulse teasing my nerve endings, sending residual tremors of pleasure through my body.

When he finally stills, he carefully slides out of me and heads for the bathroom to take care of the condom. He returns soon after with a warm, wet washcloth, which he uses to wipe me clean.

"Oh, God," he groans, falling beside me onto the bed. He pulls me into his arms and kisses my forehead. "Are you okay? I didn't hurt you, did I?"

"I'm perfectly fine," I say, feeling utterly boneless. "Way more than fine."

"That was amazing."

I'm exhausted, and I can't help the yawn that escapes me.

"Bedtime," Jake says, patting my butt cheek. "You said I could sleep with you tonight. Aiden gave me his permission to be your boyfriend and hold your hand and stuff, and you agreed, in front of witnesses. That means I get to sleep with you from now on. When he feels comfortable enough here to sleep on his own, you can move into my room. We'll be right across the hall from him if he needs us in the night. Okay?"

I smile, thinking my Jake is just as impatient now as he was in high school. "Okay. As long as Aiden's okay with the arrangements."

After resting a bit, we get up. I put my PJs back on, and Jake pulls on a pair of loose shorts to sleep in. That's it—just the shorts. The temptation of knowing I can reach out in the night and touch any part of his body is heady.

We let ourselves back into my room, careful not to wake Aiden, and I turn off the nanny cam. I climb into the middle of the huge bed, and Jake slides in beside me. Aiden's sound asleep, clutching his Stegosaurus.

Jake rolls me to my side and spoons me from behind, slipping a thigh between mine and wrapping his arm securely around my waist to anchor me to him, as if he's afraid I'll slip away in the night.

I smile when I feel his lips in my hair.

He kisses the back of my head. "Sleep well, Elliot."

I lay my arm on his and link our fingers together. "You, too, Jacob."

23

Jake

I slept well and deeply last night, probably the best sleep I've had in a long time. There was something so incredibly satisfying about sleeping with Annie in my arms.

When the first rays of sunshine slip through the crack in the drapes, I find myself wide awake and bursting with energy. I think it's the residual effect of having mind-blowing sex last night. But it also stems from sleeping with the woman of my dreams.

I lie quietly snuggling with her a while longer, just enjoying the utter peace and tranquility of having her close. The scent and feel of her skin, of her hair, soothes me. And there's probably some kind of animal pheromones involved as well.

I peer over her head at Aiden, who's still sound asleep. He's got his stuffed dino tucked beneath his arm, held close to his face. He's an adorable kid, whether sleeping or awake, and I'm excited by the prospect of becoming his dad.

I've never given much thought to having kids. When Annie was out of my reach, it just seemed pointless. Sex, sure. I had sex when I needed it, but I could never attach. I always felt a little guilty for succumbing to my baser needs. So I figured I'd die alone and childless. But now everything's changed. I have Annie in my life again, and Aiden. I'll be the best dad I can to Aiden. And hopefully, God willing, we'll give him some little brothers and sisters. I know my folks would be thrilled.

I don't want to risk waking either Annie or Aiden, so I slip out of bed and head back to my room. After a quick shower, I pull on a pair of running shorts and my running shoes. A nice long run, pounding the pavement, sounds like a good idea.

Downstairs in the foyer I find a shopping bag of bath toys—dinosaurs and a collection of cars and trucks—and a white florist's box filled with two dozen perfect, pale pink roses wrapped in cellophane and tied off with a fancy pink ribbon. Perfect! I definitely owe Cameron.

I leave the bath toys in the foyer and carry the roses into the kitchen, sure I can find a vase to put them in. I find Elly and George seated at the little kitchen table, eating breakfast.

"Have we got a vase for these?" I ask Elly, pulling the bouquet of roses out of the box.

"Oh, Jake, they're lovely." She gets up from the table. "Yes, we have plenty of vases. Hold on."

She digs around in a cupboard and pulls out a tall crystal vase. "How about this one?"

"Perfect."

She fills the vase with water. "Give them to me, dear." She unwraps the roses, trims the stems with a pair of scissors, then sets them in the vase. "I'll put these on the dining room table so Annie will see them when she comes down for breakfast."

I head outside and find Charlie on the front porch, warming up. She's obviously on the same wavelength I am because she's dressed for running too. "Mind if I join you?"

"Be my guest," she says. "I've been sitting around on my ass too much lately."

"Let's do it."

There are paved running trails that meander through the woods and around the perimeter of the grounds. I'm sure the onsite security staff monitoring the surveillance cameras will get a kick out of watching us go through our paces.

We take our time with the first mile, just warming up and stretching our legs. By the second mile, we're running pretty hard.

Charlie's pretty competitive by nature, so she keeps me on my toes. She's very agile and light on her feet. It wouldn't look good for my wingman—or rather, my wingwoman—to leave me eating her dust.

We run in silence, side by side on the paved trails, for a solid hour. I figured we've logged five miles in that hour, hardly enough to make us break a sweat, but enough to say we at least did something.

After a cool down, Charlie and I head inside, where we find Annie and Aiden eating breakfast in the dining room.

I poke my head through the dining room doorway, making eye contact with Annie. "I'll grab a quick shower and join you."

"Oh, good, breakfast!" Charlie says, heading for the buffet.

I race upstairs to take a quick shower and put on clean clothes, then return to the dining room. After filling up a plate and grabbing a cup of coffee, I sit down next to Annie. "Good morning," I say, leaning over to kiss.

She smiles at me. "Good morning to you, too."

"Hi, Jake!" Aiden says, talking around a mouthful of food.

"Hi, Aiden." Then I turn to Annie. "So, what's on the agenda for today?"

"Aiden and I are going to do some schoolwork," she says. "And, Charlie promised to give Aiden another swimming lesson today."

"Good. What else?"

"I think that's it for now. Maybe later we could all take a walk down by the lake."

Aiden gives his mother a beseeching look. "Mommy... remember? You said you'd ask him."

Annie frowns, brushing back her son's hair. "I know, sweetheart. But I also told you it's probably not a good idea right now. I'm sorry."

"But you could ask him."

"Ask me what?" I say, sipping my coffee. "What's not a good

idea?"

"Can I go to my school's carnival?" Aiden says. "It's on Saturday. They're gonna have rides and games. Can I go? Please, Jake?"

"Maybe we can go next year," Annie says, patting the kid's back.

Aiden's expression falls, and he hits me with these puppy dog eyes. "Please, Jake?"

Annie bites back a grin as she watches me. Clearly, Aiden has decided to go over his mom's head.

"So, what's this carnival?" I ask her.

"Aiden's school is having its annual carnival on Saturday. It's a fundraiser for the school. He's been looking forward to this since he started preschool."

I exchange glances with Charlie, who gives me an ambiguous shrug. I sigh, hating to be the bad guy here, especially when I'm trying to win Aiden over. "I'm sorry, pal, but going to a carnival right now isn't a good idea."

Aiden looks crestfallen. "Please?" he says. "Just for a little while? We don't have to stay long. And I'll be really good, I promise."

I look at Annie. "I have to assume that your ex knows about this event."

She nods. "He probably does. It's being advertised pretty heavily on social media."

Aiden doesn't say another word, but he's clearly disappointed. He stares at his food, picking at it with his fork.

I smile apologetically at Annie. Damn, this parenting thing is hard. You want to make the kid happy, but you've got to watch out for his safety. That has to come first.

"He's bound to expect you to be there," I say to Annie, feeling the need to justify my position.

She nods. "I know. It's not safe. We understand completely, don't we, Aiden?"

Aiden picks at his food. "I guess so."

"It would be a security nightmare." I glance at Charlie, hoping for a little support here. "A huge crowd, potentially hundreds of people milling about. Total chaos. Even if we had Cameron and Killian with us, it would still be a nightmare."

"It would," Charlie says, fighting a grin as she nods in agreement. "No doubt about it. A real nightmare." She presses her lips in a flat line and looks down at her plate. "Absolutely. It would be a terrible idea."

"It would be," I say, getting up for a coffee refill. Actually, it really would be idiotic to even attempt it. So, why do I feel so bad for saying no to the kid?

Aiden peeks up at me from beneath his dark lashes.

"What?" I say, knowing I sound more than a little defensive. Since when do I have to justify security decisions to a five-year-old?

Aiden shakes his head. "Nothing."

When Charlie chuckles, I glare at her. "Not helping."

"What did I do?" She shrugs. "Hey, I'm on your side, big guy. I totally agree it would be a security nightmare to take a little boy to his school carnival so he can ride little kiddie rides and eat cotton candy."

I return to my seat. "What do you think, Elliot?"

"Jake, no one's arguing with you on this." She lays her hand on my arm. "I agree that it would be a real challenge from a security standpoint. We all understand. Really. It's fine."

I cross my arms over my chest and stare her down. "It sure feels like everyone's arguing with me."

Annie breaks into a killer smile and leans forward to kiss me. "Jake, it's okay. Honestly."

The adults in the room might understand, but Aiden clearly doesn't. He looks crushed. This carnival seems to mean a lot to him, and I don't want to disappoint him. He's been through enough as it is. I sigh. "All right, we'll go to the carnival. But just for an hour, and not a minute longer, is that understood, young man?"

Aiden perks up instantly, a huge grin on his face. "Really? We can go?" He jumps up from his seat and runs to me, throwing his arms wide open and giving me a fierce hug. "Thanks, Jake!"

I hug him back. "You're welcome."

Annie meets my gaze over the top of Aiden's head, and she gives me a smile that makes my heart skip a beat.

"With a team of five," I say, "we should be able to keep one little boy safe."

"Five?" she says.

"I'm including you, along with Charlie, Cameron, and Killian. You're part of the team now."

* * *

After breakfast, I head to the security office and hold a video conference call with Killian so he can update me on their surveillance activities. He shows me some video footage he and Cameron have gotten on Patterson. They captured two meetings between Patterson and his dealer. They've got money exchanging hands, as well as heroin. We've got him on buying and possession, enough to put him behind bars for a while. But I want more than that. I want to get him on dealing. And according to Killian's sources, he is.

"We've also got him on prostitution," Killian says, bringing up a video clip that shows Patterson chatting up a middle-aged woman on a street corner in the dead of night. From what I can tell through the night-vision camera, the woman looks strung out.

After a brief exchange of words, and a hand-off of cash, the woman walks off with Patterson, turning the corner and disappearing down a dark alley, out of the camera's view.

I exhale harshly, scrubbing my hand over my face. I can't believe this low-life asshole was ever married to Annie. I know she said he wasn't like this early in their marriage, and I know drug addiction makes people do crazy things, but this guy... damn. Just give me five minutes alone with him. That's all I need to make sure he never darkens Annie's doorstep again. Just five minutes.

"Yeah, he's a real gem," Killian says. "So, you and Annie, huh?"

"Yeah." I guess word gets around fast.

He nods. "I'm not surprised. I saw how you reacted when you saw her at the McIntyre building. I've never seen you like that with a woman. She feels the same way?"

"Yeah, she does."

"I guess this means you're going to be a stepfather."

"Looks like it." It's a good thing Killian can't see the stupid grin on my face. He'd never let me live it down.

After we conclude our video call, I go in search of my new family. I find Annie and Aiden seated at the little table in the kitchen.

With a fat pencil clutched tightly in his hand, Aiden is in the process of painstakingly writing his name on a pad of paper, pronouncing each letter as he writes it. "A – I – D – E – N."

"That's right, honey!" Annie cups the back of Aiden's head and kisses his forehead.

Aiden has a huge smile on his face, clearly proud of himself. When he sees me standing in the doorway, he says, "Jake, come look! I spelled my name!"

"Good job, buddy," I say, walking over to them so I can admire his handiwork. The letters are crooked and about two inches tall, and the "E" is backward, but other than that, it's perfect.

I lean down to kiss Annie. "I'll be downstairs lifting iron. When you guys are free, come get me and we'll do something fun."

‿ɔ 24

Annie

J ust as Aiden and I are wrapping up our lessons for the morning, Charlie appears.

"How about a swimming lesson, Aiden?" she says. "If that's okay with Mom."

"Sure," I say, smiling as Aiden jumps up eagerly from the table. "I think we've done enough school work for today."

Charlie holds out her hand to Aiden. "Come on. Let's go get you changed into your swim trunks."

"Don't get Stevie wet!" I remind him. "And be sure to go potty *before* you get in the pool."

I remain at the table for a moment, admiring Aiden's handiwork. In addition to writing his name, he wrote the entire alphabet and his numbers from one to twenty. I drew geometric shapes for him to color. We counted and did some basic arithmetic using M&Ms so he could conceptualize the quantities. I'm excited to think about teaching my son math.

I make a note to myself to go online and order some workbooks for us to use this summer in preparation for him starting kindergarten in the fall. Of course, I don't know where we'll be in the fall or what we'll be doing. We certainly can't stay here indefinitely. Shane was kind enough to let us stay here at his estate, but we can't trespass on his generosity forever.

After putting away our school supplies, I head downstairs to find Jake. I have this overwhelming desire to see him, to be in the same room with him. To be near him.

I know it sounds like a cliché, but last night was life-changing. The way he made love to me—the intensity, the passion, the fearlessness—he shook me to the core. I think it shook him, too. It wasn't just sex. It was healing. It was bonding.

He's the same caring and attentive boy I fell in love with so many years ago, but he's also so much more now. He seems bigger than life to me now, not just figuratively, but literally as well.

Of course I find him in the fitness room. This time he's standing on a mat lifting a barbell. There are several large weights attached to each end of the bar, and he's straining, grimacing, as he raises the bar to his chest. I can't help staring at his muscles as he lifts the weights, watching them contract and flex with the effort.

I'm not ashamed to say that watching him lift weights is a real turn-on. How can it not be? Last night, having all that strength and intensity directed at me was mind blowing.

"Aren't you supposed to have a spotter when you do that?" I say, leaning in the doorway, watching him. "Those weights look pretty heavy."

He lowers the bar to the mat with a grin. "I'm not lifting enough to need a spotter. All done with school?" He glances behind me. "Where's Aiden?"

"Charlie took him to the pool for a swimming lesson." I walk into the fitness room, finding it hard to take my eyes off Jake. He's wearing black shorts and black sneakers, and nothing else. Jake brings a whole new meaning to the phrase *tall, dark, and handsome.*

He grabs a towel and wipes his face and neck. "Sorry, baby, I'm a sweaty mess."

"That's okay. I don't mind." I walk closer, standing just a foot away, and our gazes lock. Just thinking about how we made love last night kicks my pulse into overdrive. He was wild, almost animalistic. Just thinking about it makes me blush. He was fearless, intense, shameless.

And the way he marked my skin last night... leaving several small hickeys between my thighs, in a private place that only he and I will ever see.

Gazing intently at me, he walks forward, steering me backward until my back hits the mirrored wall. He looms over me, like a dark guardian angel. I can feel the heat radiating from his big body and smell him, a combination of warm male skin mixed with faint aftershave. His gaze lowers to my mouth, and when I nervously wet my bottom lip, his expression darkens and his nostrils flare.

He leans down, his mouth close to my ear. His warm breath washes over me, teasing my nerve endings. "After last night, there's no way I can ever again sleep without you. I'm just telling you." He places a warm, open-mouthed kiss on my neck, just beneath my ear. "I need you in my bed, Elliot."

I nod. "I'll talk to Aiden. He slept in his own bedroom at Mom and Dad's, so he should be fine having his own room again."

Jake cups my breast through my top, his thumb brushing against my nipple. My nerves tingle all the way down to my core, leaving me hot and needy. I reach out and cup his face, and he leans into my hand before turning his face into my palm and kissing it.

"I'll talk to him after dinner tonight," I say.

"I know I have to share you with Aiden, and I'm okay with that. And I get that Aiden's needs have to come first. After all, he's your baby."

"He's not my only baby." I lean forward to kiss him. "You're my baby too. Don't worry. I have more than enough love for the both of you."

He presses his mouth to mine, sucking gently as he seals our mouths for a kiss that makes me ache.

* * *

After supper, Jake and I take Aiden downstairs to the home theater to watch a kids' animated dinosaur movie.

This theater is amazing. It resembles a commercial movie theater, just smaller in size. Still, I bet it could seat forty people. There's a concession stand in the rear of the screening room, with a vending machine filled with cold drinks. Aiden was amazed when Jake showed him how to push a button to make his selection.

"You don't have to put money in it?" Aiden said.

"Nope. Just push a button and your drink comes out here."

There's also a candy vending machine that spits out free candy—a child's dream come true. Aiden is astounded.

The best feature, though, is the old-fashioned red-and-white popcorn machine. Aiden finds the process of making popcorn fascinating, and he asks Jake to lift him up so he can watch the first kernels pop.

It's painfully ironic that my parents disapproved of Jake when we were in high school and considered him a bad prospect for a husband. And yet, he's clearly the best thing that's ever happened, to me, and to Aiden.

It's pretty clear to me that McIntyre Security has made the family quite wealthy. I can't even imagine how much a property like this estate must be worth, but certainly it's in the millions, or maybe even the tens of millions.

But it's not just the money. It's Jake himself. He has more integrity in his little finger than Ted has in his whole body. My parents should be ashamed of what they did to us. Frankly, I'm ashamed on their behalf. I don't know how I'm going to reconcile my relationship with them knowing what I know now. For Aiden's sake, though, I'll have to figure something out. They're his grandparents. He's already lost his father. I don't want him to lose his grandparents, too.

After having made popcorn for everyone, and gotten us all soft drinks and candy, Jake goes into the control room in the back and cues up the movie. I don't remember what it's called, but he says it's rated G and that the reviews on Amazon said it was a good choice for families with very young children. The fact that Jake took the time to read the reviews ahead of time means the world to me.

Jake and I sit in the middle of the front row, and Aiden automatically climbs into Jake's lap when the opening credits begin to roll.

Aiden looks back at Jake, his expression very serious and a little sad. "I wish you were my dad."

Jake reaches for my hand and squeezes it so hard I silently wince. "So do I, pal."

"My dad's not very nice," Aiden says, his eyes filling with tears. "He hurts my mom. And sometimes he hurts me."

"I know." Jake rubs his hand up and down Aiden's back. "But he's not going to hurt either of you again. I won't let him."

Aiden nods wistfully. "I believe you. You can do anything."

Oh, my God. My throat tightens up, and I'm afraid I'm going to start bawling like a baby. I stand up. "I'll be back. I need to get something—a napkin."

"I'll get you one," Jake says, looking at me worriedly.

"No, that's all right. You guys sit. I'll be right back."

I head for the back of the theater and grab a napkin from the dispenser, dabbing at my tears. I hold back a sob, breathing through my mouth as I try to rein in my emotions. I don't know which is affecting me more... Aiden's fear of his father, or his absolute trust in Jake.

"Hey." Jake comes up behind me and wraps his arms around my waist. "It's okay. I've got you."

I turn in his arms, wrapping mine around his waist and holding on tightly. I press my face into his shirt. "I'm sorry."

"There's nothing to apologize for."

"Hey, guys!" Aiden yells, waving at us from his seat. "The movie's starting! You better hurry!"

"We're coming," Jake calls to him. "Be right there." He tilts my face up to his. "Everything's going to be fine, I promise." And then he kisses me, soppy tears and all. He takes the napkin from my hand and dabs my cheeks. "We're coming."

𝓮 25

Annie

After the movie, I take Aiden upstairs to our room. It's time for bath and bed. Thanks to Jake, Aiden has more than enough bath toys to occupy him, so bath time stretches out to nearly an hour. I finally have to make him get out of the tub, dry off, brush his teeth, and put on his PJs.

Once he's clean, warm, and tucked safely into bed, with Stevie and his favorite car beside him, I read him a couple of bedtime stories.

In between stories, I say, "Do you know how you had your own bedroom at Grandma and Grandpa's house?"

"Yeah."

"Well, how about if you have your own room here? This could be your own bedroom."

He frowns, looking a bit perplexed. "But where would you sleep?"

I sigh, not sure where to take this conversation. "Well, I was thinking—"

"I know! You could sleep with Jake," he says, very matter-of-factly. "He likes you."

I have to bite my lip to keep from smiling. "I think that's a great idea. Would you be okay with that?"

"Sure." He shrugs nonchalantly. "I think he's a great boyfriend for you. I think you should marry him. Then he'd be my dad for real."

* * *

I'm not surprised when Aiden falls asleep in the middle of our third bedtime story. He's had a busy day. I tuck him into bed, along with Stevie and his car, and kiss his sweet little forehead. "Goodnight, baby boy."

After using the restroom and freshening up, I change into the one nightgown I brought with me. It's pale blue silk and falls just above my knees. I don't know why I brought it, but I'm glad I did. It's far sexier than my PJ shorts.

After turning on the nanny cam, I let myself out of Aiden's room and slip across the hall to Jake's room. The door is ajar, so I push it open and step inside. The room is dimly lit, the only light coming from the flickering flames of three candles sitting on the fireplace mantel.

On top of Jake's dresser is a crystal vase filled with lovely pale pink roses. "My favorite flower," I say, touching the tip of my nose to the velvety-soft petals. "You remembered."

Jake's sitting at the foot of his bed, looking incredibly handsome in a pair of black trousers and a white button-up shirt that's open at the collar, exposing his strong neck and a bit of dark chest hair.

At the sight of him, my belly clenches, and I'm glad I put on the nightgown. He gazes intently at me, his expression darkening as he takes in my attire. He's all dressed up, and I'm wearing a nightgown.

I laugh nervously as I join him. "I feel a bit underdressed."

He shakes his head, chuckling. "No. My God, you look perfect." He reaches for my hand and pulls me to stand between his legs, a pleased smile on his face.

I reach out to brush back his hair. "I take it you were expecting me."

"I was hoping you'd come."

"It was actually Aiden's idea that I move into your room. He thinks you're good husband material."

Jake holds my hands tightly and pulls me close for a quick kiss. "Listen to your son. I *am* good husband material. I can provide very well for you both. I'll make sure you have everything you could possibly need."

"The only thing I need is you."

He takes my hands in his, holding them so reverently. "I love you, Annie. You stole my heart when I was a boy, and you still own it now that I'm a man. I realize you might think this is too soon..."

"Jake, are you—"

He kneels down in front of me, still holding my hands. "Annie, will you *please* marry me?"

I drop to my knees in front of him. "It's not too soon. It could never be too soon." I raise my hands to cradle his face, his soft beard tickling my palms. "I don't deserve you, but for some inexplicable reason fate has gifted me with your heart. Yes, I will marry you."

He lets out a relieved sigh. "Thank God. I don't know what I would have done if you'd said no."

"Not a chance of that happening," I say, smiling as I kiss him.

* * *

The last time Jake made love to me, it was wild and exciting. This time, when he carries me to his bed—*our bed*—and lays me down, it's slow and sweet and gentle.

He undresses me slowly, then kisses every inch of me from the top of my head to the tips of my toes. All the care he took, with the candles and the roses, and dressing up in slacks and a nice shirt, his reverence for the occasion... it shatters my heart into a million pieces.

I watch him undress, mesmerized by the sight of him. Then he climbs onto the bed, looming over me. We touch and taste, taking our time. When he finally rocks into me, it's slow and easy, generating a sweet friction that teases my body to respond.

I gasp. "Oh, God, Jake, yes. Just like that, please."

He smiles, leaning down to kiss me as he rocks into me at just the right tempo, heating me up inside. I can feel a tingling sensation growing deep in my core, swelling and unfurling as it gently crescendos. When I come, my body stiffens, my back arching and my thighs trembling. His mouth covers mine and he swallows my breathy cries.

As my sheath squeezes him tightly, practically milking him, he throws his head back with a muffled shout. He stiffens, and even with the condom between us, I can feel his erection pulsing deep inside me. His big arms are shaking as he braces himself over me in bed, careful not to crush me with his weight.

With a cry, he finally withdrawals himself and comes down beside me, pulling me into his arms. He kisses my forehead as he tries to catch his breath. "You're going to be the death of me yet, baby."

"Are you complaining?"

"Hell, no."

26

Jake

Saturday morning, Cameron and Killian show up at eight, right on schedule. I want to go over the day's itinerary with them in excruciating detail to be sure nothing is left out. I still think it's a bad idea to take Aiden to this carnival, but I hate to disappoint him.

"We'll leave at ten," I tell the guys and Charlie, who are all sitting around the conference table in the security wing of the estate. "I want every single base covered. I want contingency plans. Nothing can go wrong."

"Annie and Aiden will ride in the Tahoe with me and Charlie.

You guys follow in the Escalade. I told Aiden he can have *one hour* at the carnival—that's it. One hour. Not a minute longer. We'll just have to make the most of it."

"Do you really think Patterson will show up?" Cameron asks.

I shrug. "Honestly, I don't know. But I'm pretty confident that he knows about the carnival. We have to go on the assumption he might show. He's already made two attempts to grab Aiden in the past two weeks. I don't think he'll miss another chance. He would see a crowded event like this as a tempting opportunity."

"Why does he want to grab the kid?" Killian says. "He doesn't seem to me like the fatherly type."

"He's not," I say. "But Aiden is Annie's weakness. I think he's trying to get the kid so he can use him as leverage against Annie."

"Charlie and I will stay close to Annie and Aiden," I say to the guys. "I want you two keeping a wider perimeter, so you can alert us if you see Patterson on site. If Patterson is spotted, Charlie and I will get Annie and Aiden out of there, while you two run interference and prevent him from following."

"It sounds simple enough," Killian says, leaning back in his chair, crossing one cowboy boot over his knee. "So, why do I have a feeling it will be anything but simple?"

"I guess we'll find out soon enough." I plant my hands on the table. "Now, who's hungry?"

Killian rises to his feet. "Elly's making breakfast?"

"You bet."

"Then I'm eating," he says. "Her cooking is *almost* as good as my mama's."

When we walk into the dining room at nine, Annie and Aiden are already seated at the table, along with Elly and George.

Aiden looks up from his plate, and his eyes widen with excitement as he chews. "Hi, Jake! Are we going to the carnival today?"

"Honey, please don't talk with your mouth full of food," Annie says, laughing as she pats the kid's back.

"Yes, we're going to the carnival," I tell him. "Just as soon as everyone has had breakfast."

* * *

As soon as Annie and Aiden are done eating, she hustles him upstairs so he can brush his teeth and get ready to leave.

"Let's meet out front in twenty minutes," I tell the rest of the team.

I head upstairs to my suite, pausing for a moment outside Aiden's door. I can hear Aiden talking excitedly. I also hear an odd thumping sound which has me wondering what the hell's going on in there.

I knock on the door.

The door opens, and Annie's there looking flustered. She's holding two tops in her hands, still on hangers. I glance over her shoulder to see Aiden jumping on the bed. That explains the thumping noise.

"Everything okay?" I ask her.

"Yeah," Aiden says, answering for his mom. "She can't decide which top to wear." He rolls his eyes at me. "Girls. Am I right?"

I bark out a laugh. "Where did you hear talk like that?"

"Charlie," he says, hopping off the bed and running into the bathroom. "Brushing my teeth!" he yells back through the open doorway.

I take advantage of the momentary privacy to sweep Annie into my arms and kiss her thoroughly.

"What was that for?" she says.

"That was for last night. I came to tell you we're meeting out front in twenty minutes. Either Charlie or I will come get you."

"Okay."

I head to my room for a quick shower, and then change into jeans and a black T-shirt. I strap on my chest holster along with my Beretta and extra ammo. A black leather jacket conceals the handgun.

When I knock on Annie's door, she opens immediately. Wearing jeans and a pink top, her hair up in a ponytail, she looks so much like my Annie from high school I could cry. Aiden runs up beside her, bouncing with excitement.

"Ready?" I ask.

"We are," she says, ushering Aiden out the door.

Charlie joins us, and the four of us head downstairs, where Killian and Cameron are standing out front with George and Elly.

"Don't you look pretty," Elly says, smiling when she sees Annie. Annie blushes. "Thank you."

We're off then, our little convoy of two, as we head for Lincoln Park.

"Okay, ground rules, pal," I say, meeting Aiden's gaze in the rearview mirror. "You stay with me at *all times*. Do you hear me, young man?"

He salutes my reflection in the rearview mirror. "Yes, sir!"

"I mean it. You don't leave my sight for any reason. No running off. If you need to go to the bathroom, I'll go with you. Got it?"

"Yes! I got it. What about my mom? What if she needs to go to the bathroom?"

Charlie laughs. "If your mom needs to go to the bathroom, I'll go with her."

"Right." Aiden nods, looking so serious.

Before long, we arrive at the school and have to wait in line a few minutes before we can enter the parking lot. The parking lot is filled to overflowing, and we're directed to park on the grass. Cameron and Killian are right behind us in the Escalade, and they park beside us at the end of a row.

"Now, we four stick together like glue," I say, eyeing Aiden directly. "Got it?"

"I got it, Jake!" Aiden quickly unbuckles his seat belt and opens his door to climb out.

Charlie and I are both armed, of course, and wearing ear comms and wrist mics so we can communicate with the rest of our team. I give an ear piece to Annie, too, so she can hear our chatter.

"What about me, Jake?" Aiden says, missing nothing. "Don't I get an ear thing too?"

"Sorry, buddy, they're just for grown-ups." I hold out my hand to him, and he doesn't hesitate to take it. "Remember, you said you'd stick close to me," I remind him.

Then Aiden reaches for Annie's hand, and the three of us are holding hands, Aiden in the middle, as we head toward the carnival entrance. Charlie follows behind.

At the entrance, I buy all four of us entrance passes in the form of wristbands. It gives me an oddly pleasant feeling as I attach the wristband to Aiden's little wrist.

He gazes up at me with wide, excited eyes. "Thanks for letting us come here, Jake."

"No problem, kid." I reach out and ruffle his hair. "So, now that we're here, what do you want to do first?"

"Can we go down the slide?" he says, pointing at a forty-foot tall slide across the way.

It's one of those slides where folks sit in burlap sacks and slide down the tall, wavy slide. It seems safe enough.

"Sure, why not?" I say.

Aiden starts off for the slide, but I whistle sharply, stopping him in his tracks. I crook my finger at him, and he runs back to me. "What did I tell you about sticking close to me?"

"I forgot," he says. "Sorry."

"No need to apologize. Just remember to stay right by me at all times, okay?"

"Got it!"

Then he reaches for my hand, and we walk hand-in-hand toward the slide, Annie and Charlie following us.

Charlie and I already had a discussion this morning, before we left. Her job is to stick to Annie like glue, just as a precaution.

Aiden is a much more vulnerable target than his mother, but we need to be prepared for all contingencies.

Aiden goes down the slide once with Annie, and then he asks me to slide with him. How the hell can I refuse? "All right, pal. Come on."

I put my hand on his back and lead him up the steps to the top of the slide. While we're waiting our turn, I glance down at Annie and Charlie, who are laughing at something—probably me. As Annie looks up and catches me watching her, her laughter morphs into a smile that hits me like a punch to the gut.

Aiden grabs my arm. "Jake, it's our turn!"

"What? Okay. Right." I lay the burlap sack down on the slide and sit on it, pulling Aiden onto my lap and securing him with an arm around his waist.

Aiden latches onto my arm with both hands, holding on for dear life, and leans back against me. I push us off with my free hand, and as we're careening down the slide, he screams his head off, clearly delighted.

"Let's go again, Jake!" he crows, when we reach the bottom of the slide. "Please?" He grabs my hand and tugs me after him as he heads for the steps again.

The smile on Annie's face makes it all worth it.

৶ 27

Annie

I can't remember the last time I had so much fun. Watching Aiden run Jake ragged all over the carnival grounds is quite entertaining. Charlie must think so, too, as she hasn't stopped smiling either. Once Jake rode the slide with Aiden, Aiden decided that he had to ride all the rides with Jake.

After the slide, Jake takes Aiden on the kiddy rollercoaster, which Jake can barely squeeze into. His legs are way too long for the diminutive cars. Then they ride the merry-go-round twice and the spinning tea cups three times until Aiden says he's going to vomit. Charlie and I follow along, enjoying watching Jake run ragged by an energetic five-year-old.

"He'll make a great dad," Charlie says to me, as we're watching Jake play the ring toss game as he tries to win a stuffed Panda bear for Aiden.

"Yes, he will."

"Do you want more kids?"

I hesitate, wondering if she's asking me a hypothetical question, or if she specifically means me and Jake. "Yes, I want more kids. I'd love for Aiden to have a brother or sister."

"Or a bunch of them." She laughs. "Jake comes from a family of seven kids. I somehow don't think he'll want to stop at one or two."

As an only child, I like the idea of us having a big family. Growing up, I always wished I had siblings. "I think I could handle that."

When Aiden tries to talk Jake into letting him have some cotton candy, Jake looks to me for guidance. I smile and shrug. This is his show. Of course, he acquiesces and buys Aiden a huge bag of rainbow-colored cotton candy.

One hour has come and gone, quickly morphing into two hours, and Jake seems to be having as much fun as Aiden. Twice, I've caught glimpses of Cameron and Killian shadowing us at a distance, and they seem equally amused at Jake's role as Aiden's new best friend.

Charlie and I are standing off to the side while Jake and Aiden wait in a long line to ride the bumper cars. After downing a large lemonade, I'm in need of a restroom. "I need to pee," I whisper to Charlie.

Charlie nods and speaks into her wrist mic. "I'm taking mama bear to the ladies' room."

Jake glances back at us, his expression suddenly sharp. Then he nods and says, "Make it quick" into his mic.

"The restrooms are inside the school," I tell Charlie, and she follows me to the main entrance.

There are quite a few people milling about inside the school, looking at student art exhibits and an assortment of class displays posted on the walls. We turn left and follow the main corridor to the restrooms, but the line for the women's room is down the hall and around a corner.

While we're waiting, I feel someone tap me on the shoulder. I look back and find Aiden's preschool teacher smiling at me.

"Mrs. Patterson, hi. The line's really long. You can use the restroom in my classroom if you'd like," she says. "It's unlocked."

The preschool classrooms are close by, so I thank his teacher and we head down the hall to her classroom. Sure enough, the door's unlocked, and Charlie and I walk right in.

I flip on the light, and we walk into a room filled with little child-sized tables and chairs.

"Oh, my goodness," Charlie says, nudging one of the little chairs with her foot. "They're so tiny."

"That's preschool for you." I head across the room to the restroom, which is located in the back corner. "Be right back."

I turn on the restroom light and step inside, closing the door behind me. I hurry, not wanting to be away from Aiden for longer than necessary. Just as I'm washing my hands, I hear a loud crash coming from the classroom, followed by a muffled grunt.

I open the door. "Charlie, are you—"

Several of the kids' desks in the center of the room have been shoved aside, the chairs knocked over. On the floor, Charlie's grappling with someone—a man—for control of a handgun.

"Get back in the bathroom and lock the door!" Charlie yells, just as she does something painful to the man's wrist, making him cry out and drop the gun. She slides the gun across the floor, far out of reach, and pins the man to the floor, securing his arms behind his back.

The knit hat on the man's head slips off, and I stand frozen to the spot, horrified. I can't see his face, but I recognize that sandy-blond hair. "Ted?"

Charlie glares at me. "Get back in the bathroom and lock the fucking door, now!"

Ted heaves himself up, throwing Charlie off. She immediately moves between us, holding him away from me.

She activates her wrist mic. "We have a fucking situation in the preschool classroom!"

"Annie, we need to talk," Ted says, trying to get around Charlie.

Charlie intercepts him and motions for me to move back.

My heart is pounding. All I can think about is Aiden and Jake. Are they okay? "Ted, you shouldn't be here."

"Don't tell me what I can and can't do, you stupid bitch!" he yells. He looks terrible, his face gaunt and pale.

Ted makes an attempt to get past Charlie, and she cuts him off, putting him in a choke hold. Gritting his teeth, he strains against her hold, trying in vain to break free.

The door to the preschool room crashes open, slamming into the wall, as a deep roar fills the air. "Step away from them. Now!"

I look up just as Jake charges into the room, his thunderous gaze locked on Ted. "Charlie, get Annie out of here!"

If Jake is here with us, then where is Aiden?

"What the fuck are *you* doing here?" Ted growls, turning to face Jake. He scowls at Jake, then turns back to me, an incredulous look on his face. "Holy shit, is this your *boyfriend?* Are you fucking kidding me? As soon as I'm out of the picture, you run right back to him? I knew it! I knew you were fucking him behind my back. You whore!"

Visibly seething, Jake grabs Ted by the front of his shirt with both hands. Then he glances at Charlie. "Take Annie to the vehicle," he says, his voice deep and measured. "Aiden's there now with the guys."

My knees almost buckle in relief when I hear that Aiden is okay.

Charlie grabs my arm and marches me toward the door, making a wide swath around Ted and Jake. Just as we step out of the classroom, I glance back in time to see Jake haul off and slam his fist into Ted's abdomen. Ted folds in two and sinks to the floor, clutching his belly, groaning.

Charlie hauls me through the hallway and out the front door. We head for the parking lot, and when I see the familiar vehicles, I rush ahead, looking for Aiden. He's in the rear seat of the Escalade, sitting with Cameron.

Cameron opens the car door and lets Aiden hop out and run

to me.

"Are you okay, sweetie?" I ask Aiden, hugging him close.

He grins up at me, unfazed. "We had so much fun today!"

Clearly Aiden has no idea there's been some trouble. "I'm glad, honey."

"Where's Jake?" he says, glancing around. "He said he had to go to the bathroom."

"He'll be here soon." *I hope.*

Charlie has the Tahoe unlocked and the rear door open. I steer Aiden inside the vehicle and into his car seat, helping him strap in. Then I sit beside him, willing my body to stop shaking.

Charlie and the guys stand outside the Tahoe, clearly alert and on guard as they wait for Jake to return. I know they're all concealing handguns beneath their jackets. Aiden and I couldn't be safer than we are sitting here in the Tahoe. I'm not worried about us. But I am worried about Jake.

"Did you see all the rides we went on?" Aiden chatters happily, oblivious to the tense undercurrents all around us.

"Yes, I did."

"It was awesome!"

I finally realize that Aiden is holding a baseball glove and a stuffed Panda bear. I remember Jake playing a ring toss game for the Panda. "Where did you get the baseball glove?"

"Jake won it for me. He said he'd teach me how to throw a baseball."

I smile. Jake's been a better father figure to Aiden in less than a week than Ted ever was.

✄ 28

Jake

I haul Patterson into the bathroom and lock the door behind us. I don't want to make a mess on the classroom carpet. Blood will be much easier to wipe off these tile floors.

"Let me go!" Patterson growls, practically spitting at me as he struggles in my grip.

He can fight all he wants, but he's not getting loose. I have six inches and over a hundred pounds on this guy. It's not going to be a fair fight, but I don't give a shit. I'm not here for a fair fight. I'm here to exact vengeance on an abusive asshole who hurt the woman I love and the boy I consider my own now.

"You think you're so hot because Annie's with you now?" he hisses at me. "Well, fuck you! You can have the cunt! She was a pathetic excuse for a wife and an even worse lay. Fucking her was like sticking it in a sex doll. I'm done with her!"

I'm itching to wrap my hands around his throat and squeeze, putting an end to Annie's terror once and for all. All I can see is red, and I can't hear much over the rush of blood in my head. I just want to grind this pathetic loser to a pulp beneath my boots.

His outburst doesn't deserve a reply. Instead, I slam my fist into his face. Blood sprays from his shattered nose like a geyser, hitting me in the chest and face. I couldn't care less. I'll bathe in his blood if I have to.

Patterson chokes on his own blood, sputtering and yelling garbled obscenities. I drive my fist into his belly and release him, letting him drop to the tile floor like so much dead weight.

"This is for Annie and Aiden," I say, crouching over him so I can drive my fist into his face with a satisfying thud. "For every bruise and cut and broken bone." I let myself go, giving rein to my hatred for this lowlife, pummeling him without mercy until his face is drenched in blood. When he's reduced to a mewling, sobbing mess, I step back. "You're not so tough now, are you?"

I glance at the mirror hanging over the sink, startled at how much blood is on me. Wetting some paper towels, I wipe away the blood from the front of my jacket and from my face. My T-shirt is ruined, so I zip up my jacket to hide the mess.

Before I walk out, I give Patterson one last warning. "If I ever see you anywhere near Annie or Aiden, I will kill you. Is that crystal clear?" He might think it's an empty threat, but it's not.

Patterson's bloody face is so swollen, his response is incomprehensible, just garbled syllables that make no sense. I walk out of the bathroom, grab Patterson's discarded handgun off the floor, and tuck it into the back waistband of my jeans.

Then, using the old landline phone on the classroom wall, I dial 911 and report that there's a mess that needs to be cleaned up in the preschool bathroom.

* * *

When I approach the vehicles in the parking lot, I see the rest of my team on guard, protecting my family seated in the Tahoe. I feel a surge of relief knowing that Annie wasn't hurt, and that Aiden never even knew his dad had come to the carnival. I glance down once more to make sure there's no sign of blood on me.

My team is still on high alert, their eyes watching me intently. The Tahoe's rear passenger door opens and Annie steps out, a concerned look on her face.

She rushes past her guards and intercepts me, grabbing my arms and looking me over hastily. "Are you okay? Are you hurt?"

Her concern helps soothe the acid singeing my veins. "I'm fine." I take her arm and gently steer her back to the vehicle. "Get in, babe. We're leaving."

She frowns, but she climbs into the back of the SUV and buckles her seat belt.

Cameron and Killian fall back to the Escalade, leaning against the side of the vehicle as they watch me.

Charlie gets in my face. "Is Patterson still alive?" She keeps her voice low enough that Annie and Aiden can't hear.

I grit my teeth. "Yes. Barely. I called it in, so we'd better get going."

I signal for the guys to take off in the Escalade. Then I start for the driver's door of my Tahoe, but Charlie snags my arm.

"You'd better let me drive," she says, glancing pointedly at the knuckles of my right hand, which are already starting to turn purple and swell.

I'd managed to wipe off the blood, but the tissue damage isn't so easy to hide. Annie will see the damage to my knuckles if my hands are on the steering wheel. "Good point."

I hand my keys to Charlie, and she climbs behind the wheel as I get in the front passenger seat.

"Hi, Jake!" Aiden says, all smiles.

"Hi, buddy."

Aiden is happily occupied with Stevie, his new Panda bear, and his baseball glove, and the rest of us ride in silence.

After a few moments, Annie releases her seat belt and scoots forward in her seat, her hands coming to rest on my shoulders. She presses her lips to the back of my neck. "Are you sure you're all right?" she whispers.

The feel of her warm breath on my neck makes me shiver, and I cover one of her hands with my good one. "I'm fine, baby, honestly. Now put your seat belt back on—you're committing a security violation."

Charlie takes us home, and we arrive at the estate in the late afternoon. Elly's out front tending her potted flowers on the front steps. She waves at us as Charlie parks the Tahoe near the front doors. "How was your outing?" she asks as we disembark.

"It was awesome!" Aiden yells, jumping out of the SUV. He runs to Elly and gives her an impromptu hug. "We rode a lot of rides. And Jake won a Panda and a baseball glove for me!" He proudly shows her his new toys.

"That's wonderful!" she says, giving me a wink. "I'm sure Stevie the Stegosaurus would love to have a friend. What are you going to name the Panda?"

Aiden thinks for a moment. "Paul! His name is Paul."

"Paul the Panda," I say, nodding. "Makes perfect sense."

Elly wipes her hands on her gardening apron and draws Aiden close. "Are you hungry for a snack? I made some chocolate chip cookies. Would you like some cookies and milk?"

Annie steps behind Aiden, putting her hands on his shoulders. "That sounds wonderful, Elly. Would you mind taking Aiden inside for a snack?" She gives Elly a pointed look. "I need to talk to Jake."

"Sure," Elly says, catching on quickly. She takes Aiden's hand and leads him inside the house.

Charlie walks up the steps and opens the front door, following them inside. "I'll stay with him," she says, giving us a look. "Take your time."

That leaves me alone with Annie on the front steps.

Annie reaches for my right hand, cradling it in both of hers, staring down at the darkening bruises. "Tell me what happened." She gently strokes the back of my hand, careful not to touch my damaged knuckles.

I sigh. "I beat the fucking hell out of your ex-husband. That's what happened."

She winces at the harsh tone of my voice. "Is he—"

"Still alive? Yes. Although to be honest with you, I wanted to kill him. And I told him if I ever see him around you or Aiden again, I *will* kill him."

From the look on her face, I can tell she believes me. Good. Because I meant it.

"Come upstairs with me," she says. "Let me take care of your hand."

"It's not necessary. I've had much worse."

"Please, Jake." She squeezes my good hand.

I'm not used to being fawned over like this. I'm not used to someone caring that I'm injured. It's a nice feeling. "Okay. If it will make you feel better." I lay my arm across her shoulders and we walk inside together. Up the stairs we go, hand-in-hand, and down the corridor to my room.

I start to unzip my jacket, but freeze when I remember my T-shirt underneath is stained with blood. "On second thought, maybe this isn't such a good idea."

Her brow furrows, and she pushes my hand aside and unzips my jacket, pushing it off my shoulders. She gasps when she sees the amount of blood on my shirt. "Oh, my God! Are you sure you're not hurt? This isn't your blood?"

"None of that is mine, baby, I assure you. The day a loser like Patterson gets the drop on me is the day I need to find a new line of work." I laugh as I shrug out of my jacket.

She follows me into my walk-in closet and watches as I remove the Glock from my chest holster, securing the handgun in a small gun safe built into the wall. I also secure the gun I confiscated from Ted. Then I hang up my chest holster and whip off my ruined T-shirt, wadding it up and tossing it into a waste can.

"Come get in the shower," she says, taking my good hand and leading me into the bathroom.

I smile, suddenly feeling buoyed by the prospect of getting naked with Annie in the shower. "Only if you get in with me."

"Jake." She frowns.

"I'm serious. My hand hurts too much for me to wash myself." *Liar.* "You'll have to help me."

She rolls her eyes at my flimsy excuse for her to get naked and wet. "All right, fine."

She helps me undress, and I play up my damaged knuckles for all it's worth. She kneels on the bathroom rug to unfasten my boots and remove them, along with my socks. Then she reaches up to unsnap the waistband of my jeans. When her fingers brush my abdomen, I suck in a sharp breath. I'm already hard, and getting harder by the second. She very gingerly lowers my zipper, careful not to catch my dick. Then she tugs my jeans and boxer briefs down my legs, pulling them off.

The sublime perfection of this moment certainly isn't lost on me. *My Elliot* is on her knees in front of me, and my erection is bobbing in the air like a divining rod with a mind of its own, straining eagerly toward her mouth. She stares at the flushed head of my cock for a moment, her cheeks turning a pretty shade of pink. When she lifts her eyes to mine, I can't fucking breathe.

She wraps her hand around it, and when she licks her bottom lip, wetting it, unconsciously I'm sure, I groan. The sound echoes loudly in the bathroom. She gazes up at me from beneath incredibly long, dark lashes. *Jesus Christ!* "You're killing me here, Elliot."

She smiles. And then her pretty pink tongue slips out as she shyly licks the head of my cock. I'm sure she got a little taste of pre-come. My brain short-circuits on me, causing electrons to misfire and bounce around inside my skull. I close my eyes just for a moment, but then I have to open them so I can *watch* her drive me insane.

She smiles as she opens her mouth and draws my erection inside. I've lost the ability to breathe. She's so hesitant, seemly so unsure of herself, I have to wonder how often she went down on her dickweed of a husband, but I'm sure as hell not going to ask. Some things are better left unsaid.

When Annie gets serious, using both hands and her luscious mouth, my brain goes offline. I'm brain dead. "Ah, fuck, baby," I groan. I know I sound like a broken record, but I can't help it. I don't think I'll ever get used to this.

She wraps her fingers around me, using both hands because, yeah, my fully erect cock is a bit of a monster. Everything on me is big, so why not my dick too? She hums as she works me, gazing up at me from beneath her long lashes, and I'm already biting my tongue, trying not to come. It would be nice if I could last at least five minutes. But, damn. *Her mouth.*

Another second of this torture, and I'm gonna blow my load way too soon. I reach down and pull her up and start stripping her, methodically removing every stitch of clothing she's got on. When I tug her panties down her long, shapely legs, I ball them up and bring them to my nose, inhaling deeply. "God, that's sweet."

"Jake!" She makes a grab for the little ball of fabric. "Stop that!"

I hold them out of her reach. "Nope. They're mine now."

She laughs, swatting at me. "You don't need my panties, you idiot. You've got *me.*"

"Good point." I drop her panties and reach into the walk-in shower to turn on the water. "Grab some washcloths and towels," I tell her, pointing at the linen cupboard. The water is instantly hot, because my brother Shane doesn't spare any expenses. In fact, I have to dial down the heat a bit to make it comfortable for her.

I pull her under the spray with me. "Come here."

She wets a washcloth and pours some body wash on it, then starts washing my neck and chest and arms.

"Scrub harder, Elliot. You won't hurt me."

She concentrates as she scrubs, making sure to get every drop of blood from my neck. Once I pass her inspection, she relaxes her touch, stroking my chest and arms lovingly.

"I'm in awe of your body, Jake," she says, as she moves the washcloth down my torso. She caresses each ridge of my abdomen, moving slowly down to my belly button, and then lower.

When she reaches my cock, she discards the washcloth and lathers her hands instead. She strokes me with her soft, slippery hands, from root to tip, over and over until I throw my head back into the spray of water, grimacing because the pleasure's so intense. I swear to God, my dick is so hard I could drill through the tile wall.

Impatient, I grab the bodywash and indulge myself in washing her from top to bottom, taking special care to lavish attention on her sweet breasts and even sweeter pussy.

Finally, I can't take any more. "Okay, that's enough." I shut off the water, grab a towel to dry off and wrap it around my waist. Then I grab the other towel, wrap her up in it, and swing her up into my arms. I carry her out of the bathroom and deposit her in the middle of my bed, pulling off her towel and my own.

"I'm soaking wet," she says, laughing.

"You're about to get even wetter, I hope."

Just as I'm about to join her on the bed, she points to the door. "Is it locked?"

"Oh, shit, no." I lock the door, then return to the bed. "It would be just my luck if Aiden came looking for you when I'm face down in your honeypot."

"My *what*?" Annie bursts into laughter as I crawl my way up between her legs, kissing the tender, damp skin of her inner thighs. The hickeys I gave her previously are already fading, so I add a couple new ones.

When I reach my ultimate destination, I spread her legs wide and brace them apart with my shoulders. "You heard me." And then I lavish attention on her sweet spot until she's squirming and screeching like a she-cat in heat.

"Jake, *please!*" she gasps, trying to coax me up her body.

"All right, hold your horses, woman." I raise up and kneel between her legs. Her pussy is so pink and slick and ready for me as I slowly feed my cock into her, an inch at a time. Her hands flex on my thighs, squeezing me, then releasing. I can't tell if it's too much for her, or not enough.

I get my answer when she thrusts her hips up, driving me deep inside her. Then she reaches for my shoulders and pulls me down for a soul-stealing kiss. From there on, it's fast and hungry, almost too rough I think, but she doesn't seem to mind. She encourages me to thrust harder, so I guess she's right there with me. And then...*oh, fuck no.* "Shit!"

"What?" she cries, startled.

I press my face into the crook of her neck and grit my teeth as I try not to come in that very instant. "I forgot a condom."

"Oh." As realization dawns, she chuckles into my ear. "Well, it's a little too late now."

And she's right, because my cock is shooting load after load deep inside her body, and it feels so damn good to be bareback in her that I could die a happy man right now. My cock twitches and pulses inside her, and her sweet pussy clamps down tight on me, milking me for all I've got.

Before I collapse on her and crush her, I roll to the side, bringing her with me. I'm still buried deep and still half-hard, still reveling in the residual throbbing of my dick. She feels so good, so hot and slick, I don't ever want to leave her body.

She drapes one thigh over mine, settling in comfortably, and we lie face to face grinning at each other like fools.

"That felt really good," she says, her eyes twinkling with mischief.

"Yes, it did."

She brushes back my hair. "Don't worry. I love you, and you love me. And we're going to be a family. The rest of it is just an issue of timing."

✎ 29

Annie

My tough guy passes out on me, falling asleep almost immediately after sex. His penis softens in his sleep and slips out of me, releasing a stream of semen between my thighs. I smile. He's right. As he likes to say, there's no sense crying over spilled milk. I quickly do a mental calculation and realize that if we were actively *trying* to get pregnant, now would be the ideal time to go about it.

"Oh, well." I had always wanted Aiden to have siblings. And Jake comes from a big family. I guess an unexpected baby wouldn't be the end of the world. Jake didn't seem to be too upset over the idea.

I study his handsome face as he sleeps, his beautiful lips and slightly crooked nose. I wonder how he broke it. I run my fingers through his hair, tugging gently on the longer strands on top of his head. His beard is short and surprisingly soft, and it feels incredible when he has his face between my legs.

There's a brisk knock on the door, and then Charlie says, "This is your two-minute warning. Aiden's on his way up."

I nudge Jake's shoulder. "Wake up, sleepyhead."

His eyes open immediately, and he lifts his head. "What?"

"Aiden's on his way up."

Jake jumps out of bed and pulls on a pair of sweats that are draped over an armchair. Then he races into the bathroom and returns with my clothes, tossing them to me.

"Mommy!"

I dress in record time, and as soon as I'm decent, Jake opens his door and walks out into the hallway. "Hey, buddy."

Aiden walks into the room. "Do you know where my mom— oh, there she is. Do you guys want to play with me?"

"Sure, pal," Jake says. "What do you want to do?"

"How about playing video games downstairs?"

Jake ruffles Aiden's hair. "Let me grab a shirt and my shoes, and we'll go play video games." Once he's finished dressing, Jake kisses me. "Let's let Mommy rest. She's worn out."

* * *

Jake takes Aiden downstairs to play, giving me a chance to clean up and change clothes. I head downstairs to the kitchen, where I find Elly preparing dinner. There are chickens roasting in the oven—filling the kitchen with the most delicious aromas. She stands at the island cutting up a mountain of potatoes.

"Can I help?" I ask her, washing my hands at the kitchen sink.

She smiles. "Sure. Why don't you wash and cut up some veggies for the salad?"

While I'm working on the salad, and she's putting the potatoes on to boil, I think about how my own mother would react if she knew that Jake and I are planning to marry in March. March seems so far away, but it's really not. We'll have so much to do in the meantime... all the planning. I don't want anything fancy or complicated. Something small and intimate, just our families and Jake's friends. It saddens me to think my parents might not want to attend.

"Jake asked me to marry him," I blurt out, realizing only then that I desperately need to tell someone. And sadly, I don't have anyone to tell. Certainly not my parents, and I really don't have many close friends left. Ted scared them all off.

"And?" Elly says, looking at me expectantly. "What did you say?"

"Oh. I said yes."

"I'm so glad to hear that. I can't tell you how happy his family will be when they find out. And George and I couldn't be happier."

I wish I could expect such a warm, heart-felt reaction from my own parents. "Thank you, Elly. That means a lot. It really does. I wish my own parents could be happy for us."

Elly wipes her hands on a hand towel and holds her arms out to me. "Your parents only want the best for you. Once they realize Jake is what's best, they'll be happy for you, too. You'll see."

I take so much solace from Elly's embrace, it makes me realize how much I want my own mom to support me.

"Just give them time, sweetheart," she says. "I promise you, they'll come around."

I smile, remembering when Aiden told Jake, *I wish you were my dad*. I feel like saying the same to Elly: *I wish you were my mom*. I squeeze her tightly. "Thank you, Elly."

While Elly tends the roasting chickens and prepares the mashed potatoes and gravy, I see to the salad and cut up some fresh fruit.

Charlie breezes through the kitchen on her way out the side door. "Do you have enough food for two more?" she says to Elly. "Jake told me to tell you that his parents are coming for dinner. Mrs. M. said she's bringing a cake. They'll be here at six."

"Perfect timing," Elly says, opening the oven door to check on the chickens. "And bless Bridget's heart. That saves me from making dessert."

* * *

Right on time, Jake's parents pull up to the front of the house in a dark SUV. Just as I open the door to walk out to greet them, Jake and Aiden come running up the stairs from the lower level.

Jake grins when he sees me and takes my hand. Then he pulls both me and Aiden out the front doors and down the steps to the circular gravel drive.

"Hi, honey," Bridget says as she gives her son a hug. Then she turns to me. "Hello, darling." She pulls me into her arms.

"I told them," Jake says to me, just before he hugs his dad. "I hope you don't mind. I just couldn't keep it to myself."

"I don't mind," I say. "I told Elly."

"Told them what?" Aiden says, looking confused.

After an awkward moment of silence, Jake kneels down in front of Aiden. "Your mom and I are getting married, pal."

Aiden nods. "Good." Then he looks at Jake's mom. "Does that mean you're my grandma now?"

"Yes, sweetie." She ruffles his hair. "I am."

Dinner is a bustling, joyous affair, with everyone talking over everyone.

"Just wait until your brothers and sisters hear the news," Bridget says.

Jake's mom is sitting next to Aiden, helping him cut his chicken into bite-sized pieces. I'm amazed at how easily she slipped into grandma mode with him. Aiden is eating up the attention, regaling her with stories about our afternoon at the carnival. Thank God he doesn't know everything that happened there.

After dinner, we all move to the great room for coffee and cake. Bridget baked a delicious strawberries-and-cream cake with pink buttercream frosting.

When Elly asked her what the special occasion was, she just

shrugged and said, "Oh, no reason. I just felt like baking a cake."

But she's not fooling anyone. We all know the truth. One of her boys is getting married.

* * *

That night, as Jake and I are lying in his bed together, he says, "Where do you want to live? I have an apartment in a high-rise in The Gold Coast, right on Lake Shore Drive. It's a two-bedroom on the forty-sixth floor. It will do fine for us in the short term, but it's not an ideal place to raise a five-year-old. He needs room to play outside. He needs a swing set and a sandbox, and maybe a tree house."

"Well, we certainly can't live with my parents," I say. "Let's buy a house of our own, with a yard, maybe in Lincoln Park."

He nods. "That sounds good. I could mow the lawn on the weekends, and we could grill out and invite our families over."

Jake's phone rings, and he reaches for it, checking the screen. "It's Shane," he says, sounding surprised. He accepts the call, then listens for several long minutes as his brother does all the talking.

I don't know why, but I start to get a really bad feeling in the pit of my stomach. Just when everything is going so perfectly, why does something have to come along and ruin it?

Finally, he sighs, then says, "All right. Tell Troy I'm on my way."

He ends the call and lays his phone on the nightstand. Then he turns to me, wrapping me in his arms, and kisses me so tenderly.

"What's wrong?" I swallow hard. "And who's Troy?"

"Troy Spencer is McIntyre Security's attorney. Shane called to tell me there's a warrant out for my arrest. He advised me to turn myself in before the cops come here looking for me."

"What!" I prop myself up on my elbow, staring down at him in shock. "Why? How?"

"Ted is charging me with felonious assault with a deadly weapon."

"Deadly weapon? What weapon? Did you pull your gun on him?"

"No." He laughs. "I used my fist."

I fall back onto the mattress. "Oh, my God. How about I charge Ted with attempted assault? Or, Charlie can charge him with assault with a deadly weapon. He pulled a *gun* on her, Jake. On both of us, really. And then there are the restraining orders. One for me, and one for Aiden."

Jake kisses me, then sits up. "Don't worry. Troy will handle it— he's the best. I've got to drive back to the city now. I'm sorry. I'll be back as soon as I can."

I sit up and toss the covers aside. "I'm coming with you."

"No, you're not," he says, pushing me back onto the mattress and giving me a stern look. "You will stay right here, where I know you're safe. Charlie will stay with you. I'll be back as soon as I can, I promise."

"How long will that be?" I say, blinking back tears. "What are we talking about? Hours? Days? Weeks?"

"Just a few hours, I'm sure. Don't worry. Troy will work it out. He's one hell of an attorney. I'm sure I'll be back by morning."

* * *

I can't sleep. Jake's been gone for five hours now, without a word to me since he left. I know he wasn't lying when he said he'd be back by morning. But when the sun rises, bright light filtering through a crack in the drapes, I know it's not to be.

I cry for half an hour, alternately missing him and fearing for him. Then I get up and take a shower and dress. Aiden is still sound asleep, so I head downstairs and find Elly in the kitchen making coffee. I can tell by the look on her face that she already knows Jake is gone. I don't have to say a word. She just envelops me in her arms and holds me while I cry.

Breakfast comes and goes. Aiden and I do some schoolwork. We work on his letters and his numbers. Then he practices drawing shapes and coloring them in. After that, we play a kid's boardgame that Elly magically produces.

The worst part is finally having to explain to Aiden that Jake is gone.

"Where's Jake?" he asks after we finish our game. "He said we could play baseball today."

I tell Aiden as little as possible, just that Jake had to go back to the city today.

Aiden frowns. "He left without saying goodbye to me?"

"I'm sorry, honey. He had to leave really early, and he didn't want to wake you up."

Charlie is always close by, but she's acting rather subdued. So is Elly. Bridget calls us once just to see how we are doing. She obviously knows, too, because she never once asks to speak to Jake.

I send Jake a text message every hour, on the hour, hoping for a reply, but none comes. And the longer we go without hearing from him, the more worried I become.

Just as I'm seriously contemplating trying to get in touch with Shane, Jake finally calls with some news.

"I'm sorry I didn't call sooner." He sounds exhausted.

"It's okay."

"I really didn't know anything until just now. Plus, I was locked in a jail cell—where I spent the night—and they'd confiscated my phone as soon as I arrived at the station. I just now got it back and saw all your text messages. By the way, I love you, too."

"Do you know when you can come home?"

"I'll be home this evening, I promise. I'll explain everything then."

ℒ 30

Jake

I t's eight-thirty in the evening before I make it back to the Kenilworth estate. I couldn't get home fast enough. When I pull up to the front of the house, everyone is standing out on the steps waiting for me. Annie, Aiden, Charlie, Elly, George. God, seeing them standing there, looking worried as they wait for *me*, makes my chest ache.

I pull the Tahoe up to the front steps and get out, walking toward them. Aiden breaks free from the group and races down the steps to meet me, throwing himself into my arms and practically strangling me.

"I missed you all day, Jake," he says, kissing my cheek, and then he buries his face in the crook of my neck.

His little body shakes as I straighten, holding him in my arms. He's wearing PJs and holding both Stevie and Paul.

Annie joins us, putting her arms around both of us, and the three of us stand there for a good while, just holding each other. "Is everything okay?" she asks me.

"Yes. The charges were dropped. I'm in the clear."

Annie sighs heavily, closing her eyes in relief. "You'll have to tell me everything. Later," she says, eyeing Aiden.

I nod, then lean in to kiss her. Then, to lighten the mood, I look at Aiden. "Hey, buddy, shouldn't you be in bed by now?"

"I couldn't go to bed without you being home. Mommy said I could wait up for you."

I hug him, overwhelmed by how much this kid means to me already. The fact that he cared about my whereabouts kills me. "Well, I'm home now, pal. How about I put you to bed tonight?"

"Yeah." He yawns, then lays his head on my shoulder, his arms going around my neck as I carry him up the stairs and into the house. "Mommy, you come too," Aiden says.

Charlie's there, and she gives me a nod and holds out her hand for a fist bump as I walk past her. "It's about time you got back, bruh. I was about ready to send out a search-and-rescue team."

* * *

Upstairs, Aiden goes potty and brushes his teeth. While he's in the bathroom, I hold Annie in my arms, just gently rocking her. She clings to me, not saying much. Her death grip says it all. She was scared, and I feel bad about that.

"The charges against you have been dropped?" she says.

I guess she just needs some reassurance. "Yes, they were dropped. And Patterson was charged with illegal possession of a handgun, violating the restraining order against you, and also violating a restraining order on behalf of the school. I'm out, and he's locked up right now. Although I don't know for how long."

"I'm just so glad you're home."

Aiden comes racing out of the bathroom. "I'm ready!" he says, throwing himself onto the bed.

It takes some doing, but I finally get him to settle down long enough to cover him up. I lie beside him to read his favorite story books. Annie lies on my other side, her head on my shoulder and her arm around my waist. I could easily get used to this.

Aiden falls asleep halfway through his second bedtime story. We switch off the lights and lie there quietly with him, in no rush to leave. There's something very satisfying about the three of us being together. I think back to yesterday, when Annie and I forgot to use a condom. I'm sure the odds are low that she'll end up pregnant, but if she does, I won't be upset. We have plenty of room in our lives for more kids. *More family.*

Finally, hunger drives me to climb carefully out of Aiden's bed. Annie comes down to the kitchen with me and helps me heat up a plate of leftovers that Elly left for me in the fridge. I sit at the little table in the kitchen, and Annie sips a cup of decaf tea while

I eat.

By now, it's after ten, and we're both exhausted. I don't think either one of us slept last night. We clean up after our late-night snack, then head upstairs to my room—*our* room. I take a quick shower and join her in bed, where she's struggling to keep her eyes open.

"I'm sorry I scared you," I tell her, pulling her into my arms. "But I'm not sorry I beat the shit out of your ex. I meant what I said. If he comes near you or Aiden again, I'm going to kill him."

"Please don't say that. You spent a night in jail for beating him up. I can't imagine what would happen if you killed him."

"You let me worry about that, okay? Trust me, I'm not going to go off half-cocked and get myself convicted of murder, or even manslaughter."

She raises up on her elbow and leans over my chest. "We're a family now. You can't go off half-cocked. You have to think about us."

"I *am* thinking about you, both of you. I don't want your ex hanging over you like a dark cloud for the rest of your lives. If I have the chance to take him out, I'm going to take it. But please, don't worry. I'll be careful. I know what's permissible and what's not. Chances are, he'll make the first move, which is perfect. I can claim self-defense."

31

Annie

The next few days pass peacefully. The preschool workbooks I ordered online arrive in the mail, and Aiden and I work on schooling. Jake takes Aiden out to the barn to see the horses, and they take little hikes around the estate. Charlie resumes Aiden's swimming lessons, and Jake and I join them in the pool, starting out swimming laps, but ending up goofing off and acting like teenagers again as we splash and tickle our way across the pool.

I've never been so happy in my life, and mentally I'm making plans for us to move into Jake's downtown apartment as soon as he says it's safe for us to return to the city. Then we can start looking for a house of our own.

Our quiet little respite is shattered, though, when my mother calls me Thursday afternoon. "Annie, your father's had a heart attack. He's in intensive care at Cook County Hospital."

I run out onto the back deck, looking for Jake. He said he was taking Aiden out back to teach him how to throw a ball. When Jake sees me—sees the look on my face—he drops the ball and meets me halfway on the lawn.

"What's wrong?" he says, gripping my arms hard.

"My mother just called. Dad's had a heart attack. He's at Cook County, in the ICU."

"Oh, Christ, sweetheart, I'm sorry."

"Jake, I have to go to the hospital. Right now."

Jake shakes his head, frowning. "No. Baby, you know Ted's been using tracking devices to keep track of your family's movements. There's every reason to suspect he's still watching your parents. It's too risky for you to go to the hospital. I'm sorry. I'll go and check on him for you, and then report back. But you can't go."

My heart is racing, and even though I understand the risk, there's no way I can stay away. I grab his hands, holding them to my chest, willing him to understand how important this is. "Jake, he's my *father*. He may not be perfect, but he's still my dad. I have to go. Please, I need you to support me on this."

Jake scowls, rubbing his hand over his face as he makes an exasperated sound. "All right. But Aiden stays here with Charlie.

That's not negotiable."

I throw myself at him, reaching up on my tiptoes to wrap my arms around his neck. "Thank you!"

* * *

I frantically collect my purse and meet Jake out front at the Tahoe. It's just the two of us in the vehicle, so I can finally sit up front with him.

Aiden certainly wasn't happy about us taking off so suddenly and leaving him behind. Fortunately, Charlie was able to distract him with a promise to take him downstairs to play video games.

It's a forty-five minute drive to the hospital. We park in the public garage, and Jake escorts me inside, holding my hand and keeping me close. He's very vigilant, I can tell as he continuously scans our surroundings. We know that Ted's been released from jail, but that's about it. I think it's very unlikely that he would show up here at the hospital. And besides, even if he does show up, what can he do to us in such a public place?

I text my mom to let her know we're here, and she offers to come down and meet us in the lobby. While we wait for her, I realize this is the first time my mother and Jake are going to see each other, face to face, since Jake and I pieced together the fact that my parents were responsible for interfering in our lives. Jake said he'd deal with my parents the next time he saw them, but now hardly seems like the time for a confrontation.

"Mrs. Elliot," Jake says to my mom, when she joins us. He gives her a polite nod, and to my relief, he says nothing more.

"Hello, Jake," my mother says. She narrows her eyes at him, but doesn't say any more. Then she reaches out to touch my arm. "Hello, Annie." That's it. Just an impersonal pat on the arm, like one might give a distant friend. No hug. No kiss. No emotion at all. My throat tightens.

As if he senses my emotions, Jake puts his arm around me and draws me close, kissing the top of my head.

My mother frowns at his blatant display of affection. "It's this way." She turns and heads for the bank of elevators.

The three of us are alone in the elevator as we take it up to his floor. "Frank had a massive heart attack. He's still in the intensive care unit. We're waiting to find out if he can move to a room."

We follow her to the ICU, where my father is being closely monitored. There are so many wires attached to his body, and his bed is surrounded by beeping machines keeping track of his vitals.

Mom takes a seat in the chair beside my father's bed, while Jake and I stand at the foot of the bed, trying to take everything in.

My father looks so pale, so gaunt, as he lies sleeping. His cheeks are hollowed out, and he's lost even more weight than I remember from just a week past.

"Thank you for bringing Annie," Mom says to Jake.

He nods. "It was my pleasure, Mrs. Elliot."

For a minute, I'm relieved she's actually being cordial to him, but my hopes are dashed when she says, "There's no need for you to stay. I'll take care of Annie. You can leave."

Her rudeness makes me gasp.

"If you don't mind, I'll stay with Annie," he says sounding perfectly pleasant. He gives me a wink.

I love him so much in that moment, for being the bigger man and not sinking to her level. I lean into him, laying my head against his shoulder.

"Actually, I do mind," she says, her voice cold as ice. "This is a private family matter. You're not needed or welcome here."

"Mother!" I gasp.

Jake tightens his hold on me. "Actually, Annie is my family. So, if she needs me here, I'm going to be here. *For her.*"

Before my mother can respond, a nurse comes into the room.

"Mrs. Elliot," the woman says. "We're going to move your husband into his own room now. His vitals have stabilized, and he's out of danger."

Mother pastes a bland smile on her face. "I'm so glad to hear that," she says. "Do you have the room number?"

"Yes," the nurse says, giving her the number. "I'm preparing your husband to be moved soon."

My mother nods as she walks out of the room. Jake and I stay behind and observe as the nurse detaches my father from all the wires.

"He's better?" I say.

The nurse nods. "Much improved. He's stable now. He's going to be fine."

I'm tremendously relieved at the news.

After the nurse moves my father's bed out of the room, I sigh with relief. Then I have to deal with my mother. "I'm so sorry, Jake."

He turns me to face him, giving me a gentle kiss. "You have nothing to apologize for. You're not responsible for what comes out of your mother's mouth."

I laugh in spite of the situation. "I can't believe she's so openly hostile to you after everything you've done for me and Aiden."

"Do you want to go to your father's new room?"

I nod. "If you don't mind, yes."

"Of course, I don't mind. Your mother can say all she wants to me. I don't care. I'm here for *you*."

We step out into the hallway, and Jake checks our surroundings. For a moment, I had forgotten the possibility that Ted could show up here. I still don't think it's likely.

We head to the floor where my father's room is located, and when we go inside, we find my mother seated once more beside his bed. My father is awake, although groggy.

"Dad!" I run to his side and lean down to give him a careful hug and a kiss on his cheek. "I'm so glad you're all right."

He gives me a weak smile. "I'm fine, honey. Just a slight glitch, that's all." Then he glances at Jake, who's standing beside me. "Hello, Jake," he says, with an unexpected smile on his face.

Jake nods. "Hello, Mr. Elliot. I'm glad to see you're doing well."

"Call me Frank, please. I'm glad you're here, son. There's something I need—"

A nurse walks in. "Sorry to interrupt folks," she says. "I just need to make sure Mr. Elliot is hooked up right." She checks the wires and machines and his IV, looking everything over before giving it her approval. "Someone will be in shortly to check on you, and you'll get a light supper this evening—liquids only at this time. Doctor's orders."

The nurse comes and goes several times, bringing a pitcher of ice water and a cup, just generally making sure my father is settling in well. A little while later, someone from the dietary department stops by with my father's supper, which consists of a cup of decaf coffee, a bowl of clear chicken broth, and a gelatin cup.

"Damn, no solid food," Dad says, scowling. "And I'm so hungry I could eat a horse."

Surprisingly, my mother hasn't made any hateful comments to Jake since my father woke up. I find that rather interesting, especially as my father seems to be going out of his way to be polite to Jake.

I hear a quiet sound from the open doorway, just the barely perceptible squeak of a sneaker on the polished floor. I look up, surprised to see a stranger standing in the doorway. He looks familiar, and yet he doesn't. It takes me a minute to realize why. His bruised face is horribly swollen, his nose especially. His face is so shockingly distorted that it takes me a second to recognize him.

Ted raises a gun, pointed at *me*. "You fucking bitch! Do you really think I'd just let him have you?"

And then everything happens so fast, faster than my eyes can track or my mind can comprehend.

My mother jumps to her feet, screaming. My father's face, frozen in shock, turns a ghastly white, and he gasps for air.

Jake lunges in front of me as Ted squeezes the trigger. The resulting crack is deafening in the small room. The bullet strikes Jake, and he's knocked backwards, into me, sending me crashing into an empty guest chair.

My eyes widen in utter disbelief as a jagged hole blooms on Jake's back, up near his left shoulder. Blood, thick and viscous, streams out of the hole, running down his back.

My mind rebels, screams reverberating in my skull, as Jake staggers on his feet. He reaches into his jacket and pulls out his gun. Holding it with both hands, he fires at Ted. Ted's eyes widen in shock as a spot of blood appears in the center of his forehead. I hear a dull thud as Ted hits the floor.

A moment later, a doctor and two nurses storm into the room, followed closely by a uniformed security officer who is shouting into a comm device as he stands over Ted's body.

With a pained grimace, Jake sinks to his knees as he presses his hand to the hole in his shoulder. He turns to me and starts yelling.

I think I must be in shock, because I can't hear a thing he's saying. There's a burning chill spreading across my chest, stealing my breath.

Why can't I breathe?

Jake reaches for me, despite the agony he must be in. He looks horrified. But he shouldn't be. Ted is dead. He can't hurt us anymore.

And then blackness descends over me, and I feel nothing.

∾ 32

Jake

My mind's reeling, and my body is numb. Part of that numbness might be because of the local anesthetic they gave me before they patched up my shoulder. And then there's the pain meds, dripping through a tube into my arm, making me loopy.

After cleaning me up, they put me in a bed, in a room which is now filled with people all talking quietly at once. *My people. My family.*

There's a second bed in my room, but it's empty.

Like me.

Everyone's here, except for Beth and the baby. Shane left his wife and newborn son at home. Beth doesn't know about the shooting, because Shane doesn't want to upset her. He says she's got enough on her plate right now.

My big brother Jamie sits in the chair beside my bed and reaches toward me. When his hand comes into contact with my arm, he slides it down until he encounters my hand, which he grips hard. "Everything's going to be all right," he says. "Just hang in there."

That's easy for him to say. His woman was never shot in the chest.

I failed her.

There's a slight commotion at the foot of the bed as my youngest sister, Lia, takes a seat, making herself at home. She pats my leg. "You fucking saved her life, dude. I'm proud of you."

"I failed her."

"What part of *you fucking saved her life* did you not understand?" Lia frowns at me. "If you hadn't taken that bullet for her, and eroded its momentum, we wouldn't be sitting here right now wondering when the hell she'll finally get out of surgery. We'd be picking out her casket instead."

Mom smiles at Lia. "Watch your language please, sweetheart." Mom's sitting on the other side of my bed, holding my right hand. She looks the same as I feel right now. Gutted.

My sister Sophie rushes through the door, her dark eyes wide and frantic as she zeroes in on me. "Oh, my God, Jake." She comes to my bedside and leans down to kiss my forehead. "Thank God you're all right. You're both going to be all right."

"Hi, Soph."

Sophie looks around the room. "Any word on Annie yet?"

"She's still in surgery, honey," my dad says. "We're still waiting to hear something."

My entire family is here, except for my sister Hannah, who lives in the wilds of Wyoming, up in the mountains where there's no cell signal. No one's been able to reach her yet.

All my big, boisterous, loving family is here. Three brothers, two sisters, my parents. Jamie's girlfriend, Molly. Lia's boyfriend, Jonah. And still, I feel empty. Alone.

Shane turns his head to something happening out in the hallway. Then he pushes away from the wall he's been leaning against and walks out the door. My youngest brother, Liam, goes with him. A minute later, they return.

"I just talked to Annie's mother," Shane says. "She says Annie is out of surgery and in recovery now. She's in critical, yet stable, condition. She's going to be all right."

I pull my right hand free and cover my face with it, wanting to hide my pain and relief and tears.

"Did they say anything more?" my mom says.

"The bullet hit her left lung," Shane says. "The damage has been repaired. The concern now is for infection and the functionality of the lung. Right now, she's being kept sedated."

Shane walks up to the foot of the bed and reaches down to grasp my ankle. "Give yourself some credit, Jake. Annie's alive because of you. If you hadn't slowed the bullet, it would have destroyed her lungs, or possibly hit her heart, which would likely have been fatal."

I close my eyes, wishing I could just shut everyone out. I love my family, and I know they mean well, but right now I'm just sick inside. My heart, my mind... I just can't handle it right now. All I wanted to do was protect Annie. I swore to her that asshole would never hurt her or Aiden again, and I failed her.

And poor Aiden! My God, if Annie had died—I can't even think about it.

❧ 33

Annie

There's a comforting weight on my left arm, as well as one across my waist. Warm fingers are entwined with mine, holding me tethered to this place. Something a little rough and calloused strokes the back of my hand.

I try to open my eyes, but my lids aren't cooperating. They're too heavy, almost weighted down. I'm so tired, so drowsy, my mind and body are sluggish.

I open my mouth and attempt to speak. "Wha—" One dry, hoarse syllable is all I can manage before those comforting weights are abruptly lifted, leaving my bare arm exposed to the cool air. I would shiver, but I'm already shaking from head to toe.

A familiar male voice, low and urgent, comes from somewhere above me. "Annie? Can you hear me? Look at me, baby, please."

I blink several times, trying to clear my vision so I can see, but I can't seem to focus. I see a dark shape looming over me. "Jake?"

"Molly, can you turn up the lights, just a little? Thanks."

A faint light from somewhere behind me slowly comes up, bathing my unfamiliar bed in a soft glow. The dark shape hovering over me comes better into view, looking bulky and unkempt. I try to reach for it with my right hand, but my arm falls back numbly to the bed.

"Yes, it's me," he says. "I'm right here, baby. Can you see me?"

My vision wavers, but I focus on that dark shape. Slowly Jake's features come into view.

"She's awake," he says to someone in the room. "Get the nurse."

He leans down and kisses my forehead, then he kisses my cheeks and my chin. "Hey, sweetheart." His low voice is soft like brushed velvet. "How do you feel? Are you in pain?"

I close my eyes and sigh. "Can't... keep... my eyes...open."

"That's okay." Gentle fingers brush my cheek. "Go back to sleep. I'll be here when you wake up."

"'k." My mind drifts for a moment until an urgent thought makes my heart contract painfully. "Aiden!"

"He's fine, don't worry. He's at home with Charlie and Elly, safe and sound."

Home? I like the sound of that. "How long?"

"How long have you been out? The shooting was yesterday.

This is day two. And your dad is fine. So, there's absolutely nothing you need to worry about."

"Wrong."

"What? Why? Why am I wrong?"

"Worried...about...you." I try to reach for him, but my arm falls back to the bed. I saw that hole blossom in his back. I saw all that blood. I didn't dream that up. "Shot."

"Me? Yeah, I was shot, but it was just a graze. No big deal. I'm fine, baby. You're going to be fine, too, so there's nothing to worry about. Just sleep and rest, so you can get stronger."

"Not...a...graze. A hole. So much blood."

I feel his lips press against my forehead, vibrating with... suppressed laughter? "Trust me, honey. Mine was nothing compared to yours."

"Who...is...Molly?" I don't know anyone named Molly.

"Molly is my brother Jamie's girlfriend. She and Jamie are here. I'll introduce you later. Just rest now, okay? Before you pass out on me again."

And then the comforting weight returns as fingers link with mine, and a comforting weight settles across my waist.

* * *

When I wake up again, the room is bright, and there's a pretty brunette sitting in the chair beside my bed, reading a paperback book. From what I can see of the cover, it looks like a military thriller.

"Hello," I say, wondering if this is Molly.

The woman closes her book, laying it on my bed, and smiles at me. "Good morning, Annie. I'm Molly Ferguson. My boyfriend, Jamie, is Jake's brother."

"Hi." I glance around the room and notice we're alone. "Where's Jake?"

When I turn back to Molly, she's keying something into her phone. "He and Jamie went to check on your dad. I'll tell them you're awake." A moment later, she sets her phone down. "How do you feel? Better?"

"A little, yes. My head's not so groggy now."

"Good. I'm so glad to hear that. And I know Jake will be thrilled."

Speaking of Jake, I can hear him several seconds before I see him, as his deep voice carries down the hallway. When he comes through the door, his eyes are on me, dark and intense. His left arm is in a sling, but other than that, he looks fine. Happy even.

"Are you okay?" I ask him.

He grins at me. "Shouldn't I be the one asking you that question?"

He leans over the side of the bed and kisses me gently. Then he sits in the vacant chair at the side of my bed.

A second man wearing a pair of dark glasses walks into the room, holding the lead on a service dog—a beautiful Yellow Lab. "Go to Molly," he says, and the dog leads him right to the pretty brunette. He grips her shoulders, squeezing them gently, then leans down to kiss the top of her head.

"Do you remember my brother Jamie?" Jake says.

I nod. "Yes, I think so." I remember him vaguely from school.

"And this is his much better half, Molly Ferguson."

Molly laughs. "Well, it's debatable that I'm the better half." She reaches out to pat my leg. "Annie and I were just chatting before you guys got back."

"You went to see my dad?" I ask Jake.

"Yes. He's doing well. He'll probably be released tomorrow."

I sigh. That's such a relief. He looked so sickly when I first saw him right after his heart attack. "And what about you? Your shoulder? You're okay, really?"

"Perfectly fine. It was a clean shot, in and out. Just needed a bit of duct tape to patch it up. You're the one who got shot in the chest and nearly died." He scowls at me. "Don't ever do that to me again."

Gradually, everything starts coming back to me. Dad in his hospital room. Jake standing beside me. Someone in the doorway, holding a gun. *Ted.* His face...so horrible. Jake lunging in front of me, and then the deafening crack of the gun. "Oh, my God, Jake! You threw yourself in front of me! Are you crazy?"

He grins. "Well, I am your bodyguard, aren't I? It's my job."

Hot tears start streaming down my cheeks, and I close my eyes as pain knifes through me. What if he hadn't been okay? *What if he'd died?*

"Please don't cry, baby," he says, grabbing a tissue from a box on the cart beside my bed. Gently, he dabs my cheeks. "After the past couple of days, my heart just can't take it." His phone chimes with an incoming message, and he grins when he checks the screen. "I have a surprise for you."

"What?"

"Wait for it..." he says, holding up a finger and gesturing toward the door. "Wait for it..."

A moment later, my son comes barreling through the open door, Charlie close on his heels.

"Gee, slow down, tiger," Charlie says.

"Mommy!" Aiden makes a run for my bed.

Jake intercepts him with his good arm, snagging him around the waist and pulling him onto his lap. "Slow down, pal. Mommy is really sore, so you have to be super careful, okay?"

"Okay," Aiden says, hugging Stevie to his chest. He slides off Jake's lap. "Mommy, I missed you," he whispers, inching cautiously toward the bed.

I reach out with my good arm—the one not connected to the IV line. "Oh, sweetie, I missed you too. Can I have a kiss?"

Aiden glances back uncertainly at Jake.

Jake stands. "Yes, you can kiss her. Just be really gentle, okay?" He picks Aiden up and holds him over my bed, lowering Aiden's face just enough for him to kiss me on my cheek.

Aiden's eyes tear up. "When are you coming home?"

I look up at Jake, wondering if he can answer that question. I have no clue.

"Not for a few more days," he says more to me than to Aiden. "And only then if everything continues to go well."

There's a knock on the door, and Jake says, "Come in."

Bridget and Calum walk into my room, Calum holding a bouquet of lovely pale pink roses in a glass vase. *My favorites.* Jake must have told them.

Aiden runs to Bridget, throwing his arms around her. "My mommy got hurt and she's sore. You have to be very gentle."

Bridget kisses the top of Aiden's head. "Yes, I know, darling. I promise to be gentle."

Jake's mother lifts her head and looks at me with teary eyes. Then, holding Aiden by the hand, she comes to the side of my bed and kisses my cheek. "Thank God," she breathes.

I suspect she's too choked up to say more.

Calum picks Aiden up, holding him while Bridget hugs Jake. Then she moves to the other side of the bed and hugs Jamie and Molly.

The love in this room is palpable. I'm envious of Bridget and Calum's children. I want Aiden to grow up like they did, with lots of siblings and lots of unconditional love.

34

Annie

More of Jake's family members stop by. His sister Lia and her boyfriend, Jonah. Another sister, Sophie. Shane stops by for a short visit just to say hello. He doesn't stay long, saying he needs to get back to his wife.

Everyone leaves after about an hour so I can rest. Everyone except for Aiden and Charlie. Someone—I suspect it was Jake's mom—left behind a dinosaur coloring book and a box of crayons for Aiden.

Jake helps me eat the lunch I'm brought—mashed potatoes, a grilled chicken breast, and a roll—treating me like I'm an invalid, cutting up my meat into bitesize pieces and feeding me himself.

"Jake I can do it."

He shakes his head. "You need to let me take care of you."

* * *

Later in the afternoon, Charlie takes Aiden back to Kenilworth. At first, he doesn't want to go, and I'm afraid he's going to throw a tantrum. But Charlie defuses the situation by bribing him with the promise of a swimming lesson as soon as they get home.

After they leave, I doze for a while, while Jake reads the paperback book Molly left behind. Apparently, Jamie is an author now. He writes military thrillers based on his exploits as a Navy SEAL. I didn't realize that he was one before losing his eyesight in an explosion in Afghanistan.

Later that evening, there's a knock at the door, and Jake gets up to answer it. He opens the door wide, and I'm surprised when I see my mother wheeling my father into the room. My father's looking much better than he did right after his heart attack. His color is returning to normal, and he looks much more alert.

Mother pushes his wheelchair up to the foot of the bed. Based on the pinched expression on her face when she glances at Jake, I'm guessing she doesn't actually want to be here.

Dad reaches over the footboard and squeezes my foot gently. "I'm so glad you're okay, sweetheart," he says, sounding a little choked up.

"I could say the same to you." I smile. "You look much better than you did the last time I saw you."

"Well, I have a lot to be grateful for," he says. Then his gaze goes to Jake, and he smiles before turning back to me. "Jake told me the good news, that you two are getting married in March. I couldn't be happier, sweetheart."

I glance at Jake, shocked to hear he told them. But I'm even more shocked by my father's reaction. "Really?"

He nods, looking rather embarrassed. "Yesterday, before Ted barged in and all hell broke loose, I had planned to tell you both that I hired McIntyre Security on purpose. It was my fervent hope that Jake would get wind of the trouble you were in, sweetheart, and that he'd get personally involved. I thought if I could get the two of you in a room together, you might be able to sort things out and maybe even get back together." He laughs. "I just didn't expect it to happen quite so quickly. At that initial meeting, when Jake took one look at you and cleared the room, I was both elated and terrified. I thought we were meeting with Shane first. I didn't expect Jake so soon. I didn't know how he would react. I was afraid he might blame you for what happened, when the truth is, it's my fault. Well, mine and your mother's. We interfered in your lives when we had no right. We were wrong." He looks at my mother, who's stone faced. "Well, *I* was wrong anyway, and *I'm* sorry."

I don't think my mother is one bit sorry.

"Dad." I'm not sure what to say. Jake and I had already figured out what they'd done, but to hear my father confirm it shakes me to the core. And, to hear him apologize for it... frankly, I couldn't be more surprised.

"It's okay," my father says. "You don't have to say anything. I know it's a painful issue, on many levels. I *am* sorry. I very deeply regret my part in it. And I don't expect you to just forgive me. I know it's not that easy. Just let me say that I'm truly happy you two are back together."

My dad looks at Jake, who's sitting silently by my side, offering his steadfast support, as always.

Dad looks back my way. "You and Aiden couldn't be in better hands, honey." Then, to Jake, he says, "Welcome to the family, son."

* * *

I'm shaken to the core when my parents leave. Shaken because my father actually admitted to his part and apologized. Shaken because my mother never said a word. I've been offered more love and support in the past week from Jake's family than from my own mother.

The next couple of days pass quite uneventfully. Jake's family members take turns stopping by. Charlie brings Aiden to visit me once a day. Elly comes with them once.

My pulmonologist is monitoring my lung function and watching for signs of infection. So far, so good. I feel stronger each day, and by the fifth day, I'm so ready to go home.

Home.

Jake and Aiden both refer to the Kenilworth estate as home.

I've even begun to think of it that way. But the truth is, it was meant to be a temporary safe haven. It was our safe house when Ted was a threat. As Ted's no longer an issue, we can leave the Kenilworth house whenever we want.

But the thought of leaving that house hurts. I have so many wonderful memories of our time there… Jake and I coming together and reconnecting both emotionally and physically. Spending quality time with Elly. Spending time with Jake's parents. And Aiden has had the time of his life there, with the horses, the pool, the movie theater. And then there's Charlie. He thinks the world of Charlie. I do too. I feel like she's part of the family.

"Tell me what you're thinking about," Jake says, slowly running his index finger up and down my arm. "You look preoccupied."

"I'm thinking about Kenilworth, and the wonderful times we've had there. Thinking about having to leave. I know we can't stay there forever."

He reaches carefully with his sore arm—he stopped using the sling a couple of days ago—and brushes back my bangs. "We don't have to leave Kenilworth. Shane wouldn't mind if we decided to live there. It's up to you."

As tempting as the idea is, I know we need to return to Chicago. Aiden will start kindergarten in the fall. I want to return to work, and Jake has his own work to think about. Kenilworth is a bit far for us to commute every day. "We should live in Chicago."

"Let's move you and Aiden into my apartment downtown, for the time being, while we think about house hunting."

"What about Charlie? She's like a member of our family. Aiden will be heart broken when she leaves us."

"Honey, she lives in my apartment building, just down the hall from me. Aiden can see her any time he wants." He squeezes my hand. "I bet she'll even babysit for us when we need a little quality alone time."

* * *

My doctor clears me to be released from the hospital. While Jake is making arrangements and handling the follow-up paperwork, I have some quiet time alone in my room to think about Ted. There's been such a maelstrom of activity and emotions lately that I haven't had a lot of time to process his death. But I have to face it sooner, rather than later. I still have to tell Aiden that his father is dead. Jake and I decided it would be best to wait until I was home before we told him. And that time is almost upon us.

When I think back to the day of the shooting, my memories are a bit fuzzy. I remember seeing Ted in the doorway of my father's room. I remember seeing him pointing a gun at me. I recall that he yelled something hateful at me right before he pulled the trigger.

And Jake... my God. He threw himself in front of me. I still have trouble wrapping my mind around that. He moved so fast, without thinking, he just acted on impulse. His impulse was to save me, no matter what it cost him. That kind of selfless love is... extraordinary.

And Ted? He wanted to shoot me. He did shoot me, in fact.

While Jake's thick musculature slowed down the bullet's momentum significantly, the bullet still punched through his body and into mine.

Either one of us could have died. Instead, Ted died. Jake did warn Ted that if he saw his face near me or Aiden again, he would kill him. Well, Jake kept his word. There was a brief police investigation at the hospital, but no charges were filed against Jake as he clearly acted in self-defense.

My ex-husband wanted to kill me, and my future husband risked his life to save me.

There's a light knock on my partially open door. "Come in," I say.

The door swings open and Cameron walks in. "Hey, Annie." He sits on the chair beside my bed. "How are you feeling?"

"Much better, thank you. What brings you here?"

"I wanted to check in on you, see how you're doing. Jake's getting all the paperwork in order for you to be released. When you're ready to leave, I'll go down and get the Tahoe."

I study Cameron for a moment. "I assume you heard that Jake threw himself in front of a bullet for me."

Cameron laughs. "Of course he did. This is Jake we're talking about. What else would you expect? He waited fourteen years for you, Annie. Do you really think he'd lose you to a jealous and strung-out drug addict?"

"Damn right I waited fourteen years for her," Jake says as he strolls into the room. He heads straight for my bed and gives me a sweet kiss. "Pack your bags, Elliot. We're goin' home."

Home. "That is music to my ears," I say.

35

Annie

A
s Cameron waits out front with the Tahoe, Jake wheels me to the vehicle and deposits me gently onto the front seat of his SUV. Cameron stows my small overnight bag in the back of the vehicle.

"Ready to go home?" Jake says, once he's behind the steering wheel. He leans over and kisses me. "Well, to our temporary home that is, until we move to my apartment. Which is also temporary." He's got a big grin on his handsome face. Obviously, he's in a very good mood.

"Yes, I'm ready. I miss Aiden desperately, and Elly and Charlie."

And as excited as I am about moving into Jake's apartment and eventually finding our own home, I hate the thought of leaving Elly.

"Well, I'm sure the feeling is mutual," he says. "I'm sure Aiden misses the daylights out of you. I know I would."

The drive back to Kenilworth is very therapeutic. Once we're on the property, I feel myself relaxing into my seat. *I'm home.* Maybe not at the permanent place of our residency, but I'm with my new family, and that's all that matters.

Speaking of my new family, there's a small crowd of people gathered on the front steps, awaiting our arrival. Aiden, Charlie, Elly, George. Even Bridget and Calum are here to welcome me home.

Jake makes me wait in my seat until he can walk around the vehicle and open my door, then scoop me up into his arms. He carries me to the front steps, but we don't make it any farther than that.

"Why is Jake carrying you?" Aiden says. "Can't you walk?"

I laugh. "I can walk, honey. Jake's just being chivalrous."

Aiden frowns. "What's a chiv-walrus?"

"Chiv-al-rous. It means he's being a gentleman."

"Oh."

After lots of hugging and hello's, Jake carries me inside the house and up the staircase, taking me directly to his room, where he lays me down gently on his big bed. I guess this is officially *our* room now.

"Welcome home," he says, leaning down to give me a very

warm and welcoming kiss.

Aiden climbs up on the bed next to me. Charlie and Elly join us too.

Charlie sits at the foot of the bed. "I'm so glad you're home. We all missed you."

"I missed you guys, too. All of you! And I *really* missed your cooking, Elly."

Elly puts her arm around Jake and leans her head against his arm. "We missed you, too, honey," she says to him, and I could swear he's blushing.

Aiden gets as close to me as he can without actually climbing on top of me. Someone must have coached him on being careful. My chest is still very sore post-surgery. I have a three-inch scar on my chest from where they opened me up, removed the bullet, and repaired the damage to my left lung.

"I'm so glad you're home," Aiden says, laying his arm gingerly across my belly.

"I am too, sweetie." I lean over and kiss the top of his head.

Just that short trip home from the hospital wore me out, and I'm sleepy. Aiden lies down with me while I take a little cat nap. Jake joins us, entertaining Aiden with a kids' movie playing quietly on the big TV screen in the room.

When I wake up, Aiden's movie is over and he's playing a game on Jake's phone. Jake's lying on the other side of Aiden, his head propped on his hand as he watches me.

There's a soft knock on the door.

"Come on in," Jake says.

Elly pushes a food cart into the room. "Dinner in bed, honey," she says, parking the cart beside the bed. "Chicken and dumplings, steamed veggies, and a freshly-baked apple pie for dessert. I brought enough for all three of you."

"You guys are spoiling me," I say, when Jake props pillows behind me so I can sit up against the headboard.

"Did you have fun with Charlie and Elly while I was gone?" I ask Aiden as we're eating.

"Yes. But I still missed you." His eyes light up suddenly. "I almost forgot! I have a surprise to show you!"

"What's that?"

"I can't tell you. I have to *show* you, downstairs in the pool room. Can we go down to the pool after we eat? Charlie too."

"I think we can manage that," I say, looking at Jake for confirmation. "After we rest our bellies."

"Sure," he says. "If Mommy is very careful and lets me carry her downstairs."

After dinner, Aiden rounds up Charlie, and we all walk down to the lower level. Well, three of us walk. Jake makes good on his promise to carry me. I think he's just showing off again.

We walk into the pool room, hit with the familiar scent of chlorine and the feel of warm, humid air.

Jake sets me down on one of the loungers beside the pool. Then he drags a chair close to mine and sits beside me. "All right, buddy. Show us this big surprise."

Charlie takes Aiden with her into the locker room so they can change into their swimming suits.

"Do you know what the big surprise is?" I ask Jake while we're waiting.

"Not a clue." He leans over to kiss me. "How do you feel? You have to be careful not to do too much too soon."

"I'm fine. I hardly call being carried around the house doing too much."

Charlie and Aiden come out of the women's locker room wearing their swimming gear. I fully expect them to step into the shallow end of the pool and demonstrate Aiden's progress in learning how to swim. To my surprise, they bypass the shallow end of the pool and walk down to the deep end.

"What's he doing?" I manage to keep my voice low, but my heart starts pounding.

Jake's entire demeanor changes instantly as he tenses in his chair. "I have no idea."

"Watch what I can do!" Aiden yells from across the cavernous room.

My breath stalls in my chest as Aiden climbs the ladder to the low diving board and walks all the way out to the end. Charlie is standing at the edge of the pool, near the ladder. There's no one in the pool who can swim!

"All right, buddy," Charlie says to Aiden with a grin on her face. "Show your mom and Jake what you can do."

"Jake, he's not ready for that," I murmur, about ready to get up from my chair. Before I can take a breath to tell Aiden not to jump, he bounces once on the flexible diving board and leaps into the water, his little arms and legs flailing all around him. He hits the water with a sizable splash and goes right under, disappearing from sight.

Jake is already on his feet, racing toward the deep end of the pool, pulling off his boots. But before he can dive in, Aiden surfaces, sputtering and laughing as he treads water.

"Did you see me?" he yells, a huge grin on his face. "Did you?"

Jake stops to catch his breath, and I head down to the other end of the pool, my heart still careening inside me.

Aiden doggy paddles over to the ladder and climbs out of the pool. "I can jump all by myself now," Aiden says, looking incredibly proud of himself. "Charlie taught me. I wanted to surprise you."

"Oh, we were surprised all right," Jake says, standing there with his hands on his hips, panting as he recovers from his flight-or-fight response. "Okay, let's see you do it again!"

Watching Jake's reaction, it dawns on me how quickly he has stepped into the parenting role. He's a natural. He's great with Aiden, and he'll be great with our kids. He'll be there to catch them should they fall, and he'll encourage them to strive for their best.

I smile when I realize I'm using the plural *they*... as if I'm already assuming we'll have kids of our own. Then I look at him. Of course we will.

While Aiden jumps off the diving board a second time, Jake quickly strips down to his black boxer briefs, then dives into the pool, surfacing just a few feet from Aiden.

Jake holds out his hands toward Aiden. "Can you swim to me,

buddy? That's it. Keep coming. Good job!"

* * *

That night, we're lying in bed, just the two of us, both naked, our limbs entwined. The flickering candles on the fireplace mantel are the only light in the room. It's warm and cozy and magical.

Jake leans close and kisses the side of my neck. "It would be completely irresponsible for us to have sex so soon after your surgery."

I laugh. "My doctor did tell me to take it easy for another couple of weeks. No strenuous physical activity until I feel back to normal."

"Right. No strenuous physical activity." He shoves the bedding aside and slides down the bed, making himself comfortable between my legs. "Lie very still, Elliot. No strenuous movements, got it?"

More laughter. "Jake!"

"What? I told you not to move. I'll do all the moving. You just lie there and take it."

And then my breath escapes me in a gasp when he licks his way up my slit with no warning, from my opening to my clit.

He lifts his head, gazing up the length of my body at me. "Shh. Don't overexert yourself. You're resting, remember?"

"It's kind of hard to rest when your face is *down there*." I'm trying to think back to when I had my last shower.

"Down where?" He grins. "In your honeypot?"

"You are an evil man, Jacob McIntyre."

"Lie back and close your eyes. Just relax."

And then he proceeds to lick me, in no particular rush, taking his sweet time as he explores every inch of me. My body heats up quickly, and I feel myself growing slick and warm down there. Now I'm practically panting. I figure this will be a good test of my lung functionality. That thought makes me laugh.

Jake raises his head. "What's so funny?"

"Nothing. Continue what you're doing. Don't mind me."

Suddenly, a finger joins in, slipping deep inside my opening. That diabolical finger wastes no time finding my sweet spot, and now it's a one-two punch down there, his finger and his tongue, both competing to see which can make me come first.

My orgasm sneaks up on me, creeping quietly like a cat stalking its prey. My entire body feels like a live wire, all the nerve endings singing. My muscles grow taut, tightening and coiling in preparation. When my climax hits, I see stars behind my eyelids. My back bows off the bed as I soundlessly gasp out my pleasure.

He continues licking until my body relaxes, melting onto the mattress. Then he crawls up the length of me, careful to keep his weight off, and lies beside me. I can taste myself on his lips as he covers my mouth with his.

"That wasn't too strenuous, was it?" he whispers.

"No. I hardly moved a muscle the entire time."

"Good."

"What about you?"

"What about me?"

"You didn't come."

"Oh. Don't worry about that. I'm not keeping score. Tonight was about you, and me wanting to make you feel good."

"Well, you succeeded. Beautifully."

"Good."

He wipes his face on the sheet, then pulls the bedding over us as we snuggle down to sleep. After that orgasm, I'm struggling to keep my eyes open.

"Go to sleep, Elliot," he says, his voice low and quiet.

Jake

It's moving day. After relaxing at Kenilworth for a few days, giving Annie a little more time to rest and recuperate, we decide it's time to move to my apartment in downtown Chicago.

There's not much to pack at Kenilworth because we didn't bring a lot with us. So, we pack up our stuff, Charlie too, and after saying an emotional good-bye to Elly and George, we head back to the city.

I pull the Tahoe into the underground parking garage and park near the elevators to make the trip upstairs as easy as possible for Annie. She's walking fine, but I don't want her to overdo it.

Aiden jumps out of the vehicle, Stevie tucked beneath one arm and Paul the Panda tucked beneath the other. He's excited about seeing his new place of residence. "I can't believe we're going to live with you, Jake!" he says, practically bouncing in his sneakers.

Charlie takes him by the hand as we head for the elevators. I bring up the suitcases.

"My apartment is on the forty-sixth floor," I tell Annie as we ride up in the elevator. "So is Charlie's apartment, and my sister Lia's. Shane and Beth live two floors above us in the penthouse apartment."

The elevator doors open, and I lead Annie down the hall to my apartment. I have an electronic keypad, so I show her how to use it to let herself in.

Charlie parts from us, to go to her own apartment and unpack.

I usher Annie and Aiden inside my—*our*—apartment. The place has been closed up for a couple of weeks now, and the air is stale. I flip on all the lights and open the windows to get some fresh air.

"Our bedroom is down the hall," I tell her, pointing. "We have our own bathroom, and there's also one in the hallway. Aiden can have the spare bedroom, here."

While I carry the suitcases to their perspective destinations, Annie tours the apartment, checking out the bedrooms, the bathrooms, the kitchen and laundry room, and the living room. There's a sliding glass door off the living room that leads to a balcony overlooking Lake Shore Drive, with Lake Michigan not too far beyond that. It's definitely a million dollar view.

It's clean at least—I have a cleaning company come by week-ly—but otherwise, it's nothing fancy. It's certainly nothing compared to her parents' palatial home. And I'm sure the house she shared with Patterson was probably pretty nice, too. This is just a bachelor pad.

"I know it's not much, but it's just temporary," I tell her, following her as she looks things over.

She turns and slides her arms around my waist. "It's perfect."

I wrap my arms around her, holding her close, thinking it's pretty damn satisfying to have her here under my roof. I never in my wildest dreams thought this would ever happen.

Aiden comes running down the hallway into the living room. "My room is awesome," he says, throwing his arms around our legs as he joins in our hug.

There's a brisk knock on the door and then I hear the beep of the keypad as someone lets himself or herself in. The door opens and Lia walks in, followed by Jonah.

"Hey, guys," Lia says. "Welcome home."

Annie has met Lia before, so I'm sure she remembers her. Lia and Jonah came a couple of times to the hospital to see Annie, but Annie was either asleep or pretty out of it to remember much.

Annie takes one look at Jonah, and then she looks at me, her eyes wide as saucers. "Is that who I think it is?" she whispers.

"Yeah, my boyfriend is a big, famous rock star," Lia says, apparently having overheard Annie's comment. "Whoop-dee-doo. Don't fawn over him or he'll get a big head."

Laughing, Jonah pulls Lia into his arms and kisses her. "You already give me a big head, tiger."

Lia swats at Jonah. "For crying out loud, behave! There are children present."

"Hi," Aiden says, walking right up to Lia. "Who are you?"

"I'm Lia. I'm his sister." She points at me of course. "Who are you?"

"I'm Aiden." Aiden points at me, too. "I guess he's like my dad now."

"I guess you're right," Lia says. "Nice to meet you, Aiden." Lia offers her hand to the kid and they shake. Then to Annie, she says, "Welcome to the neighborhood."

* * *

After unpacking, we head out to buy groceries and stock up on some things Annie and Aiden will need. Then we come home and cook dinner together for the first time in our kitchen.

We eat in the living room, sitting around the coffee table, and watch the animated dinosaur movie again, because apparently, you can never watch too many dinosaur movies.

After dinner, we pop over to Charlie's apartment to say hello. Aiden's happy to hear that there's a private pool on the roof of the building, and yes, he can go swimming up there.

Finally, we head back to our apartment and give Aiden a bath. Then he puts on his PJs and climbs into bed. I sit on the bed and take turns with Annie reading him stories.

"Do you think my dad will find us here?" he asks.

Annie looks at me, her eyes wide with panic. We've been waiting for the right time to tell Aiden that his father is dead. It looks like the time has come.

"Well, Aiden," Annie says, fishing for the right words.

How can there ever be the right words in a situation like this? Despite all the horrible things Ted did, he was still the boy's father.

Annie puts her arm around Aiden's shoulders and pulls him close. "Sweetie, I have some sad news to tell you."

"What?"

"Your dad... he won't be finding us here."

"Oh. Well, that's good news, right?"

Annie blows out a breath. "Sweetie..." And then she stalls, looking like she's on the verge of tears.

I get down and kneel at the side of the bed, taking Aiden's hands in mine. "Aiden, I'm very sorry to tell you this, but your father passed away."

"Passed away? What do you mean?"

"I mean... he died."

"Oh."

"Do you know what that means? When someone dies?"

"Yeah."

But I can tell by the look on Aiden's face that he doesn't. "It means he's gone, and he won't be coming back."

"Ever?"

"Right. He won't ever come back."

Aiden's brow furrows, and he looks so damn confused. He

looks to me, and then back to his mom. "He's never coming back?"

"That's right, honey," Annie says.

Aiden presses his face into Annie's chest, and he clutches her tightly as he starts sobbing.

Annie glances at me, looking like she's ready to bawl too.

I stand and scoop both of them into my arms and carry them to the master suite, depositing them in my big bed. "I think we all need to sleep here together tonight."

Annie nods, her eyes swimming with tears.

I strip down to my boxers and climb into bed. Annie and I tuck Aiden between us. Aiden clings to Annie, seeming a bit lost at the moment.

I have a feeling it's going to be a long night.

✌ 37

Jake

Once my little family is comfortably settled in to the apartment, I make arrangements to meet Cameron and Killian at Annie's parent's house. Killian rents a small moving truck, and we load all of the boxes and furniture that Annie had stored in one of the empty garages at her parents' house.

Frank comes out to watch us load the truck. "Hello, Jake. I'm glad to see your shoulder is doing well."

I rotate my left arm. "Yeah, the shoulder's fine. No permanent damage."

"How's Annie? I called her this morning. She said she's doing well."

I nod as I carry a stack of three cardboard boxes to the truck. "Yeah. She's doing great."

"Look, Jake—"

I stop on my way back for more boxes. "Frank, I appreciate what you said back at the hospital. I accepted your apology then. You don't need to say anything more."

"I know. But I—"

"Give it some time, okay? Annie and I are working hard on rebuilding our lives. We lost a lot of time, precious time that we'll never get back. You don't just get over that in a few days. It takes time."

Frank nods. "I understand." He's quiet for a moment. "All right. I'll let you get back to it. Thanks for helping Annie move her belongings. If there's anything I can do, please don't hesitate to ask."

I nod. "I'll keep that in mind."

As Frank walks away, heading back into the house, I catch a glimpse of Annie's mother watching me from an upstairs window. When she sees me looking her way, she immediately steps back out of sight.

I believed Frank when he said he was sorry for interfering in our lives. But the mother? *Damn.* That woman is a witch. I don't think she's sorry for anything. Not even for almost wrecking her daughter's life.

If she wants to be part of Annie's and Aiden's lives going forward, she'd better do some serious thinking.

Once the truck is packed, the guys drive it to the storage facility. I stay behind. When I ring the front doorbell, the door opens, and there's the dragon lady herself.

"Yes?" she says, eyeing me coldly.

Damn. She doesn't give an inch. "Look, lady. I don't give a flying fuck if I never see you again. But Annie does. She's your daughter. If you want to be part of her life going forward, you need to make an effort to be civil. If you want to be part of Aiden's life, you need to make an effort. And trust me, there will be more kids. I guarantee it. Do you want to be part of their lives?"

Her lips flatten, but she says nothing.

"Think it over. The ball's in your court." And then I turn and walk away.

For Annie's sake, and Aiden's, I hope she comes around.

* * *

After stowing all of Annie's belongings in a storage unit, I head home bringing Chinese carry-out with me. I grab a quick shower, and then the three of us sit down around the coffee table in the living room to eat and watch Aiden's favorite car movie. Again.

After we're done eating, as we're cleaning up, my phone chimes with an incoming text. "It's from Beth. She's inviting us to come up for a meet and greet. Do you feel up to it? I'd like to introduce you to my sister-in-law. I think you and she will be good friends."

"Sure." She dabs at her mouth with a napkin. "I'd love to." Her eyes light up. "We can see their new baby."

ꗍ 38

Annie

After we clean up our dinner mess, Jake takes us down the hall to show me the penthouse's private elevator. "You have to enter a code to use this elevator," he says, punching it in and summoning the elevator.

We ride up two floors to the penthouse apartment which, according to Jake, takes up the entire top floor of the building. I can't even imagine how many tens of thousands of square feet that must be.

The elevator doors open into a foyer with fancy black-and-white checkerboard floor and a stunning crystal chandelier hanging high overhead.

"Right through that door," Jake says, taking my hand. Aiden follows closely behind us, clutching Stevie closely.

Jake opens the foyer door and we step right into the great room, which is huge. The entire back wall is glass, providing a stunning panoramic view of the Chicago night sky. As far as the eye can see, buildings are lit up like Christmas trees under a blanket of stars.

A strikingly handsome man with close cropped gray hair greets us, holding a tiny infant to his shoulder. "Jake! Great to see you, man."

Jake laughs. "I'd shake your hand, but you seem to be a little busy at the moment."

"Yep. Tryin' to get this little guy to burp. He's being stubborn."

Jake puts his arm around my shoulders and pulls me close. "This is Cooper, babe. He's Shane's right-hand man and business partner. Cooper lives here in the penthouse, too. Cooper, this is Annie."

The man nods, giving me a warm smile. "It's an honor to make your acquaintance, young lady."

I return his smile. "Thank you. It's a pleasure."

Aiden sidles up to me, one arm wrapped securely around my leg as he gazes up at Cooper. "Is that your baby?"

Cooper laughs. "You must be Aiden. It's a pleasure to meet you, son. This is my grandson, Lucas Samuel McIntyre."

A much younger man with red hair twisted up into a bun and a matching red beard walks up to Cooper, putting his arm around

Cooper's waist. "I'm going to go change now," he says to Cooper. "It's almost seven."

"We have dinner reservations tonight," Cooper says. "Annie, this is Sam Harrison, my better half."

Sam gives me a quick smile. "Nice to meet you, Annie. I hate to be rude, but we have to leave soon, and I'm not dressed."

Sam kisses the top of the baby's blond head. Then he kisses Cooper right on the lips. "Be back soon."

I'm afraid I might be blushing because my face feels suddenly hot.

"Sam lives here with me," Cooper says as he pats the baby's back. "He works for McIntyre Security, too. He's Beth's bodyguard."

"Hi, Annie. I'm Beth." A stunningly gorgeous blonde in flannel PJ shorts and a tank top joins us. Her hair is slightly damp and up in a ponytail. She hugs Jake, then me. "I'm so glad to finally meet you. And this must be your son, Aiden. Hello, Aiden." Then to me, she says, "Would you like to come sit down and relax?"

We all follow her to a comfortable seating area in front of an impressive brick fireplace.

"I can't tell you how happy I am to meet you," Beth says to me. "We're all thrilled that you and Jake are together again."

I smile at her. "Thanks for inviting us up. Your home is lovely."

"I'm sorry we're so informal this evening. I just took a shower, and Shane's in his office on the phone with work. He'll be out in a minute to say hello."

The baby burps loudly, and everyone gets a chuckle out of that.

"Mission accomplished," Cooper says with a grin as he hands

the baby to Beth.

"I hear you're going to be living in our building for a while, Aiden," Beth says as she settles the baby into the crook of her arm.

Aiden nods. "I am. Mommy and I are going to live with Jake. Is that your baby?"

Beth smiles. "Yes, he is. His name is Luke. Maybe you two could be friends."

"Sure." Aiden offers the baby his dinosaur. "He can play with Stevie."

Beth laughs. "I'm afraid Luke's too young to play with toys, but when he's older, I'm sure he'd love to."

Sam reappears, dressed in a pair of dressy black trousers and a white button-down shirt. He has a towel draped across his shoulders and a pair of clippers in his hand. He walks over to where Cooper is sitting in an armchair and hands him the clippers. "Would you trim my undercut? It's getting kinda long."

"Excuse us, ladies and gentlemen," Cooper says as he stands. "I'm needed elsewhere." The two men disappear around the corner.

Shane walks into the room, heading straight for his wife. "Hi, everyone. Sorry for the delay." He leans over the back of the sofa to kiss her cheek. Then he gently brushes his hand over the sleeping baby's head.

Shane McIntyre is a very good looking man. He's probably in his mid-thirties. Short brown hair and a closely-trimmed beard. And the brightest blue eyes I've ever seen on a man. He's wearing jeans and a Navy blue T-shirt that hugs his muscular arms. Good grief. Are all the McIntyre men ripped?

Shane clasps Jake's shoulder, giving it a squeeze. "I couldn't be happier for you, man."

Jake smiles, and oh, my goodness, I think he's blushing.

Shane offers me his hand. "Annie, it's a pleasure. I saw you in the hospital a few times, but you weren't up to socializing quite yet."

Shane joins his wife and son on the sofa.

Beth cradles Luke in her arms, rocking him gently as he dozes off. "I had an ulterior motive for inviting you guys up this evening—besides wanting to meet Annie and Aiden," she says. "We're having a little family get-together tomorrow afternoon at two. I hope you'll join us."

"We'd love to," I say, glancing at Jake for confirmation. The smile on his face says it all.

* * *

The McIntyre family get-together is scheduled for two o'clock this afternoon. Ten minutes before, Jake and Aiden and I ride up in the penthouse elevator. The elevator doors open, and we step out into a foyer lavishly decorated with crystal vases filled with pale pink roses and a colorful bouquet of helium balloons that say *Welcome Home!* This isn't just a simple get-together. This is a party—*for me.*

I stop dead in my tracks, suddenly feeling ten times more nervous than I already was. I think Aiden is picking up on my mood, because he grabs my hand and holds on tightly.

When I glance up at Jake, he just smiles and shrugs. "Come on. Don't be afraid. They don't bite." Then he takes my hand and pulls me to the door that leads into the apartment.

Before he opens the door, he leans close and kisses me, and then he whispers, "I love you."

Jake ushers me through the door first, and when I step into the great room, there's a sizable crowd of smiling faces to greet us.

"Surprise!" they cheer.

Bridget comes forward, her arms open wide, and pulls me into a crushing embrace. "Welcome home, darling," she says, sounding more than a little choked up. She gives me a teary smile and kisses my cheek. Then she tucks a strand of my hair behind my ear. "We're so glad you found your way back to us."

"All right, Mom, let her breathe," Jake says, pulling me out of her arms. He lays his arm across my shoulder and draws me close. "Hey, everyone. In case you didn't know, this is the love of my life, Annie Elliot. See, she's real. I didn't make her up, as some of you have suggested over the years."

Ignoring all the laughter, Jake leans down to kiss my cheek. And then he picks Aiden up and props him on his hip. Hiding from the crowd, Aiden presses his face into the crook of Jake's neck and shoulder and wraps his arms around Jake's neck. "And this little guy is Aiden. He's a bit shy at first, but once he gets to know you, he'll charm your pants off. Did I mention I'm a dad now, too?"

And that pronouncement is followed by another round of cheering.

I'm starting to pick out familiar faces in the crowd. Charlie stands out, and Cameron and Killian. Elly and George are here, too! Along with Jake's parents. I recognize Jake's blind brother, Jamie, and his girlfriend, Molly. Beth and her baby, of course. The two guys I met last night, Cooper and Sam. Jake's sister Lia and her boyfriend, Jonah. Jake's sister Sophie. And Jake's other two brothers, Shane and Liam. Good grief, they have a big family!

Beth comes up to me, Luke cradled in her arms, and gently touches my arm. "Luke needs a diaper change. Would you like to come with me to the nursery?"

"Yes, thank you." Bless her heart, she's a mind reader. I could use a few quiet moments to process all of this.

Jake picks up Aiden while I follow Beth down a hallway that leads to a small, cozy nursery. There's a crib in here, a changing table, and a padded rocking chair and footstool.

"He sleeps in our room," she says, "in a bassinette, but we do diaper changes in here. And I nurse him in here."

Beth lays a very tiny newborn baby on the padded changing table and proceeds to unsnap the bottom half of his sleeper.

"How's he doing?" I ask. Jake told me about the traumatic events Beth went through recently. How she went into premature labor in the attic above a convenience store, where an armed robbery was taking place. His sister Lia helped her through the ordeal, as did Shane.

Beth smiles as she removes his wet diaper. "He's doing really well. His lungs are fine now, and he's eating well and gaining weight."

The baby has pale blond hair, like his mama, and bright blue eyes, like is daddy. Right now, the little guy is busy sucking noisily on his fist and looking at the colorful shapes dangling from the mobile that hangs over the changing table.

"He's adorable," I say, reaching out to hold his other little hand.

"I think so, but then I'm biased." She laughs. "How is your son doing?"

"He's doing okay. It was hard telling him that his father was dead. We didn't go into a lot of detail. He doesn't need to know his father shot both Jake and me and would have killed me if Jake hadn't gotten between us. How in the world do you explain that to a child?"

Beth lays her hand on my arm, frowning. "I'm so sorry." Then she brightens with a smile. "We're all thrilled that you and Jake are together again."

I feel tears pricking behind my eyes. "Everyone's been so nice, so accepting." I swallow, my throat tight. "I wasn't sure what to expect. Jake and I have a long history, and some of it's very painful. My parents—" I stop before I start crying. I don't want to blubber like a baby in front of Jake's sister-in-law.

"It's okay," she says gently. "You don't have to explain anything. We know, and we understand. Jake's family doesn't blame you or hold grudges. Everyone is simply happy that you're back together, and that Jake is happy. That's all that matters."

The baby starts fussing, sucking furiously on his tiny fist, doing his best to cram it into his mouth.

I laugh. "I think someone is hungry."

She grins as she picks up her son and rests him against her shoulder. "Yes, he is."

The door opens, and Shane and Jake walk in. Jake's gaze goes right to me. "Doing okay?"

"Yes, fine," I say.

"Perfect timing, gentlemen," Beth says. "I'm going to nurse Luke now."

"Great," Jake says, pulling me into his arms. "I can have my Elliot back then."

Jake and I return to the great room, leaving Shane behind with his wife and son. The nursery door closes quietly behind us, and I have to smile. Maybe someday Jake and I will celebrate the birth of a new child.

Back in the great room, Aiden is at the center of attention. He's sitting on Calum's lap, with Bridget and Charlie seated on either side of him. Aiden is regaling everyone with the tale of his exploits jumping off the diving board at Kenilworth.

Jake ushers me over to a dining table covered with hot and cold hors d'oeuvres. At the center of the table is a breath-taking, three-tiered cake decorated with tiny pale pink roses made from icing and tiny little gold candy beads. He pours me a glass of freshly-made lemonade, then one for himself.

"I have an announcement to make," he says, raising his glass and easily garnering everyone's attention with his deep baritone voice. He holds me at his side. "You should already know this by

now, but in case you don't... the love of my life—Annie Elliot—
has done me the great honor of agreeing to put up with me for
the rest of our lives. We're getting married in March and you're
all invited."

Their response makes me blush. With all the whooping and
hollering and applause, I feel so incredibly blessed. I'm amazed
that they really don't seem to be holding a grudge against me.
"Thank you, everyone."

I step forward, out from under Jake's sheltering support, both
emotionally and physically. "Many of you remember me back in
high school, when Jake and I were first together. You also know
that we went our separate ways, for lack of a better term, shortly after I left for college." I explain what happened. "I want you
all to know how sorry I am, for not being stronger, braver, more
self-assured. For letting myself be manipulated. For letting my
doubts and insecurities affect my behavior."

Jake pulls me back to his side. "The same goes for me," he says.
"But those days are behind us now."

I swallow hard. "I just want you all to know that I love Jake
with all my heart, and that I'm going to spend the rest of my
life with him, making up for lost time. I hope you will give me a
chance to become part of your family, because there's nothing I'd
like better."

When I'm done speaking, there's not a dry eye in the room,
and I don't even realize I've got tears running down my face until
Molly brings me a tissue.

Aiden jumps down from Calum's lap and runs to me, wrapping his arms around my legs as he hugs me. I pick him up, and he buries his face in the crook of my neck.

"Why are you crying, Mommy?" he asks, his voice muffled against my neck.

"I'm crying because I'm happy, sweetie."

"I'm happy, too," he says, sniffling.

Jake wraps his arms around the both of us. "Make that three."

Epilogue

Annie

It's five in the morning, and I'm standing at the bathroom counter staring at my reflection in the mirror when Jake walks in behind me, naked.

"What are you doing up so early?" he asks, squinting at the bathroom light. "Is everything okay?"

"Yes, fine."

He comes up behind me and wraps his arms around my waist. I'm wearing one of his humongous T-shirts, which is long enough to cover my rear end. That doesn't stop him, though, from sliding his warm hand up beneath the hem of the shirt and palming my naked butt cheek.

I didn't sleep well last night thanks to some crazy dreams, and then I found myself wide awake well before dawn, unable to go back to sleep. My mind was racing too much to allow me to doze off again, so I figured I might as well get this over with.

He finally notices the little blue stick I'm holding. "Is that what I think it is?"

"Yes." My cheeks heat up. "I'm two weeks late, Jake. I'm never late."

"Shit. That time I forgot to grab a condom."

"Yeah. The timing was sort of spot on then, if one was actually *trying* to get pregnant."

He peers over my shoulder to get a better look at the stick. "Well? What does it say?"

"It's not done yet. Two more minutes."

He exhales heavily, running his fingers through his sleep-mussed hair. Then, after kissing the side of my neck, he walks to the toilet and raises the seat so he can empty his bladder.

The alarm on my phone goes off, making me jump. The requisite wait time is over.

"Well?" he says.

I stare at the indicator, my mind racing.

"Elliot, for crying out loud, tell me. If we're pregnant, that's great." He does a quick mental calculation and laughs. "Jeez, you'd be nine months pregnant at our wedding."

Finished with his business, he washes his hands at the sink and dries them on a towel. Then he takes the stick from me, glancing at it briefly before setting it down on the countertop. He pulls me into his arms. "I love you."

"That's good," I say, laughing shakily. "Because we're having a baby."

When I look up at him to gauge his reaction, there are tears in his eyes. He covers his face with his hand.

"Jake? What's wrong?"

He shakes his head, not trusting himself to speak.

"You're happy, right?" I say. "I mean, we're having a baby. I need you to be happy about this."

He sweeps me up into his arms. "Of course I'm happy. I'm freaking ecstatic. I'm also scared shitless. Promise me you'll hold onto me and never let go."

"I promise."

And then he carries me back to our bed so we can properly celebrate our second chance at a new beginning.

The end... for now.

Coming Next!

Stay tuned for more books featuring your favorite McIntyre Security characters! Watch for upcoming books for Tyler Jamison, Sophie McIntyre, Charlie, Killian and Hannah McIntyre, Chloe and Cameron, Liam McIntyre, and many more!

Erin and Mack's long-awaited book, *Regret*, is coming in early 2019!

Please Leave a Review on Amazon

I hope you'll take a moment to leave a review for me on Amazon. Please, please, please? It doesn't have to be long... just a brief comment saying whether you liked the book or not.

Reviews are vitally important to authors! I'd be incredibly grateful to you if you'd leave one for me. Goodreads and BookBub are also great places to leave reviews.

Stay in Touch

Follow me on <u>Facebook</u> or <u>subscribe to my newsletter</u> for up-to-date information on the schedule for new releases.

I'm active daily on Facebook, and I love to interact with my readers. Come talk to me on Facebook by leaving me a message or a comment. Please share my book posts with your friends. I also have a very active <u>reader group</u> on Facebook where I post weekly teasers for new books and run lots of giveaway contests. Come join us!

You can also follow me on Amazon, <u>BookBub</u>, <u>Goodreads</u>, and <u>Instagram</u>!

Acknowledgements

As always, I have so many wonderful people to thank for their support on this journey.

I owe a huge debt of gratitude to my sister, Lori, for being there with me every step of the way. She's read *Redeemed* so many times, she must surely be sick of it by now. Her support and encouragement are priceless.

Thank you to Sue Vaughn Boudreaux for her tremendous assistance and support. With her many excellent skills, Sue is an invaluable help and instrumental at keeping me on track.

I want to thank Becky Morean, my dear friend and writing buddy, and author extraordinaire, for her invaluable feedback and critique. Thank you, Becky, for your amazing friendship and camaraderie.

Thank you to my beta readers: Sue Vaughn Boudreaux, Julie Collier, Sarah Louise Frost, Lori Holmes, Keely Knutton, Tiffany Mann, Becky Morean, and Brooke Smith.

Finally, I want to thank all of my readers around the globe and the members of my reader group on Facebook. I am so incredibly blessed to have you. Your love and support and enthusiasm feed my soul on a daily basis. Many of my readers have become familiar names and faces greeting me daily on Facebook, and I feel so blessed to have made so many new friends. I thank you all, from the very bottom of my heart, for every Facebook like, share, and comment. You have no idea how thrilled I am to read your comments each day.

I wouldn't be able to do the thing that I love to do most—share my characters and their stories—without your amazing support. Every day, I wake up and thank my lucky stars for you all!

With much love to you all... April